ANOTHER CASTLE

ONI PRESS

AN ONI PRESS PUBLICATION

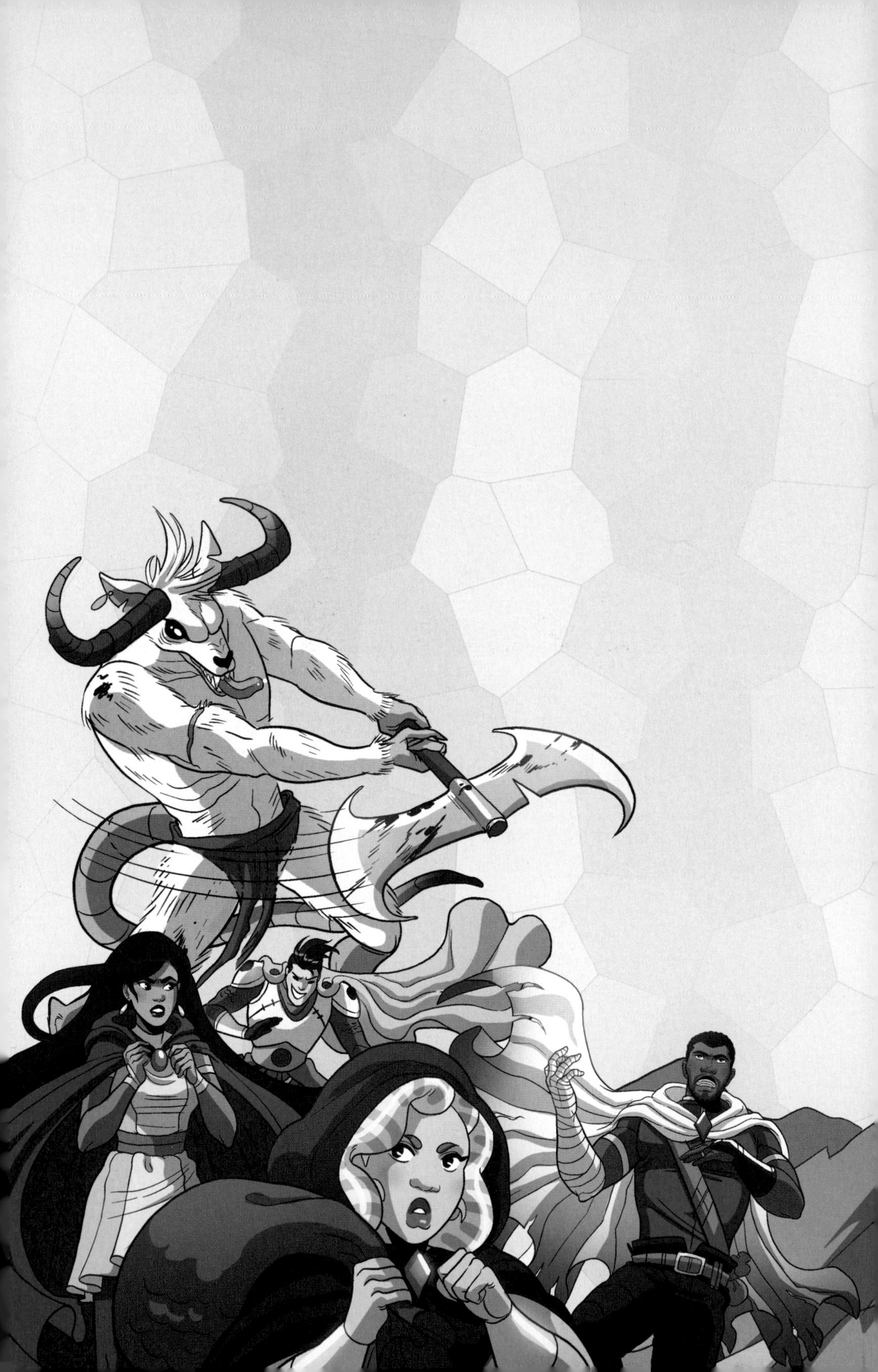

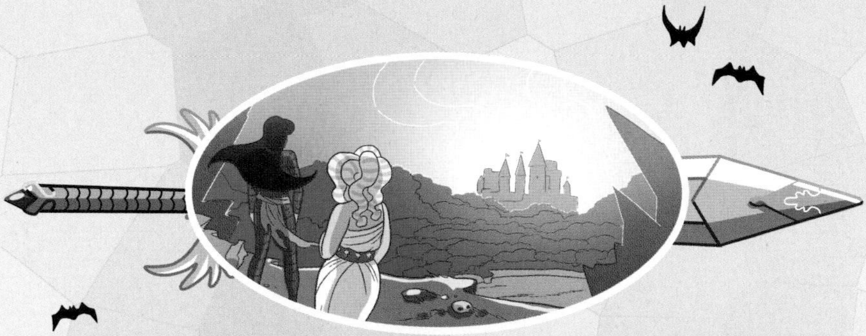

ANOTHER CASTLE

WRITTEN BY **Andrew Wheeler**

ILLUSTRATED AND COLORED BY **Paulina Ganucheau**

LETTERED BY **Jenny Vy Tran**

COVER BY **Paulina Ganucheau**

ORIGINAL EDITION EDITED BY **Ari Yarwood**

NEW EDITION EDITED BY **Desiree Rodriguez**

DESIGNED BY **Hilary Thompson**

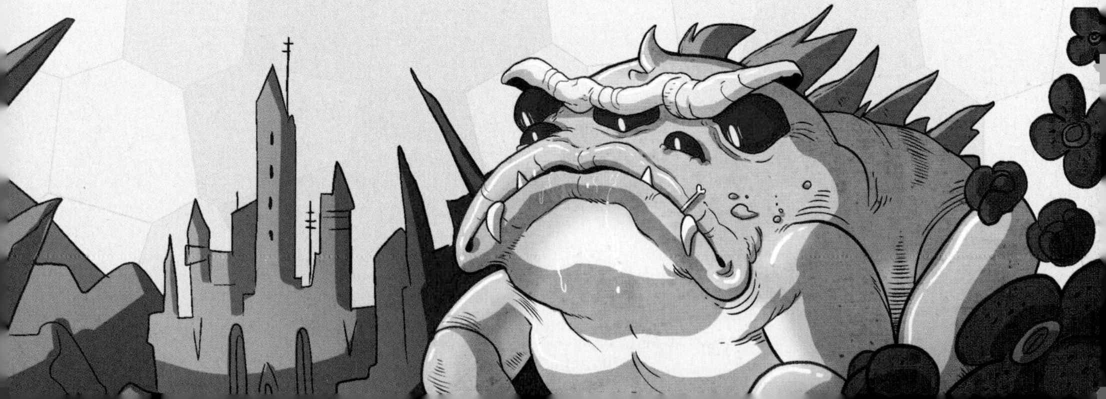

PUBLISHED BY ONI-LION FORGE PUBLISHING GROUP, LLC.

James Lucas Jones, president & publisher
Charlie Chu, e.v.p. of creative & business development
Steve Ellis, s.v.p. of games & operations
Alex Segura, s.v.p. of marketing & sales
Michelle Nguyen, associate publisher
Brad Rooks, director of operations
Amber O'Neill, special projects manager
Margot Wood, director of marketing & sales
Katie Sainz, marketing manager
Tara Lehmann, publicist
Holly Aitchison, consumer marketing manager
Troy Look, director of design & production
Angie Knowles, production manager
Kate Z. Stone, senior graphic designer
Carey Hall, graphic designer
Sarah Rockwell, graphic designer
Hilary Thompson, graphic designer
Vincent Kukua, digital prepress technician
Chris Cerasi, managing editor
Jasmine Amiri, senior editor
Shawna Gore, senior editor
Amanda Meadows, senior editor
Robert Meyers, senior editor, licensing
Desiree Rodriguez, editor
Grace Scheipeter, editor
Zack Soto, editor
Ben Eisner, game developer
Jung Lee, logistics coordinator
Kuian Kellum, warehouse assistant

Joe Nozemack, publisher emeritus

ORIGINALLY PUBLISHED AS ISSUES #1–5
OF THE ONI PRESS COMIC SERIES *ANOTHER CASTLE*.

onipress.com
facebook.com/onipress
twitter.com/onipress
instagram.com/onipress

@wheeler • andrewwheeler.co.uk
@plinaganucheau • paulinaganucheau.tumblr.com
@jenvyjams • jenvyjams.com

FIRST EDITION: APRIL 2022
ISBN 978-1-62010-986-1
eISBN 978-1-62010-312-8
1 2 3 4 5 6 7 8 9 10

LIBRARY OF CONGRESS CONTROL NUMBER: 2021937401

PRINTED IN CHINA.

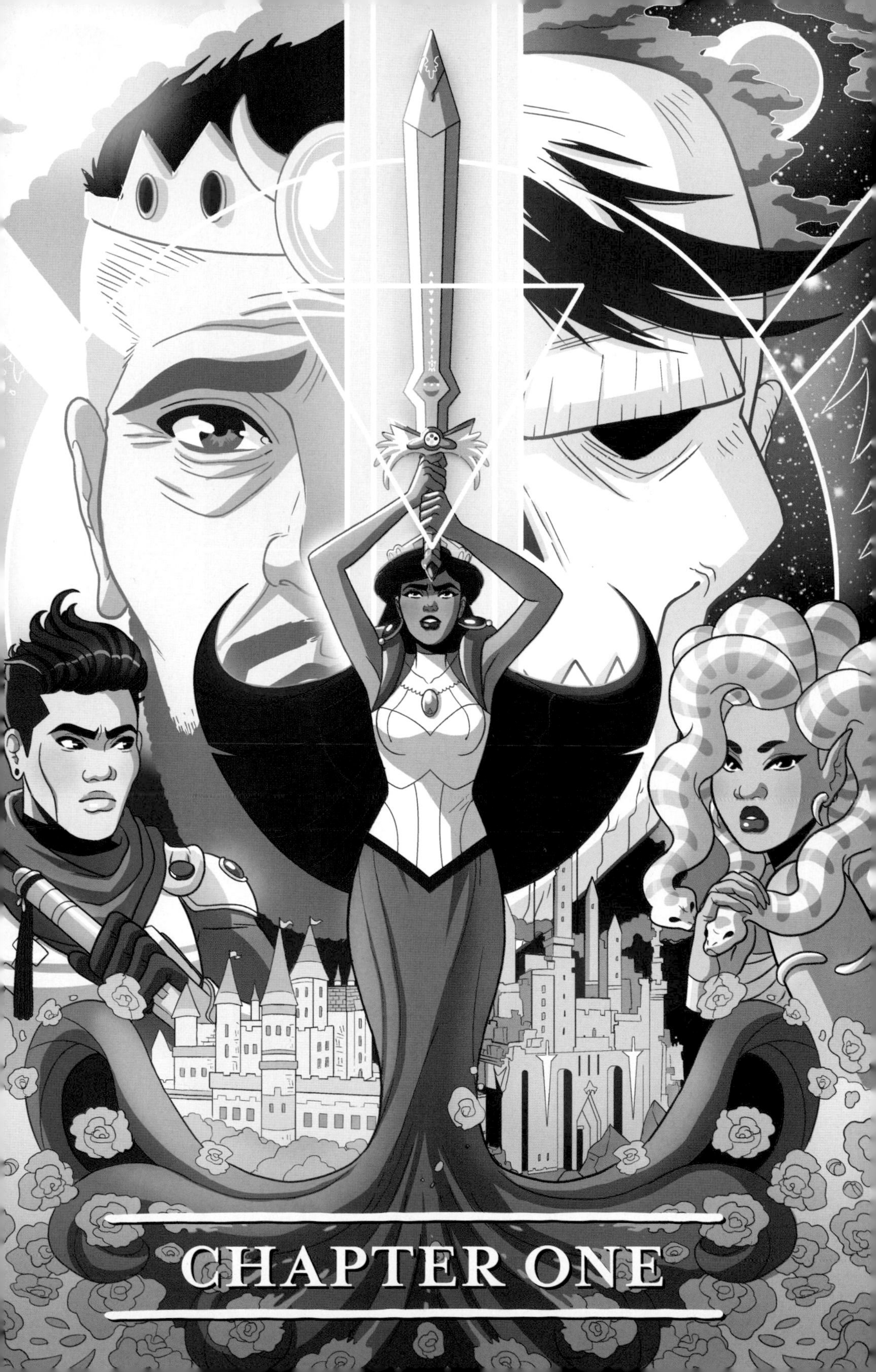
CHAPTER ONE

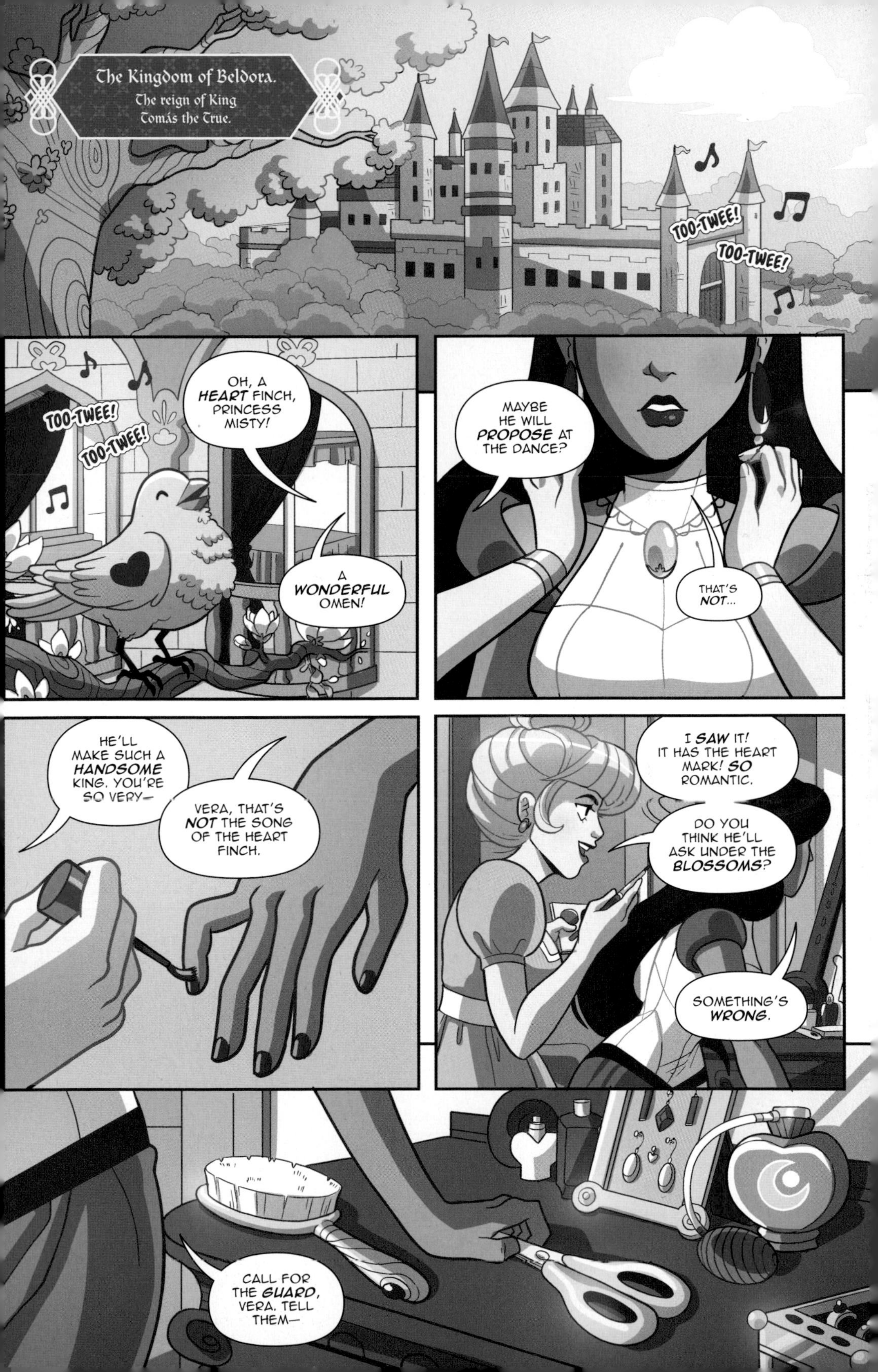

The Kingdom of Beldora.
The reign of King Tomás the True.
TOO-TWEE!
TOO-TWEE!
TOO-TWEE!
TOO-TWEE!
OH, A HEART FINCH, PRINCESS MISTY!
A WONDERFUL OMEN!
MAYBE HE WILL PROPOSE AT THE DANCE?
THAT'S NOT...
HE'LL MAKE SUCH A HANDSOME KING. YOU'RE SO VERY—
VERA, THAT'S NOT THE SONG OF THE HEART FINCH.
I SAW IT! IT HAS THE HEART MARK! SO ROMANTIC.
DO YOU THINK HE'LL ASK UNDER THE BLOSSOMS?
SOMETHING'S WRONG.
CALL FOR THE GUARD, VERA. TELL THEM—

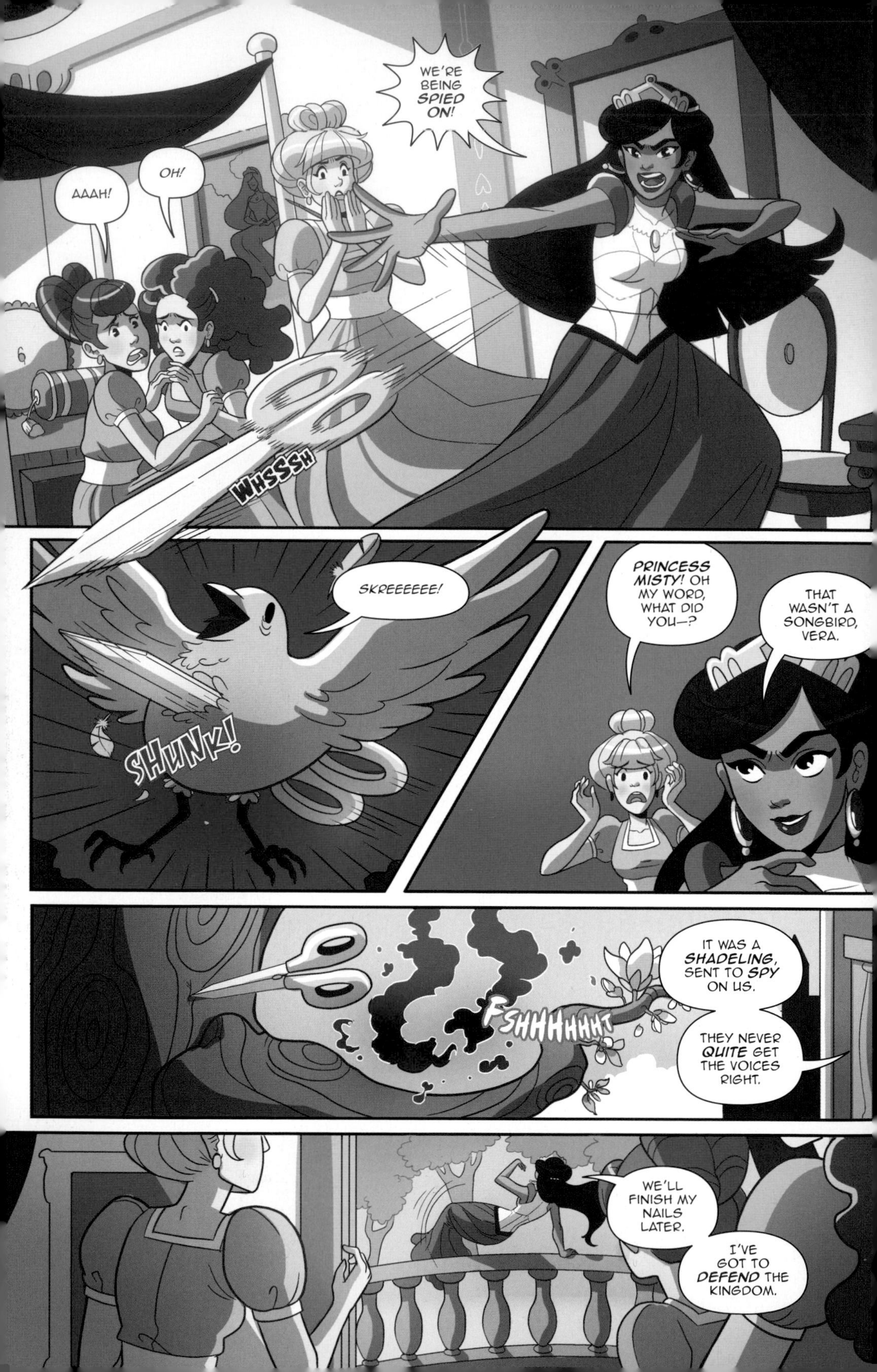
WE'RE BEING SPIED ON!
AAAH!
OH!
WHSSSH
SKREEEEEE!
SHUNK!
PRINCESS MISTY! OH MY WORD, WHAT DID YOU—?
THAT WASN'T A SONGBIRD, VERA.
IT WAS A SHADELING, SENT TO SPY ON US.
FSHHHHHHT
THEY NEVER QUITE GET THE VOICES RIGHT.
WE'LL FINISH MY NAILS LATER.
I'VE GOT TO DEFEND THE KINGDOM.

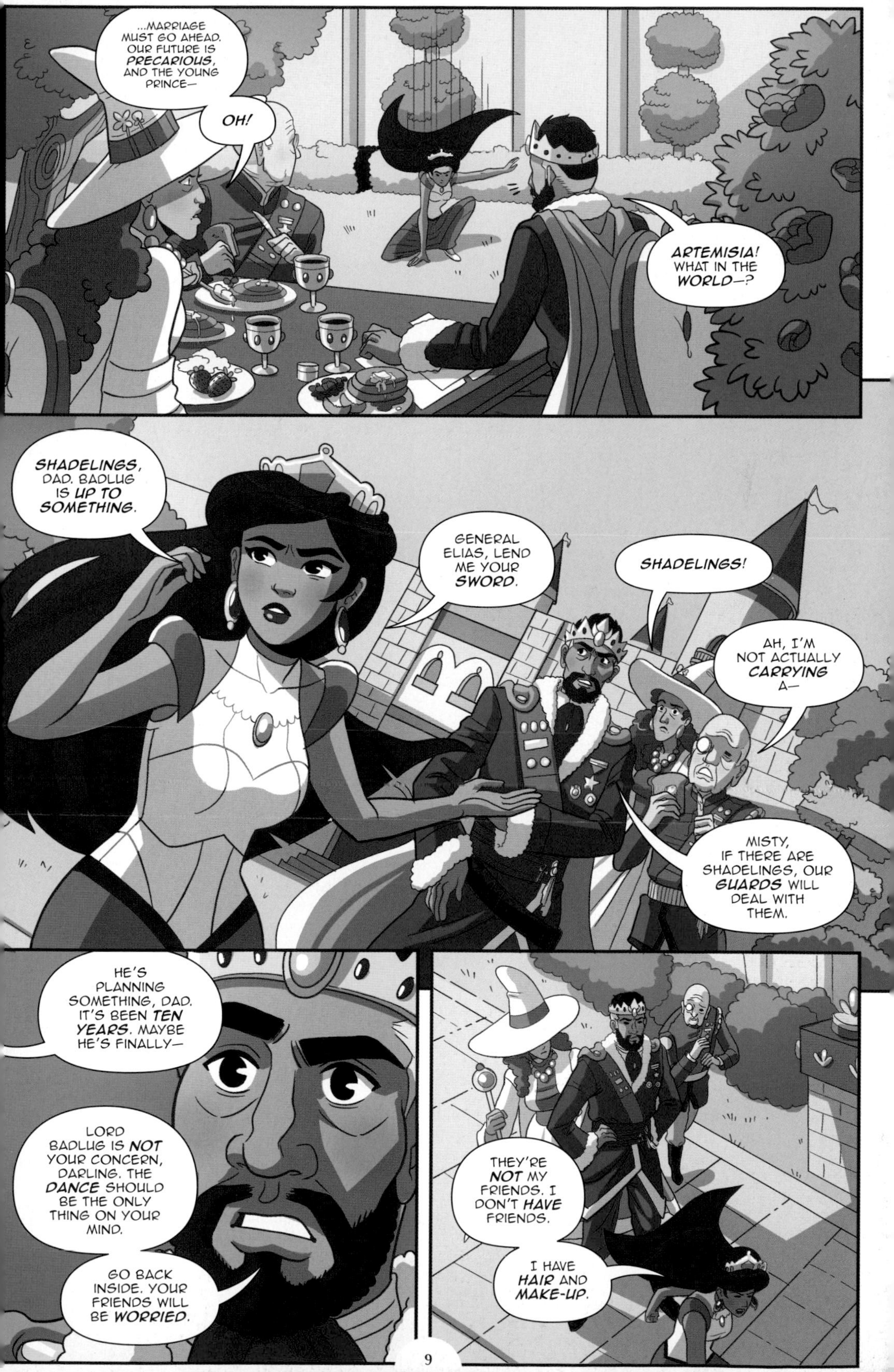

...MARRIAGE MUST GO AHEAD. OUR FUTURE IS PRECARIOUS, AND THE YOUNG PRINCE—
OH!
ARTEMISIA! WHAT IN THE WORLD—?
SHADELINGS, DAD. BADLUG IS UP TO SOMETHING.
GENERAL ELIAS, LEND ME YOUR SWORD.
SHADELINGS!
AH, I'M NOT ACTUALLY CARRYING A—
MISTY, IF THERE ARE SHADELINGS, OUR GUARDS WILL DEAL WITH THEM.
HE'S PLANNING SOMETHING, DAD. IT'S BEEN TEN YEARS. MAYBE HE'S FINALLY—
LORD BADLUG IS NOT YOUR CONCERN, DARLING. THE DANCE SHOULD BE THE ONLY THING ON YOUR MIND.
GO BACK INSIDE. YOUR FRIENDS WILL BE WORRIED.
THEY'RE NOT MY FRIENDS. I DON'T HAVE FRIENDS.
I HAVE HAIR AND MAKE-UP.

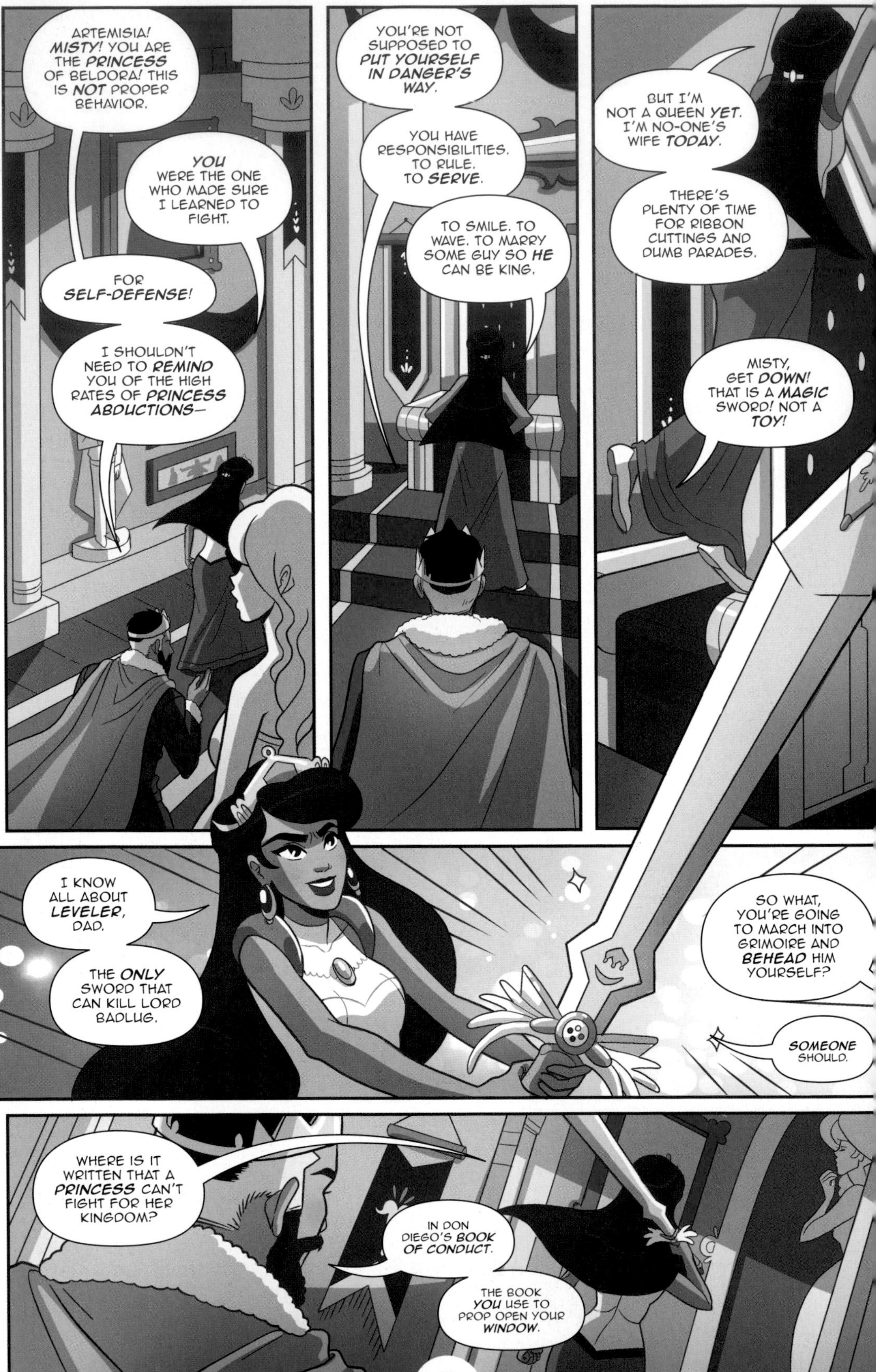

ARTEMISIA! MISTY! YOU ARE THE PRINCESS OF BELDORA! THIS IS NOT PROPER BEHAVIOR.
YOU WERE THE ONE WHO MADE SURE I LEARNED TO FIGHT.
FOR SELF-DEFENSE!
I SHOULDN'T NEED TO REMIND YOU OF THE HIGH RATES OF PRINCESS ABDUCTIONS—
YOU'RE NOT SUPPOSED TO PUT YOURSELF IN DANGER'S WAY.
YOU HAVE RESPONSIBILITIES. TO RULE. TO SERVE.
TO SMILE. TO WAVE. TO MARRY SOME GUY SO HE CAN BE KING.
BUT I'M NOT A QUEEN YET. I'M NO-ONE'S WIFE TODAY.
THERE'S PLENTY OF TIME FOR RIBBON CUTTINGS AND DUMB PARADES.
MISTY, GET DOWN! THAT IS A MAGIC SWORD! NOT A TOY!
I KNOW ALL ABOUT LEVELER, DAD.
THE ONLY SWORD THAT CAN KILL LORD BADLUG.
SO WHAT, YOU'RE GOING TO MARCH INTO GRIMOIRE AND BEHEAD HIM YOURSELF?
SOMEONE SHOULD.
WHERE IS IT WRITTEN THAT A PRINCESS CAN'T FIGHT FOR HER KINGDOM?
IN DON DIEGO'S BOOK OF CONDUCT.
THE BOOK YOU USE TO PROP OPEN YOUR WINDOW.

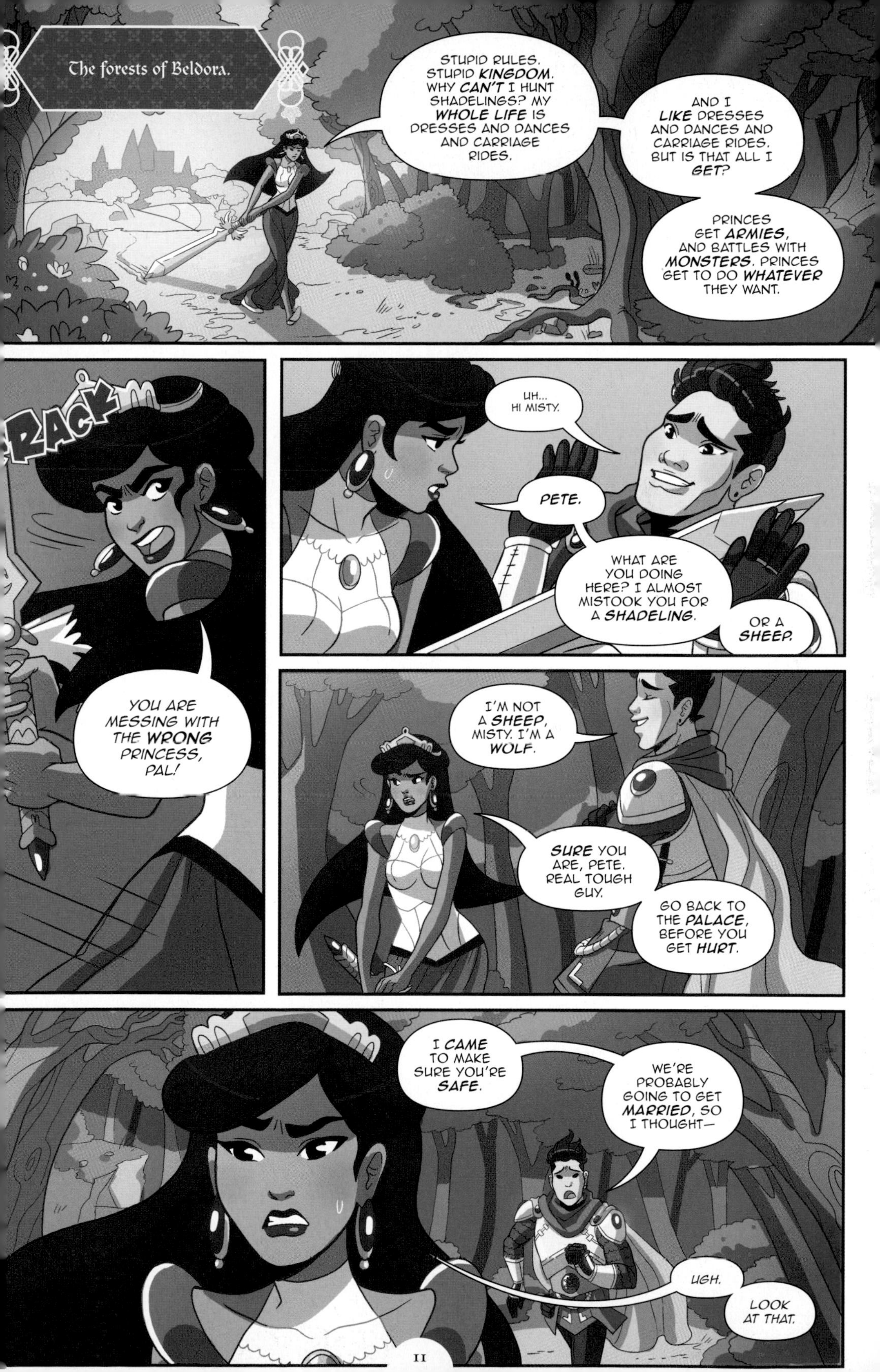

The forests of Beldora.
STUPID RULES. STUPID KINGDOM. WHY CAN'T I HUNT SHADELINGS? MY WHOLE LIFE IS DRESSES AND DANCES AND CARRIAGE RIDES.
AND I LIKE DRESSES AND DANCES AND CARRIAGE RIDES. BUT IS THAT ALL I GET?
PRINCES GET ARMIES, AND BATTLES WITH MONSTERS. PRINCES GET TO DO WHATEVER THEY WANT.
CRACK
YOU ARE MESSING WITH THE WRONG PRINCESS, PAL!
UH... HI MISTY.
PETE.
WHAT ARE YOU DOING HERE? I ALMOST MISTOOK YOU FOR A SHADELING.
OR A SHEEP.
I'M NOT A SHEEP, MISTY. I'M A WOLF.
SURE YOU ARE, PETE. REAL TOUGH GUY.
GO BACK TO THE PALACE, BEFORE YOU GET HURT.
I CAME TO MAKE SURE YOU'RE SAFE.
WE'RE PROBABLY GOING TO GET MARRIED, SO I THOUGHT—
UGH.
LOOK AT THAT.

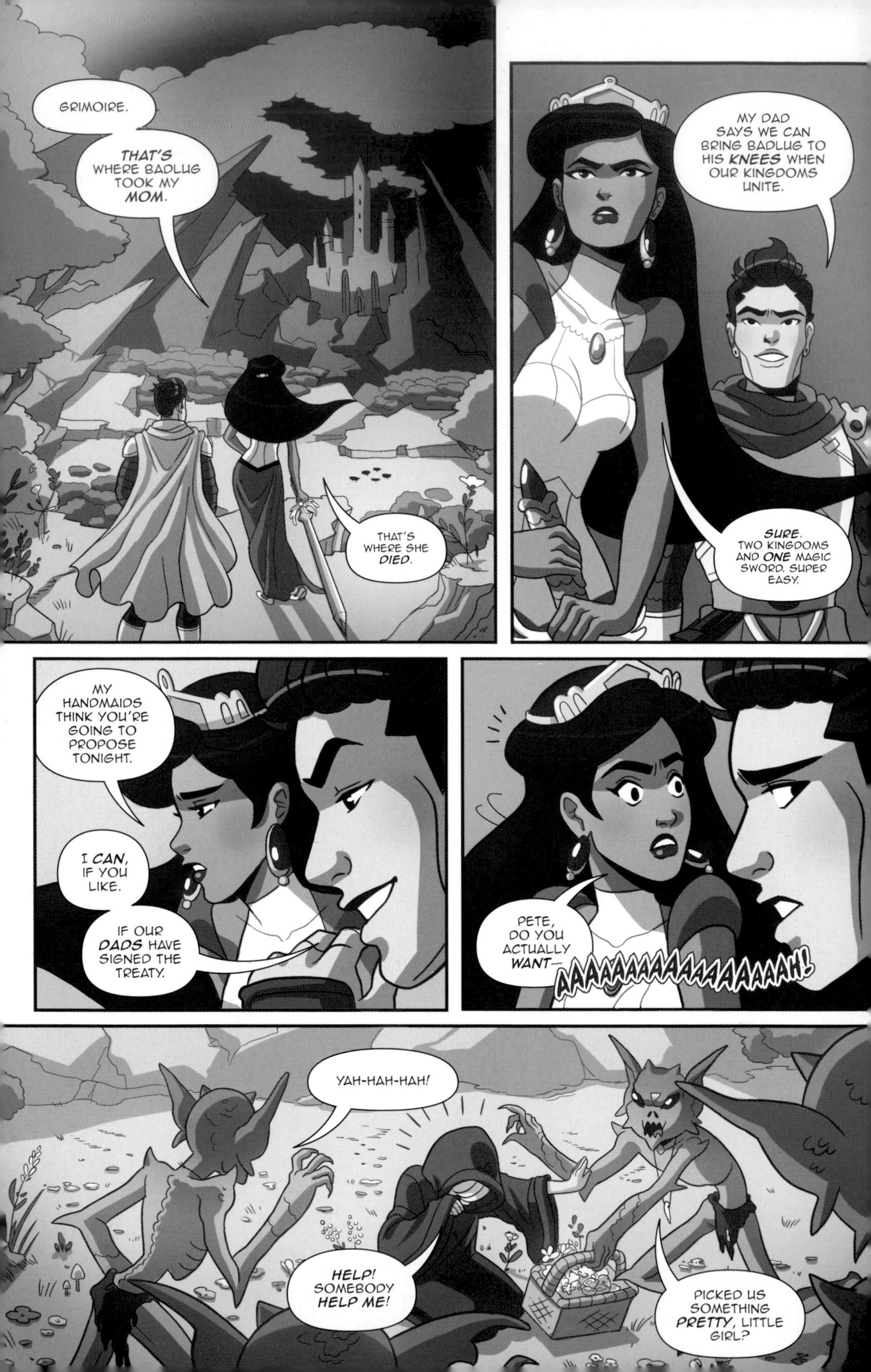
GRIMOIRE.
THAT'S WHERE BADLUG TOOK MY MOM.
THAT'S WHERE SHE DIED.
MY DAD SAYS WE CAN BRING BADLUG TO HIS KNEES WHEN OUR KINGDOMS UNITE.
SURE. TWO KINGDOMS AND ONE MAGIC SWORD. SUPER EASY.
MY HANDMAIDS THINK YOU'RE GOING TO PROPOSE TONIGHT.
I CAN, IF YOU LIKE.
IF OUR DADS HAVE SIGNED THE TREATY.
PETE, DO YOU ACTUALLY WANT—
AAAAAAAAAAAAAAAAAH!
YAH-HAH-HAH!
HELP! SOMEBODY HELP ME!
PICKED US SOMETHING PRETTY, LITTLE GIRL?

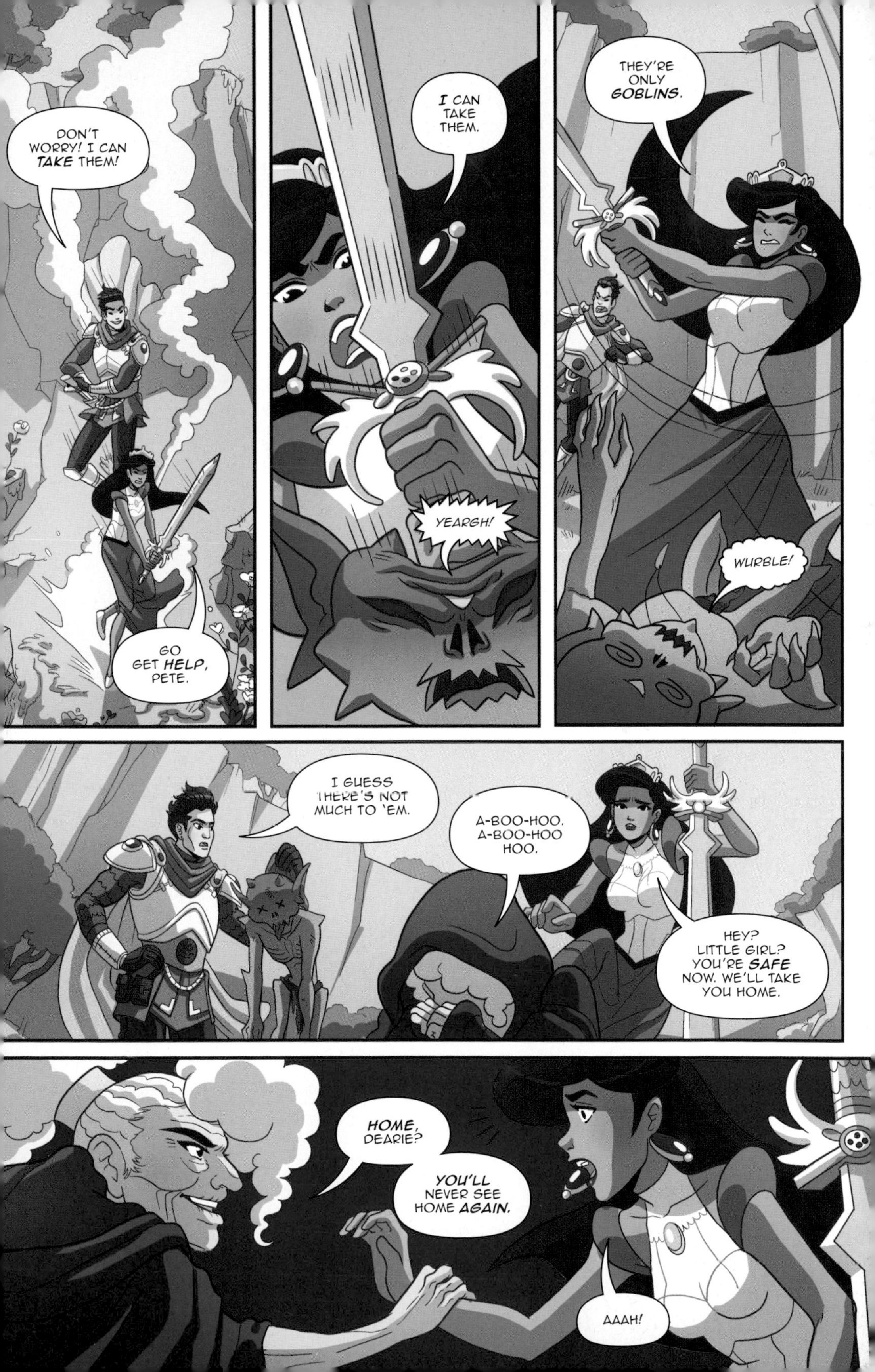
DON'T WORRY! I CAN TAKE THEM!
GO GET HELP, PETE.
I CAN TAKE THEM.
YEARGH!
THEY'RE ONLY GOBLINS.
WURBLE!
I GUESS THERE'S NOT MUCH TO 'EM.
A-BOO-HOO. A-BOO-HOO HOO.
HEY? LITTLE GIRL? YOU'RE SAFE NOW. WE'LL TAKE YOU HOME.
HOME, DEARIE?
YOU'LL NEVER SEE HOME AGAIN.
AAAH!

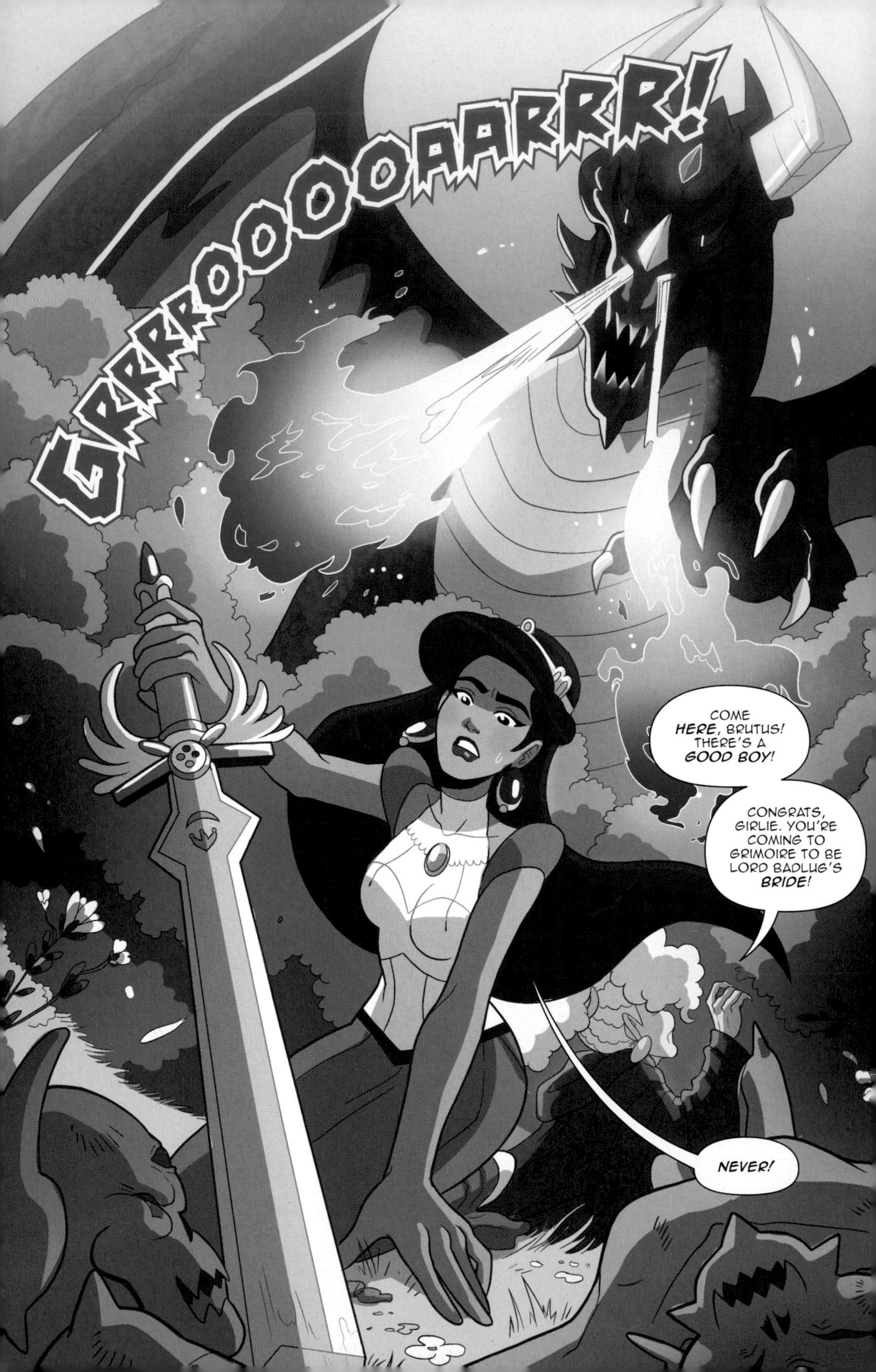
GRRROOOOAARRR!
COME HERE, BRUTUS! THERE'S A GOOD BOY!
CONGRATS, GIRLIE. YOU'RE COMING TO GRIMOIRE TO BE LORD BADLUG'S BRIDE!
NEVER!

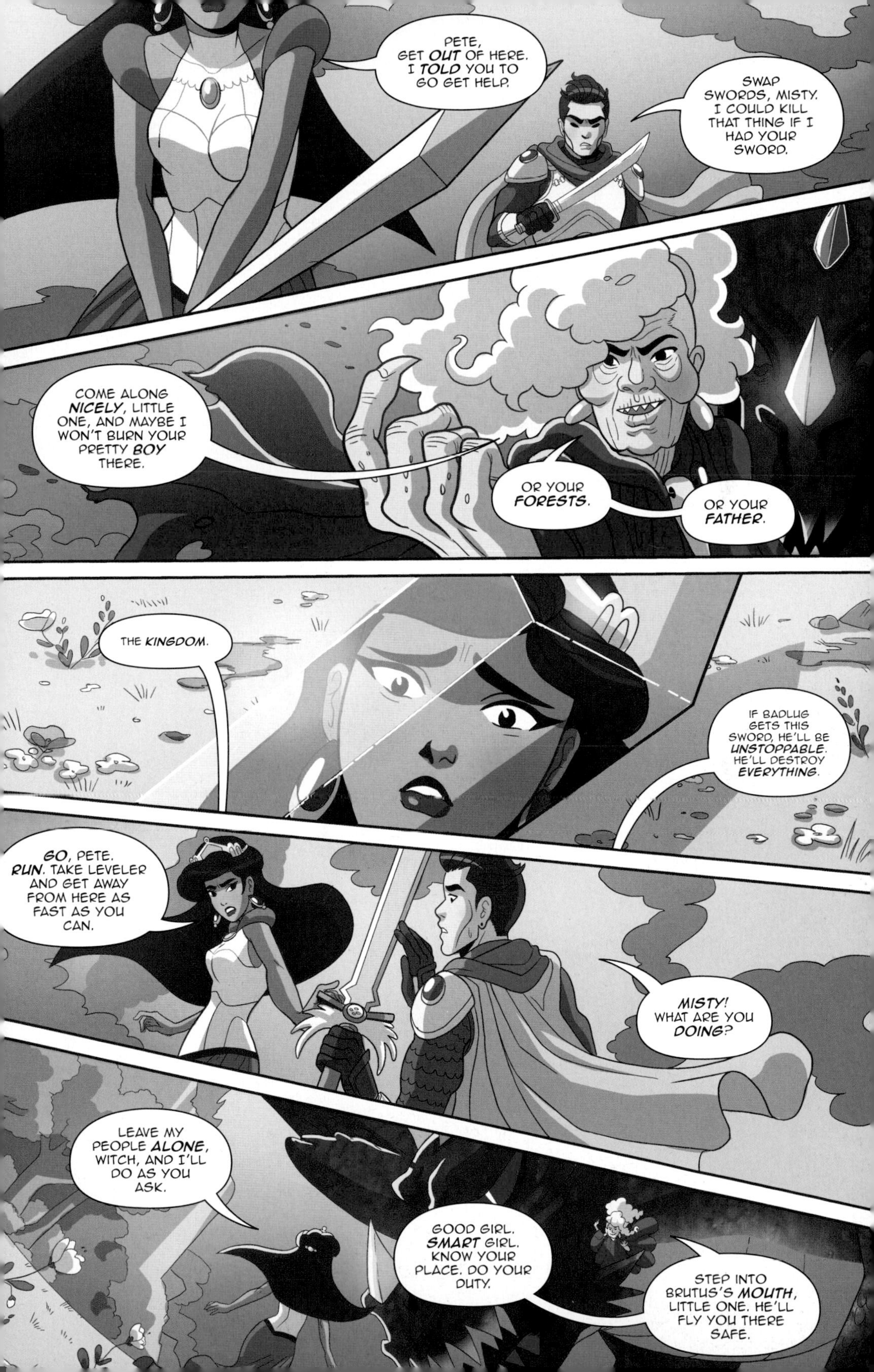
PETE, GET OUT OF HERE. I TOLD YOU TO GO GET HELP.
SWAP SWORDS, MISTY. I COULD KILL THAT THING IF I HAD YOUR SWORD.
COME ALONG NICELY, LITTLE ONE, AND MAYBE I WON'T BURN YOUR PRETTY BOY THERE.
OR YOUR FORESTS.
OR YOUR FATHER.
THE KINGDOM.
IF BADLUG GETS THIS SWORD, HE'LL BE UNSTOPPABLE. HE'LL DESTROY EVERYTHING.
GO, PETE. RUN. TAKE LEVELER AND GET AWAY FROM HERE AS FAST AS YOU CAN.
MISTY! WHAT ARE YOU DOING?
LEAVE MY PEOPLE ALONE, WITCH, AND I'LL DO AS YOU ASK.
GOOD GIRL. SMART GIRL. KNOW YOUR PLACE. DO YOUR DUTY.
STEP INTO BRUTUS'S MOUTH, LITTLE ONE. HE'LL FLY YOU THERE SAFE.

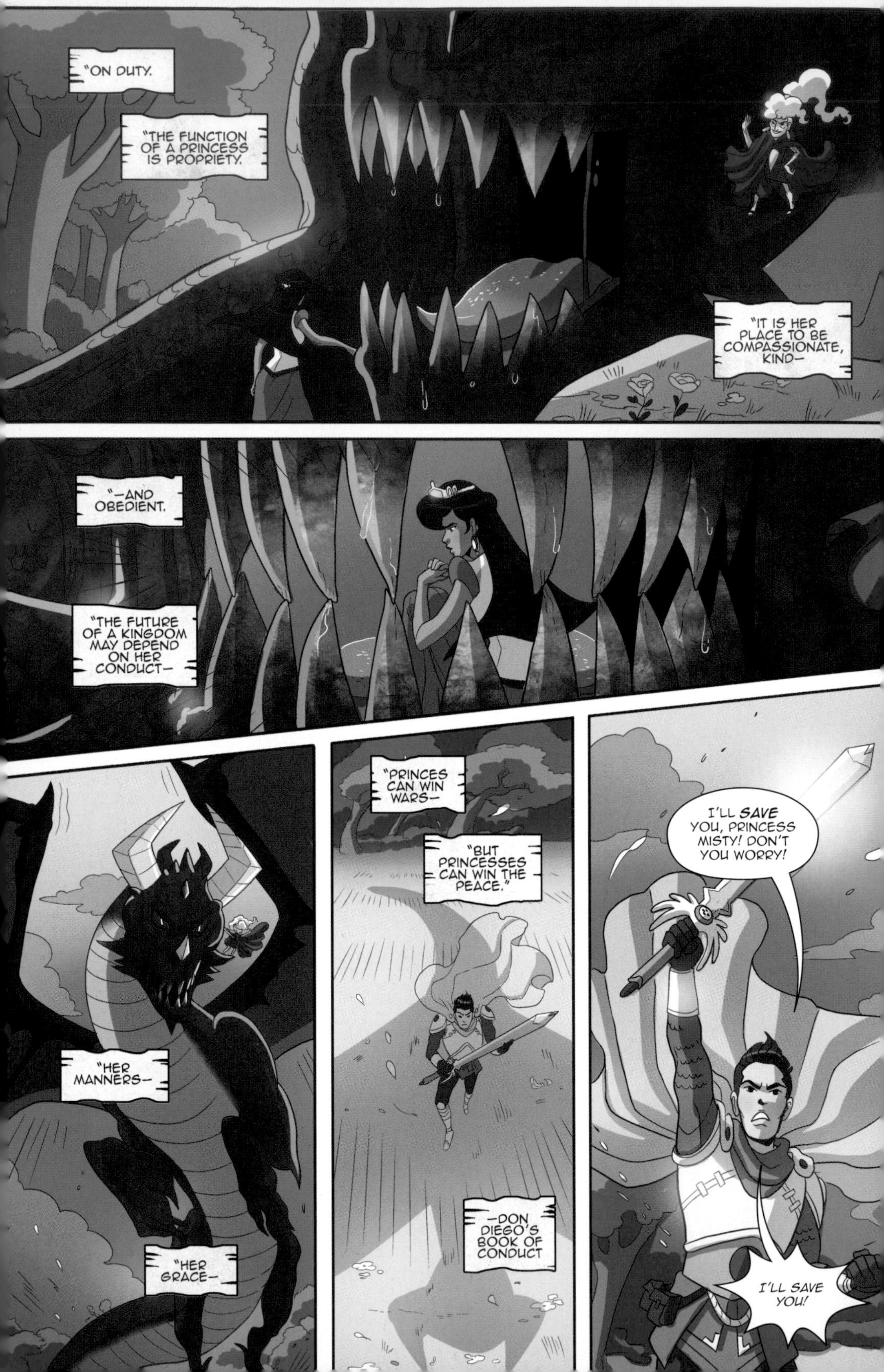
"ON DUTY.
"THE FUNCTION OF A PRINCESS IS PROPRIETY.
"IT IS HER PLACE TO BE COMPASSIONATE, KIND—
"—AND OBEDIENT.
"THE FUTURE OF A KINGDOM MAY DEPEND ON HER CONDUCT—
"HER MANNERS—
"HER GRACE—
"PRINCES CAN WIN WARS—
"BUT PRINCESSES CAN WIN THE PEACE."
—DON DIEGO'S BOOK OF CONDUCT
I'LL SAVE YOU, PRINCESS MISTY! DON'T YOU WORRY!
I'LL SAVE YOU!

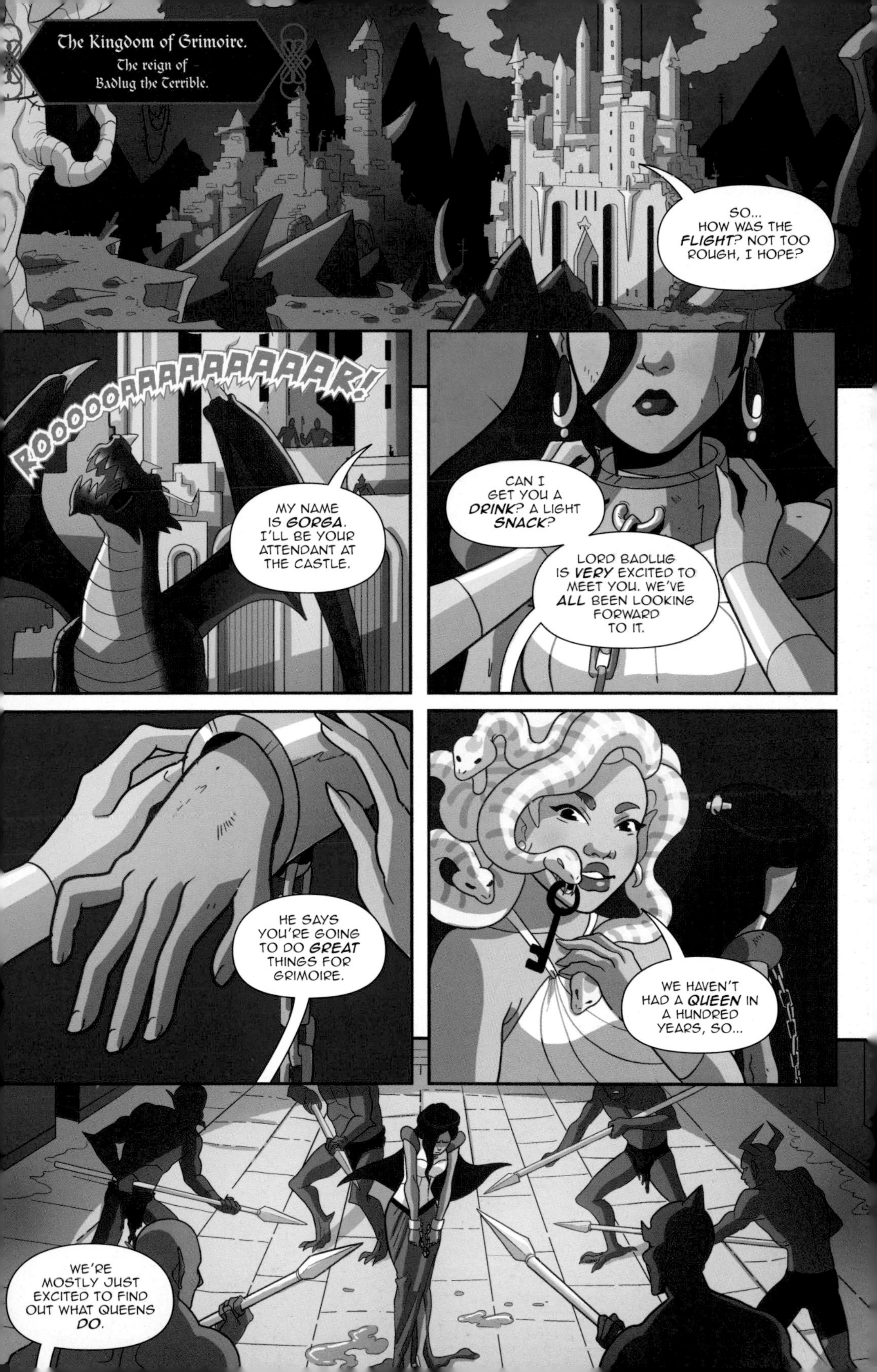
The Kingdom of Grimoire.
The reign of Badlug the Terrible.
SO... HOW WAS THE FLIGHT? NOT TOO ROUGH, I HOPE?
ROOOOOOAAAAAAAAAAAAR!
MY NAME IS GORGA. I'LL BE YOUR ATTENDANT AT THE CASTLE.
CAN I GET YOU A DRINK? A LIGHT SNACK?
LORD BADLUG IS VERY EXCITED TO MEET YOU. WE'VE ALL BEEN LOOKING FORWARD TO IT.
HE SAYS YOU'RE GOING TO DO GREAT THINGS FOR GRIMOIRE.
WE HAVEN'T HAD A QUEEN IN A HUNDRED YEARS, SO...
WE'RE MOSTLY JUST EXCITED TO FIND OUT WHAT QUEENS DO.

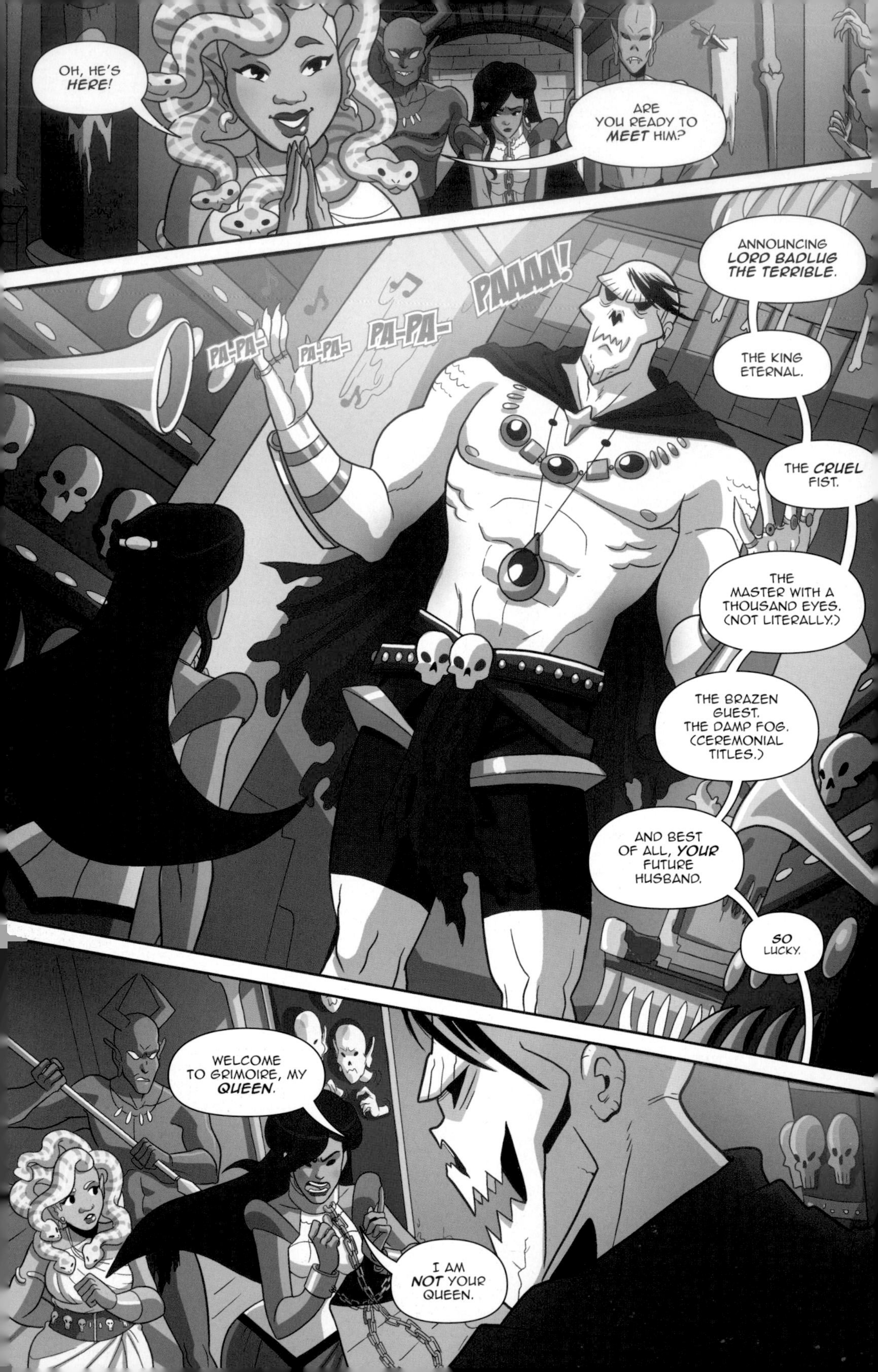
OH, HE'S HERE!
ARE YOU READY TO MEET HIM?
PA-PA-
PA-PA-
PA-PA-
PAAAA!
ANNOUNCING LORD BADLUG THE TERRIBLE.
THE KING ETERNAL.
THE CRUEL FIST.
THE MASTER WITH A THOUSAND EYES. (NOT LITERALLY.)
THE BRAZEN GUEST. THE DAMP FOG. (CEREMONIAL TITLES.)
AND BEST OF ALL, YOUR FUTURE HUSBAND.
SO LUCKY.
WELCOME TO GRIMOIRE, MY QUEEN.
I AM NOT YOUR QUEEN.

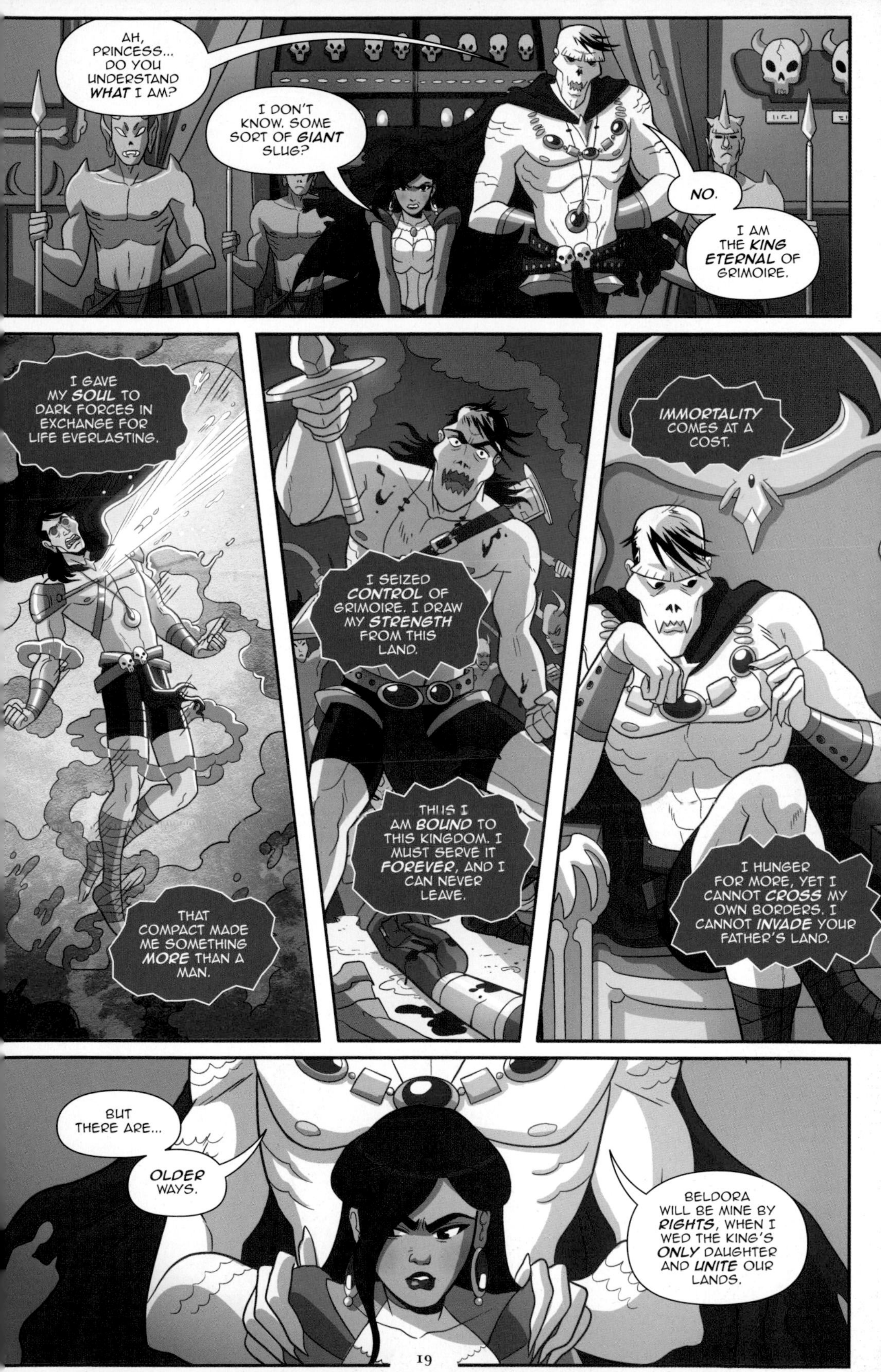

AH, PRINCESS... DO YOU UNDERSTAND WHAT I AM?
I DON'T KNOW. SOME SORT OF GIANT SLUG?
NO.
I AM THE KING ETERNAL OF GRIMOIRE.
I GAVE MY SOUL TO DARK FORCES IN EXCHANGE FOR LIFE EVERLASTING.
THAT COMPACT MADE ME SOMETHING MORE THAN A MAN.
I SEIZED CONTROL OF GRIMOIRE. I DRAW MY STRENGTH FROM THIS LAND.
THUS I AM BOUND TO THIS KINGDOM. I MUST SERVE IT FOREVER, AND I CAN NEVER LEAVE.
IMMORTALITY COMES AT A COST.
I HUNGER FOR MORE, YET I CANNOT CROSS MY OWN BORDERS. I CANNOT INVADE YOUR FATHER'S LAND.
BUT THERE ARE...
OLDER WAYS.
BELDORA WILL BE MINE BY RIGHTS, WHEN I WED THE KING'S ONLY DAUGHTER AND UNITE OUR LANDS.

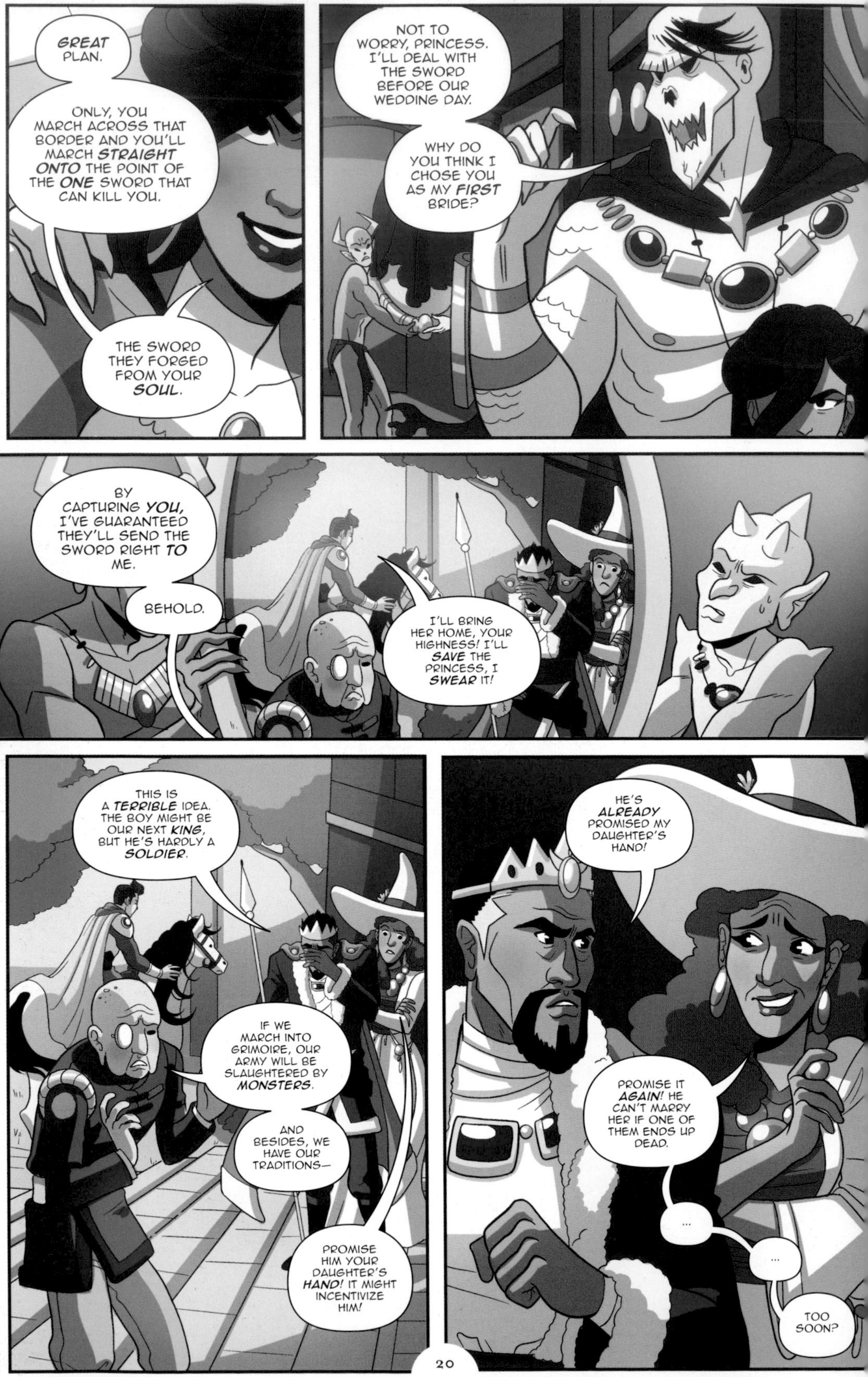
GREAT PLAN.
ONLY, YOU MARCH ACROSS THAT BORDER AND YOU'LL MARCH STRAIGHT ONTO THE POINT OF THE ONE SWORD THAT CAN KILL YOU.
THE SWORD THEY FORGED FROM YOUR SOUL.
NOT TO WORRY, PRINCESS. I'LL DEAL WITH THE SWORD BEFORE OUR WEDDING DAY.
WHY DO YOU THINK I CHOSE YOU AS MY FIRST BRIDE?
BY CAPTURING YOU, I'VE GUARANTEED THEY'LL SEND THE SWORD RIGHT TO ME.
BEHOLD.
I'LL BRING HER HOME, YOUR HIGHNESS! I'LL SAVE THE PRINCESS, I SWEAR IT!
THIS IS A TERRIBLE IDEA. THE BOY MIGHT BE OUR NEXT KING, BUT HE'S HARDLY A SOLDIER.
IF WE MARCH INTO GRIMOIRE, OUR ARMY WILL BE SLAUGHTERED BY MONSTERS.
AND BESIDES, WE HAVE OUR TRADITIONS—
PROMISE HIM YOUR DAUGHTER'S HAND! IT MIGHT INCENTIVIZE HIM!
HE'S ALREADY PROMISED MY DAUGHTER'S HAND!
PROMISE IT AGAIN! HE CAN'T MARRY HER IF ONE OF THEM ENDS UP DEAD.
...
...
TOO SOON?

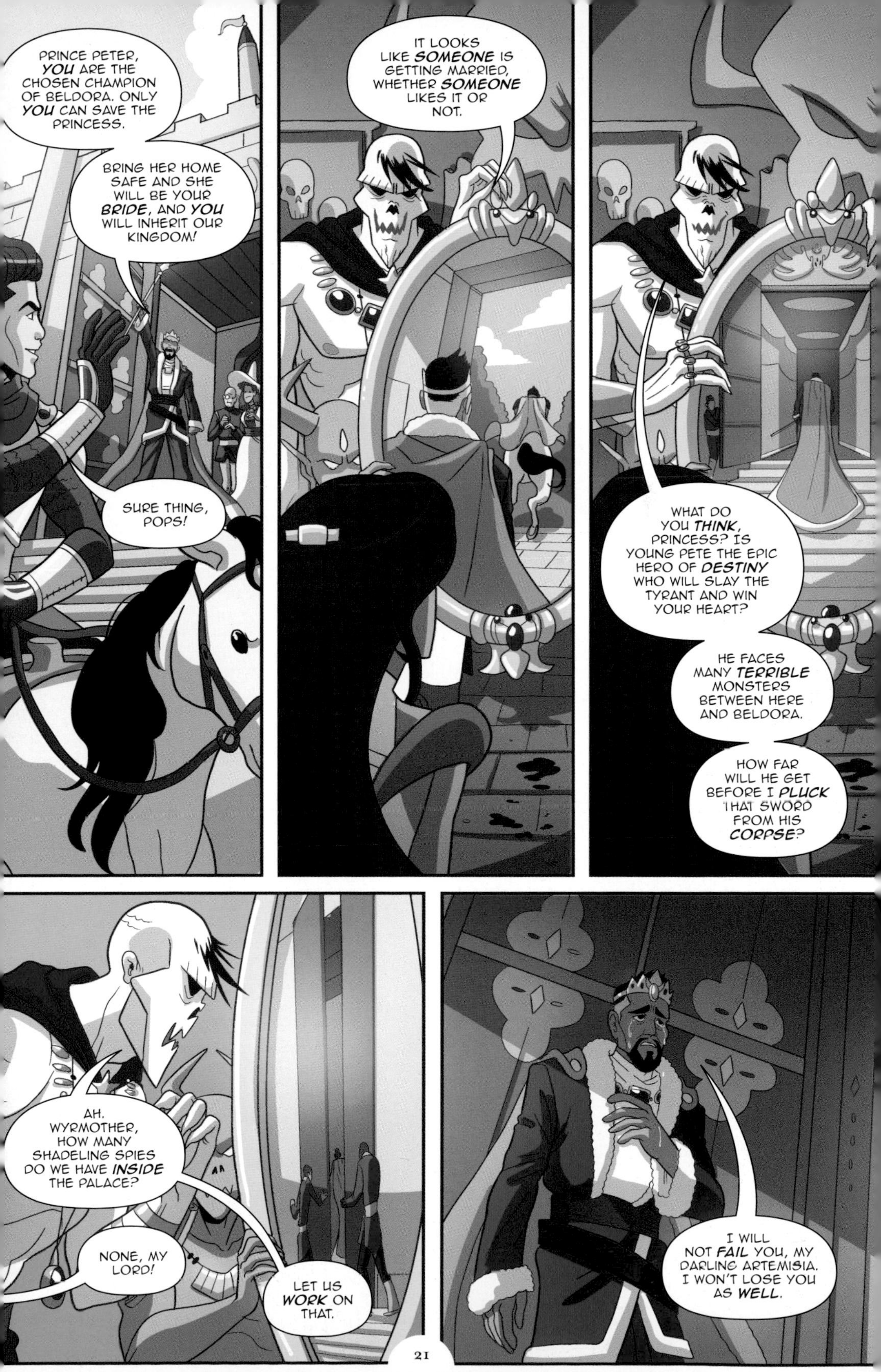
PRINCE PETER, YOU ARE THE CHOSEN CHAMPION OF BELDORA. ONLY YOU CAN SAVE THE PRINCESS.
BRING HER HOME SAFE AND SHE WILL BE YOUR BRIDE, AND YOU WILL INHERIT OUR KINGDOM!
SURE THING, POPS!
IT LOOKS LIKE SOMEONE IS GETTING MARRIED, WHETHER SOMEONE LIKES IT OR NOT.
WHAT DO YOU THINK, PRINCESS? IS YOUNG PETE THE EPIC HERO OF DESTINY WHO WILL SLAY THE TYRANT AND WIN YOUR HEART?
HE FACES MANY TERRIBLE MONSTERS BETWEEN HERE AND BELDORA.
HOW FAR WILL HE GET BEFORE I PLUCK THAT SWORD FROM HIS CORPSE?
AH. WYRMOTHER, HOW MANY SHADELING SPIES DO WE HAVE INSIDE THE PALACE?
NONE, MY LORD!
LET US WORK ON THAT.
I WILL NOT FAIL YOU, MY DARLING ARTEMISIA. I WON'T LOSE YOU AS WELL.

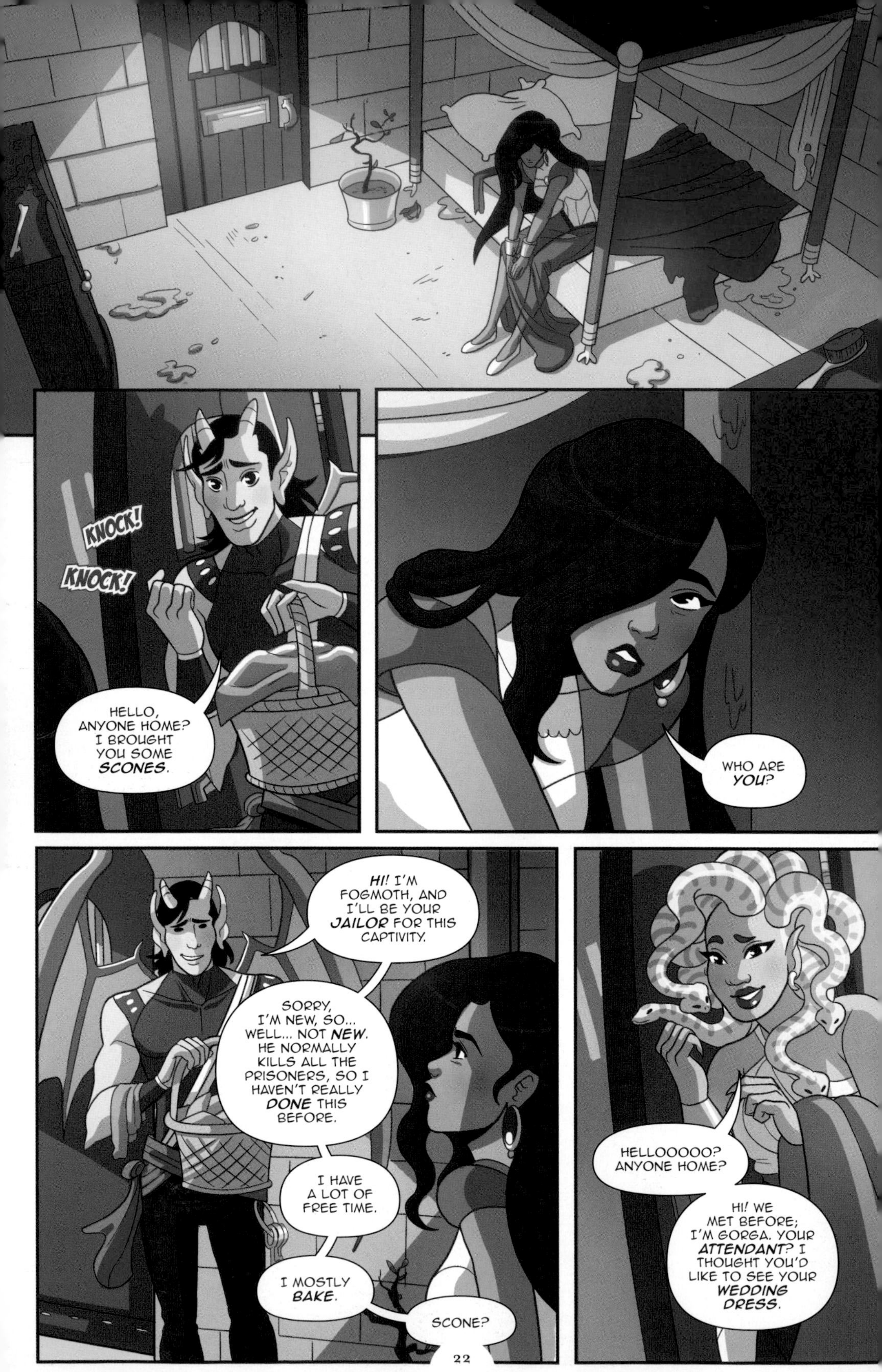
KNOCK!
KNOCK!
HELLO, ANYONE HOME? I BROUGHT YOU SOME SCONES.
WHO ARE YOU?
HI! I'M FOGMOTH, AND I'LL BE YOUR JAILOR FOR THIS CAPTIVITY.
SORRY, I'M NEW, SO... WELL... NOT NEW. HE NORMALLY KILLS ALL THE PRISONERS, SO I HAVEN'T REALLY DONE THIS BEFORE.
I HAVE A LOT OF FREE TIME.
I MOSTLY BAKE.
SCONE?
HELLOOOOO? ANYONE HOME?
HI! WE MET BEFORE; I'M GORGA. YOUR ATTENDANT? I THOUGHT YOU'D LIKE TO SEE YOUR WEDDING DRESS.

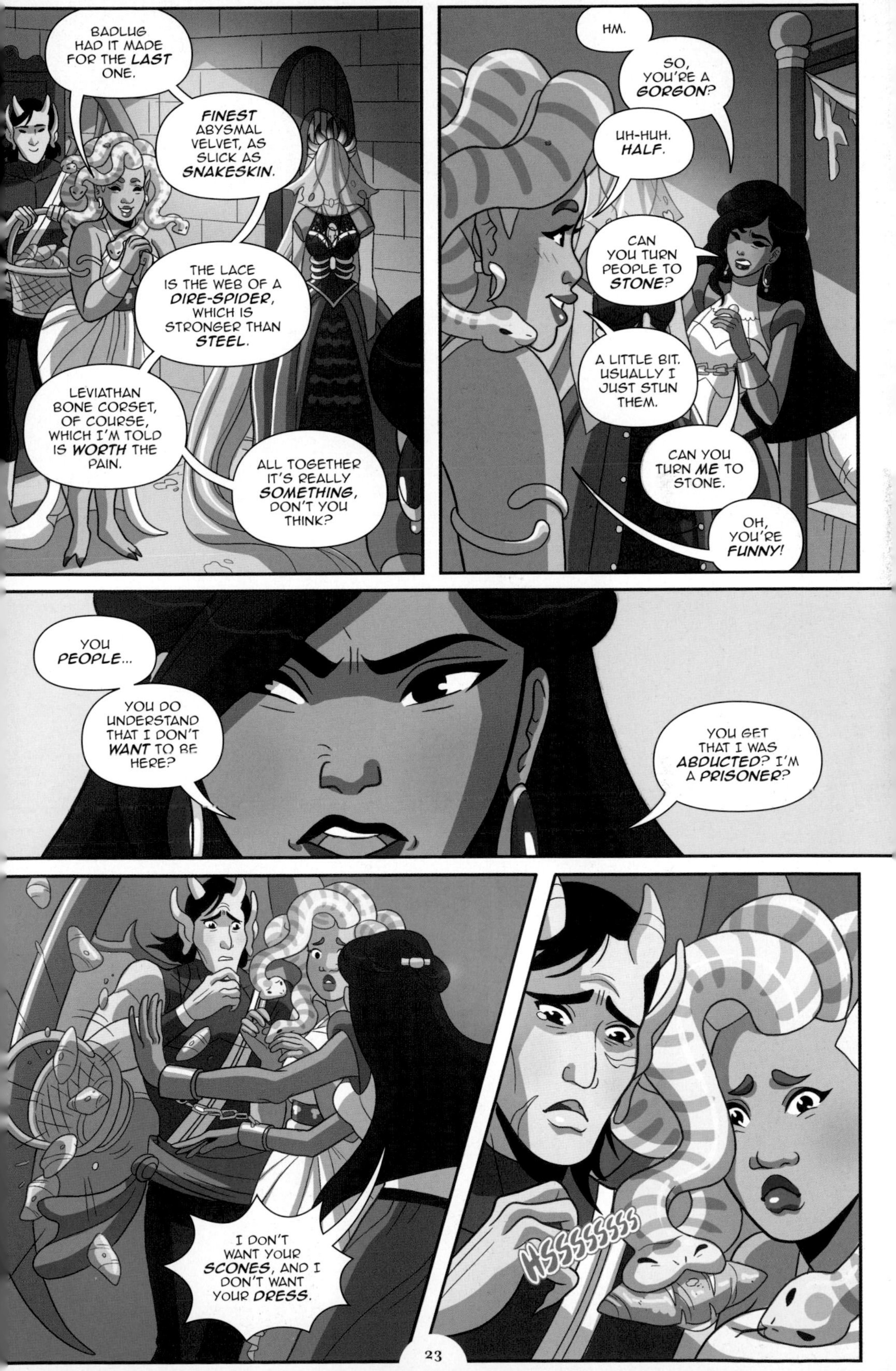
BADLUG HAD IT MADE FOR THE LAST ONE.
FINEST ABYSMAL VELVET, AS SLICK AS SNAKESKIN.
THE LACE IS THE WEB OF A DIRE-SPIDER, WHICH IS STRONGER THAN STEEL.
LEVIATHAN BONE CORSET, OF COURSE, WHICH I'M TOLD IS WORTH THE PAIN.
ALL TOGETHER IT'S REALLY SOMETHING, DON'T YOU THINK?
HM.
SO, YOU'RE A GORGON?
UH-HUH. HALF.
CAN YOU TURN PEOPLE TO STONE?
A LITTLE BIT. USUALLY I JUST STUN THEM.
CAN YOU TURN ME TO STONE.
OH, YOU'RE FUNNY!
YOU PEOPLE...
YOU DO UNDERSTAND THAT I DON'T WANT TO BE HERE?
YOU GET THAT I WAS ABDUCTED? I'M A PRISONER?
I DON'T WANT YOUR SCONES, AND I DON'T WANT YOUR DRESS.
HSSSSSSSS

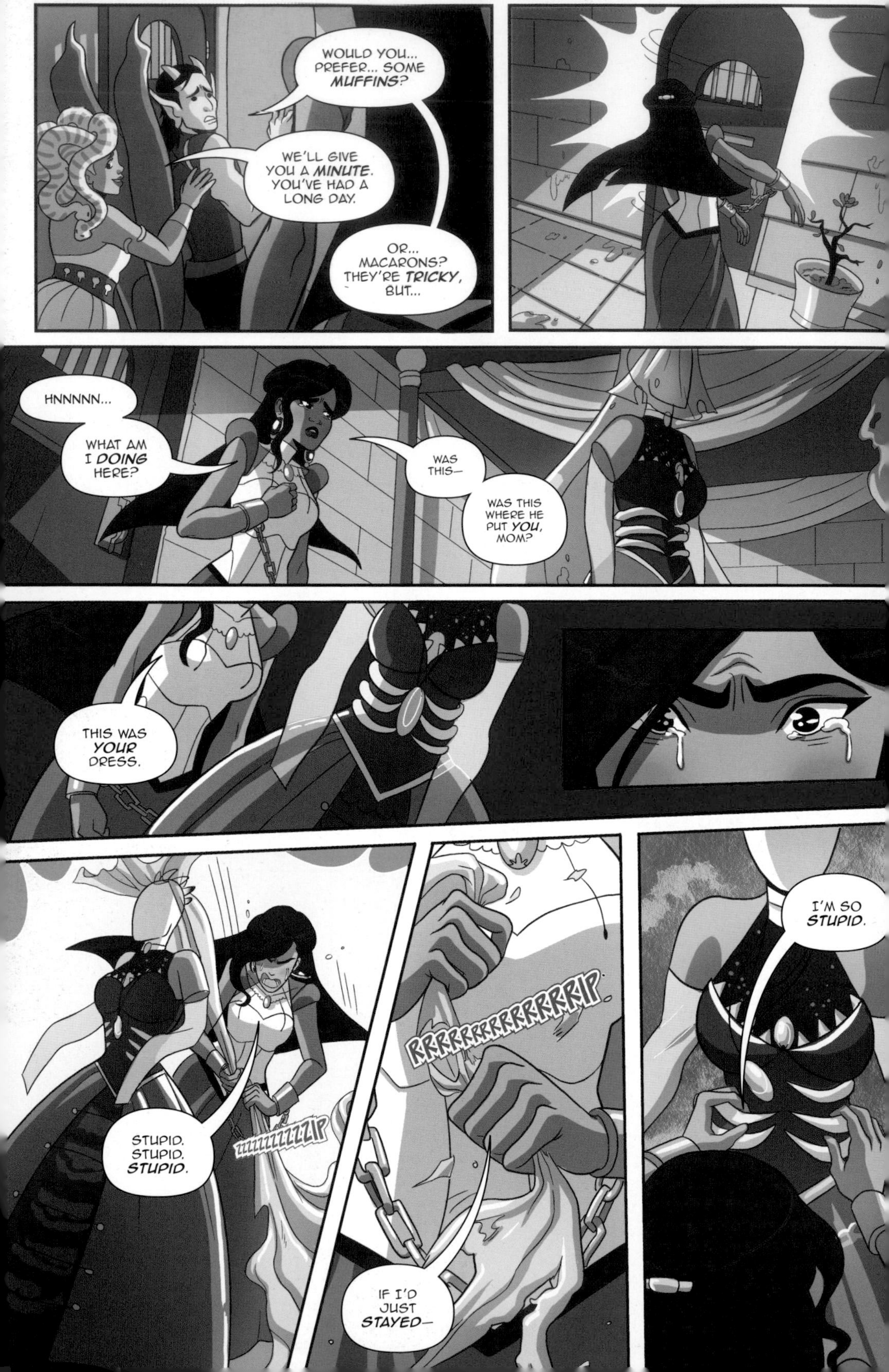
WOULD YOU... PREFER... SOME MUFFINS?
WE'LL GIVE YOU A MINUTE. YOU'VE HAD A LONG DAY.
OR... MACARONS? THEY'RE TRICKY, BUT...
HNNNNN...
WHAT AM I DOING HERE?
WAS THIS—
WAS THIS WHERE HE PUT YOU, MOM?
THIS WAS YOUR DRESS.
STUPID. STUPID. STUPID.
ZZZZZZZZZZZIP
RRRRRRRRRRRRRRIP
IF I'D JUST STAYED—
I'M SO STUPID.

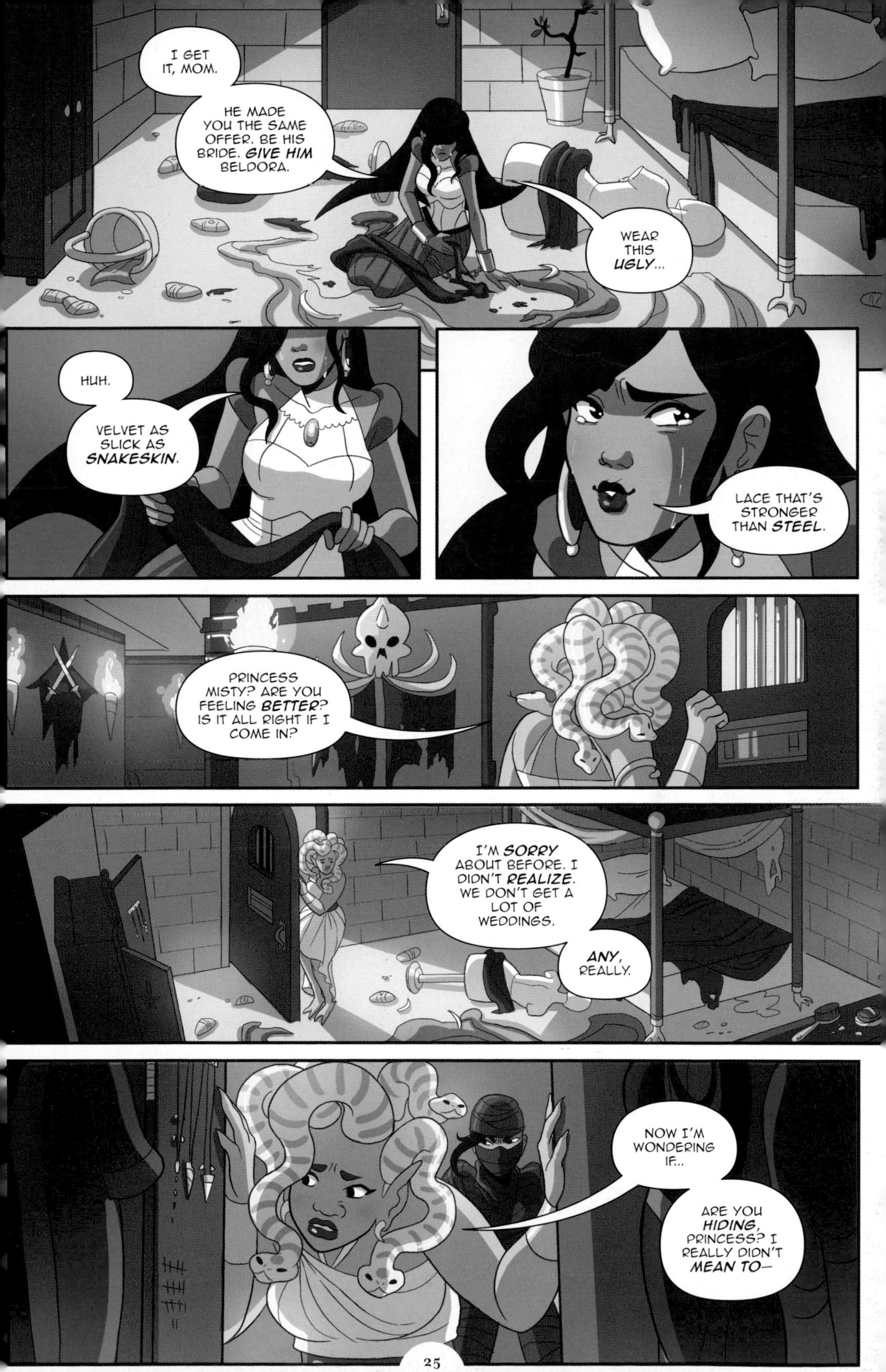
I GET IT, MOM.
HE MADE YOU THE SAME OFFER. BE HIS BRIDE. GIVE HIM BELDORA.
WEAR THIS UGLY...
HUH.
VELVET AS SLICK AS SNAKESKIN.
LACE THAT'S STRONGER THAN STEEL.
PRINCESS MISTY? ARE YOU FEELING BETTER? IS IT ALL RIGHT IF I COME IN?
I'M SORRY ABOUT BEFORE. I DIDN'T REALIZE. WE DON'T GET A LOT OF WEDDINGS.
ANY, REALLY.
NOW I'M WONDERING IF...
ARE YOU HIDING, PRINCESS? I REALLY DIDN'T MEAN TO—

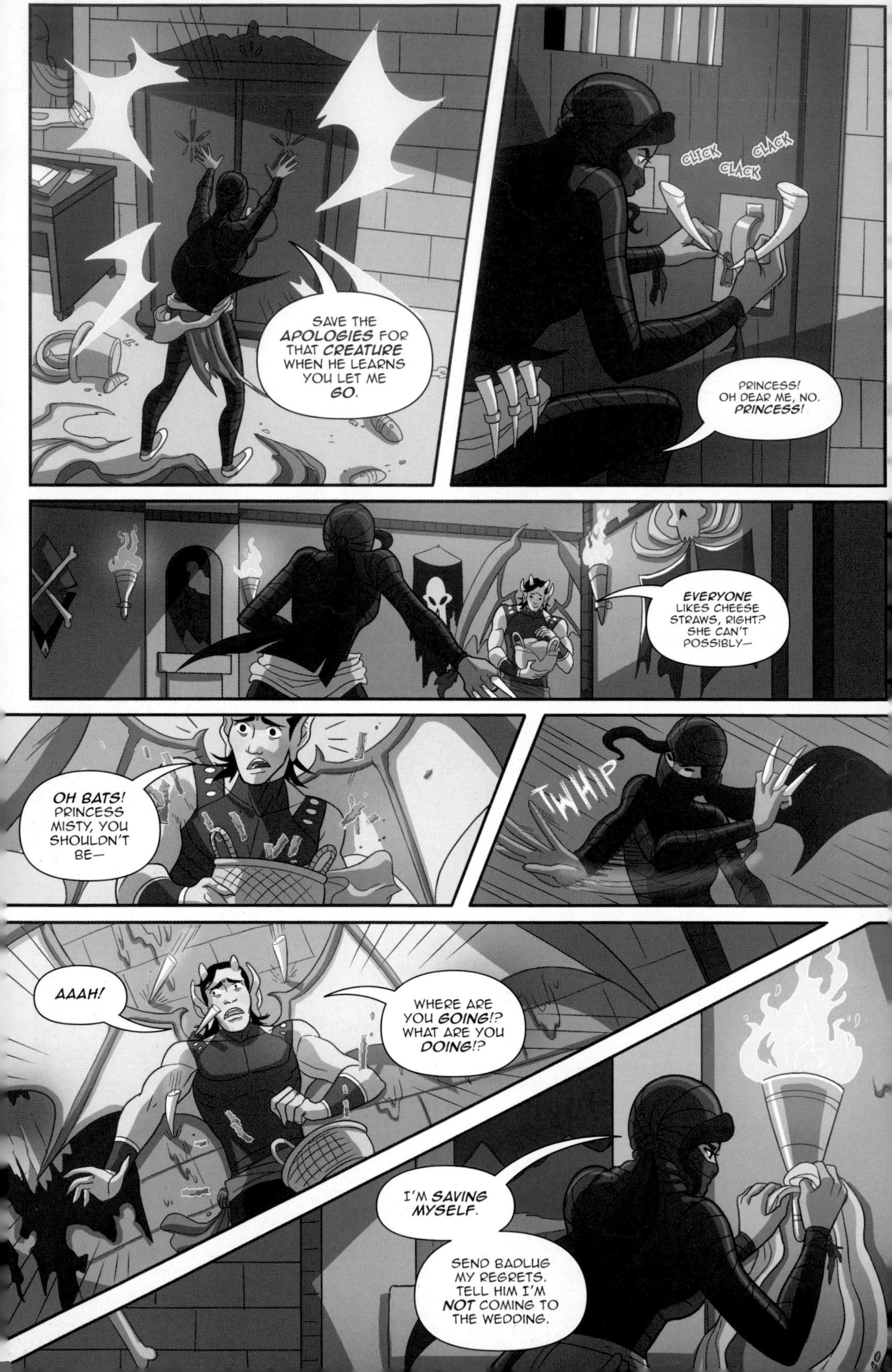
SAVE THE APOLOGIES FOR THAT CREATURE WHEN HE LEARNS YOU LET ME GO.
CLICK CLACK CLACK
PRINCESS! OH DEAR ME, NO. PRINCESS!
EVERYONE LIKES CHEESE STRAWS, RIGHT? SHE CAN'T POSSIBLY—
OH BATS! PRINCESS MISTY, YOU SHOULDN'T BE—
TWHIP
AAAH!
WHERE ARE YOU GOING!? WHAT ARE YOU DOING!?
I'M SAVING MYSELF.
SEND BADLUG MY REGRETS. TELL HIM I'M NOT COMING TO THE WEDDING.

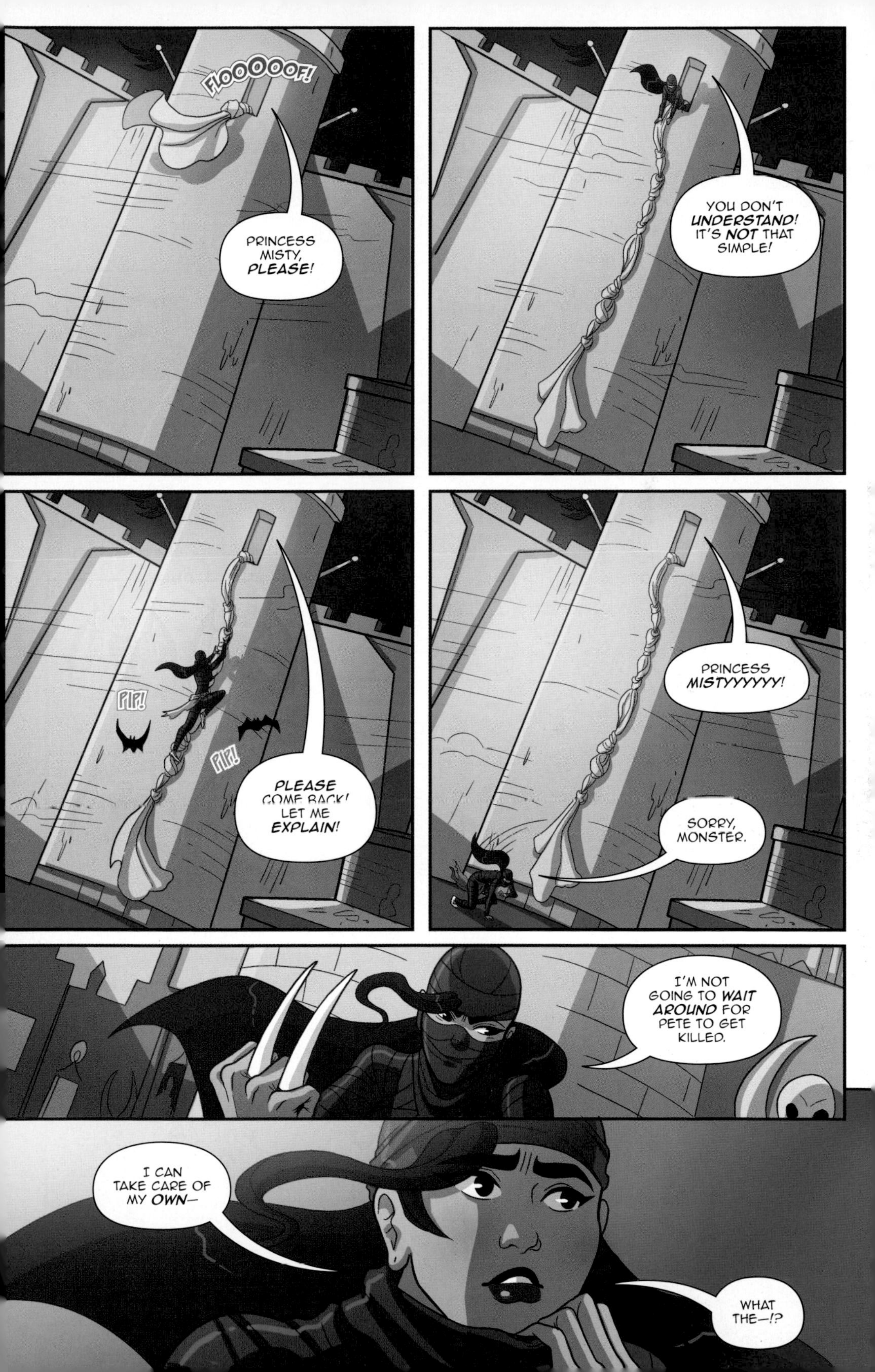
FLOOOOOF!
PRINCESS MISTY, PLEASE!
YOU DON'T UNDERSTAND! IT'S NOT THAT SIMPLE!
PIP!
PIP!
PLEASE COME BACK! LET ME EXPLAIN!
PRINCESS MISTYYYYYYY!
SORRY, MONSTER.
I'M NOT GOING TO WAIT AROUND FOR PETE TO GET KILLED.
I CAN TAKE CARE OF MY OWN—
WHAT THE—!?

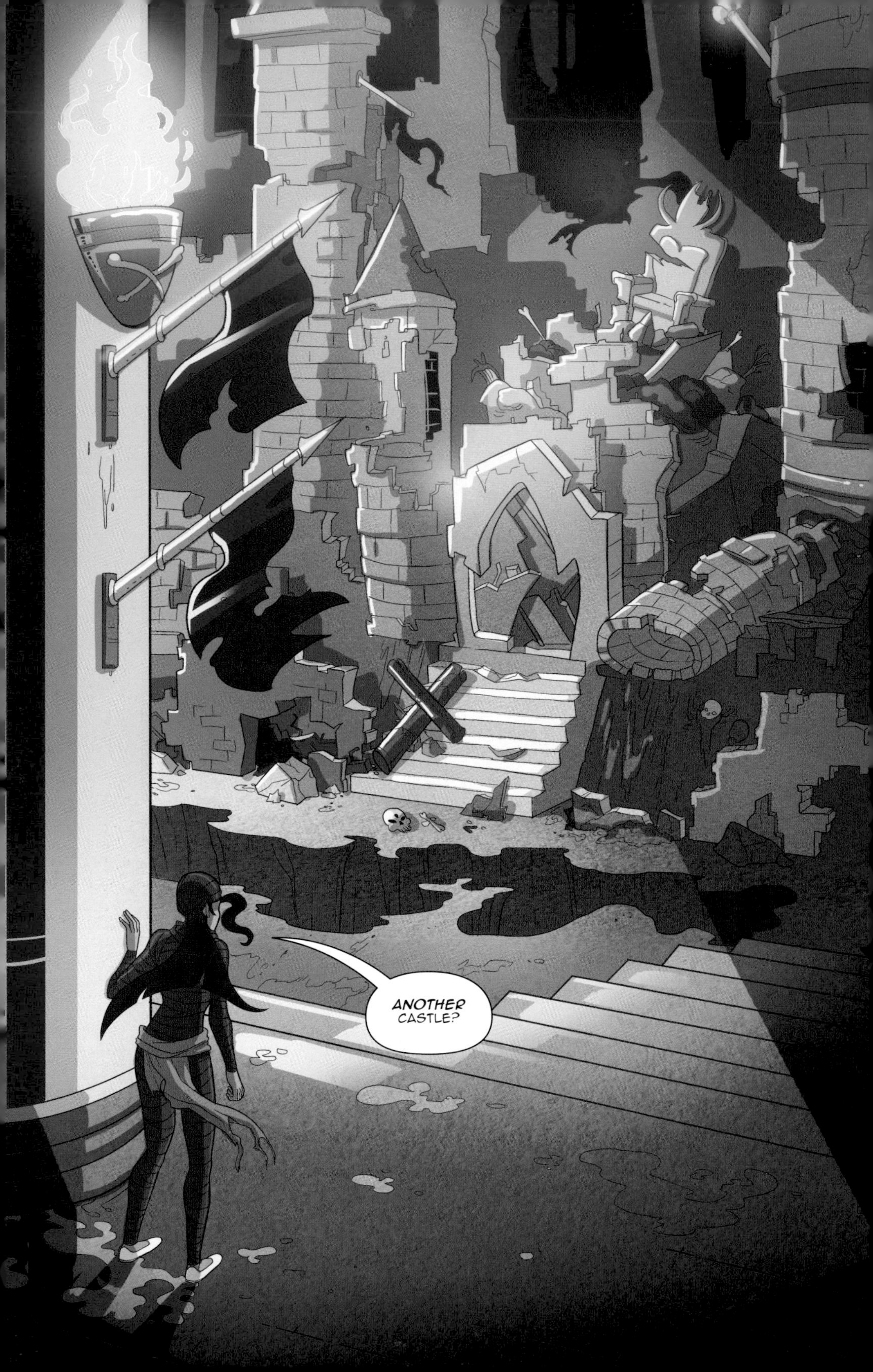
ANOTHER CASTLE?

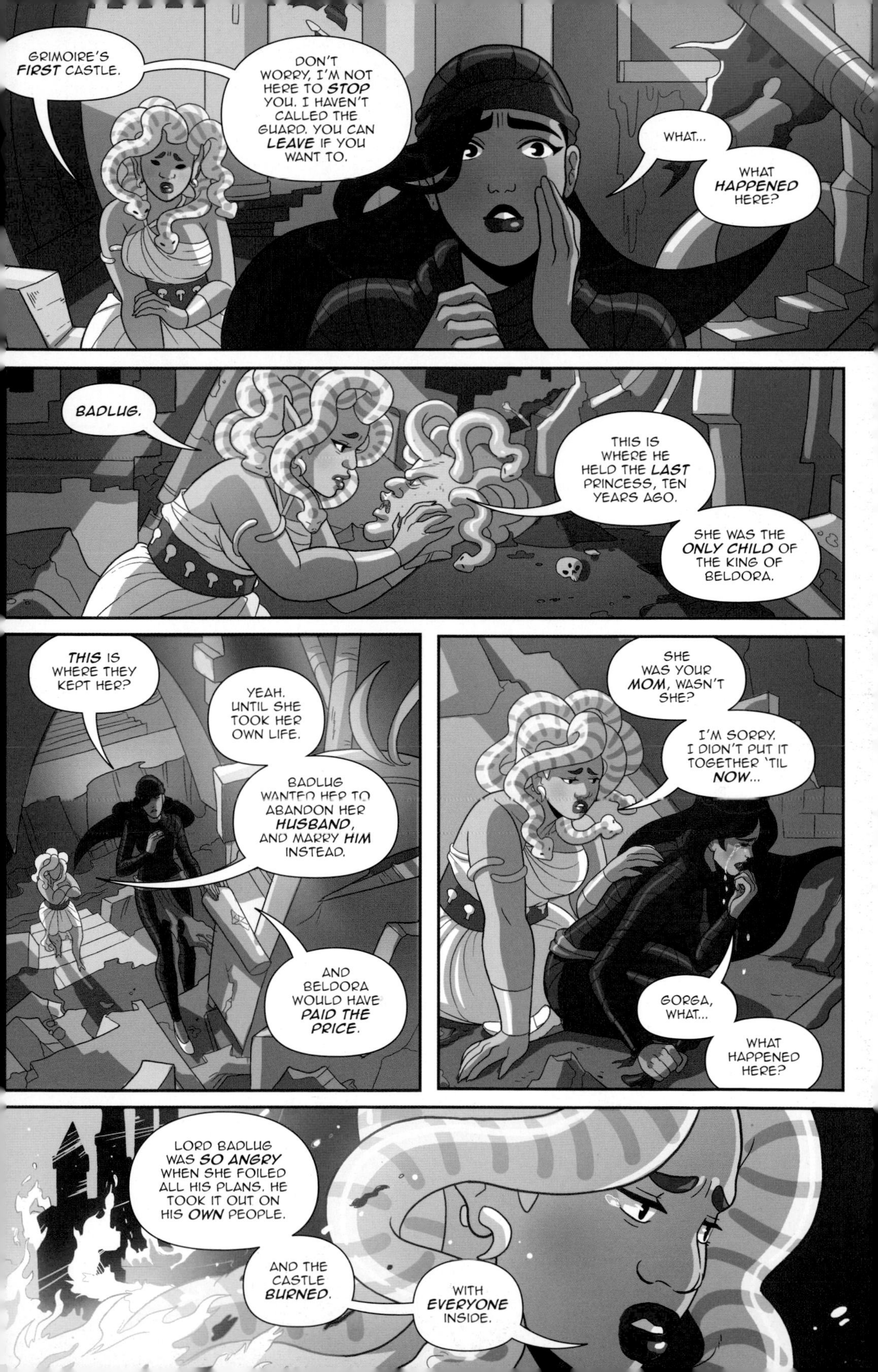
GRIMOIRE'S FIRST CASTLE.
DON'T WORRY, I'M NOT HERE TO STOP YOU. I HAVEN'T CALLED THE GUARD. YOU CAN LEAVE IF YOU WANT TO.
WHAT...
WHAT HAPPENED HERE?
BADLUG.
THIS IS WHERE HE HELD THE LAST PRINCESS, TEN YEARS AGO.
SHE WAS THE ONLY CHILD OF THE KING OF BELDORA.
THIS IS WHERE THEY KEPT HER?
YEAH. UNTIL SHE TOOK HER OWN LIFE.
BADLUG WANTED HER TO ABANDON HER HUSBAND, AND MARRY HIM INSTEAD.
AND BELDORA WOULD HAVE PAID THE PRICE.
SHE WAS YOUR MOM, WASN'T SHE?
I'M SORRY. I DIDN'T PUT IT TOGETHER 'TIL NOW...
GORGA, WHAT...
WHAT HAPPENED HERE?
LORD BADLUG WAS SO ANGRY WHEN SHE FOILED ALL HIS PLANS. HE TOOK IT OUT ON HIS OWN PEOPLE.
AND THE CASTLE BURNED.
WITH EVERYONE INSIDE.

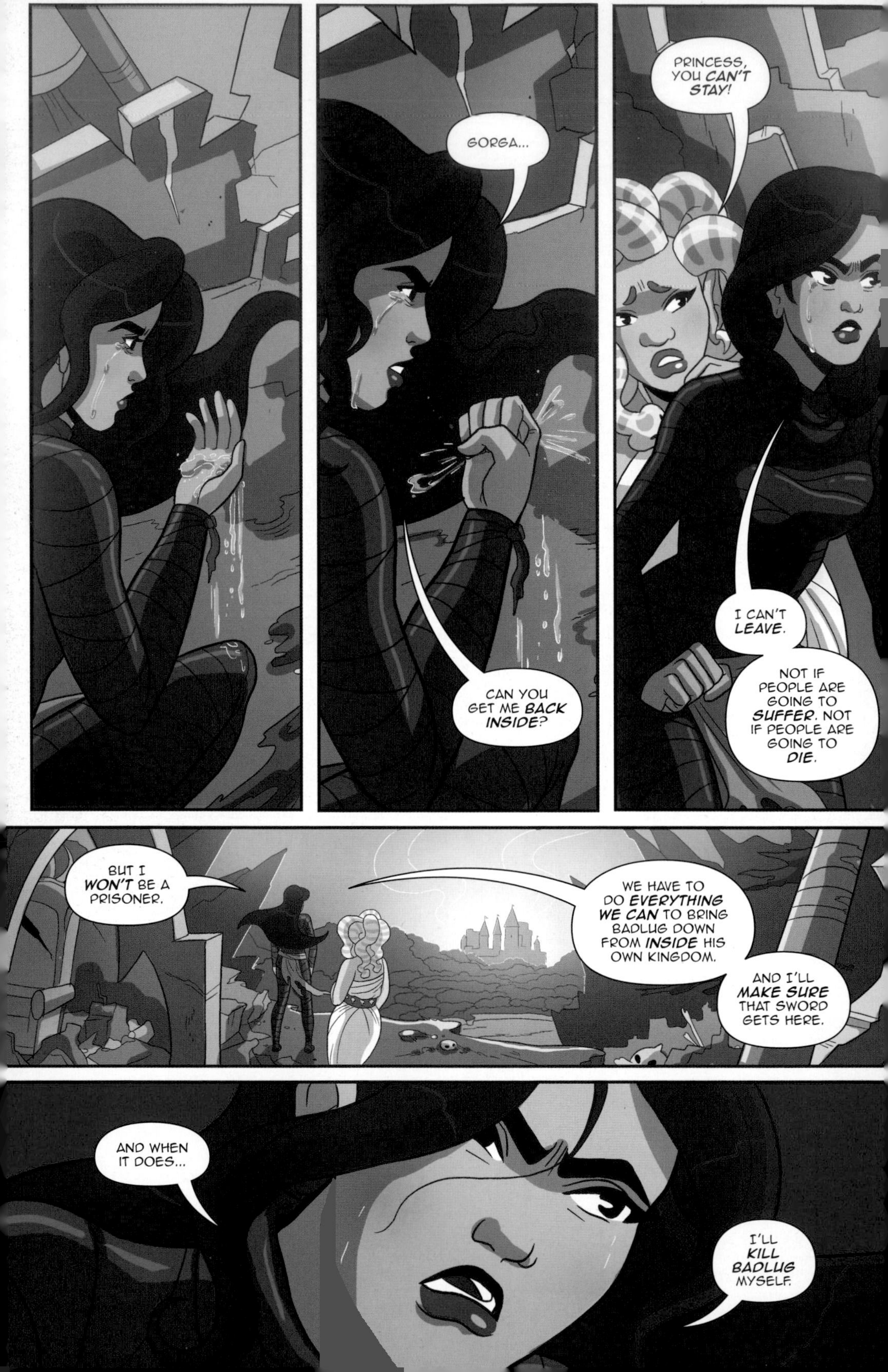
GORGA...
CAN YOU GET ME BACK INSIDE?
PRINCESS, YOU CAN'T STAY!
I CAN'T LEAVE.
NOT IF PEOPLE ARE GOING TO SUFFER. NOT IF PEOPLE ARE GOING TO DIE.
BUT I WON'T BE A PRISONER.
WE HAVE TO DO EVERYTHING WE CAN TO BRING BADLUG DOWN FROM INSIDE HIS OWN KINGDOM.
AND I'LL MAKE SURE THAT SWORD GETS HERE.
AND WHEN IT DOES...
I'LL KILL BADLUG MYSELF.

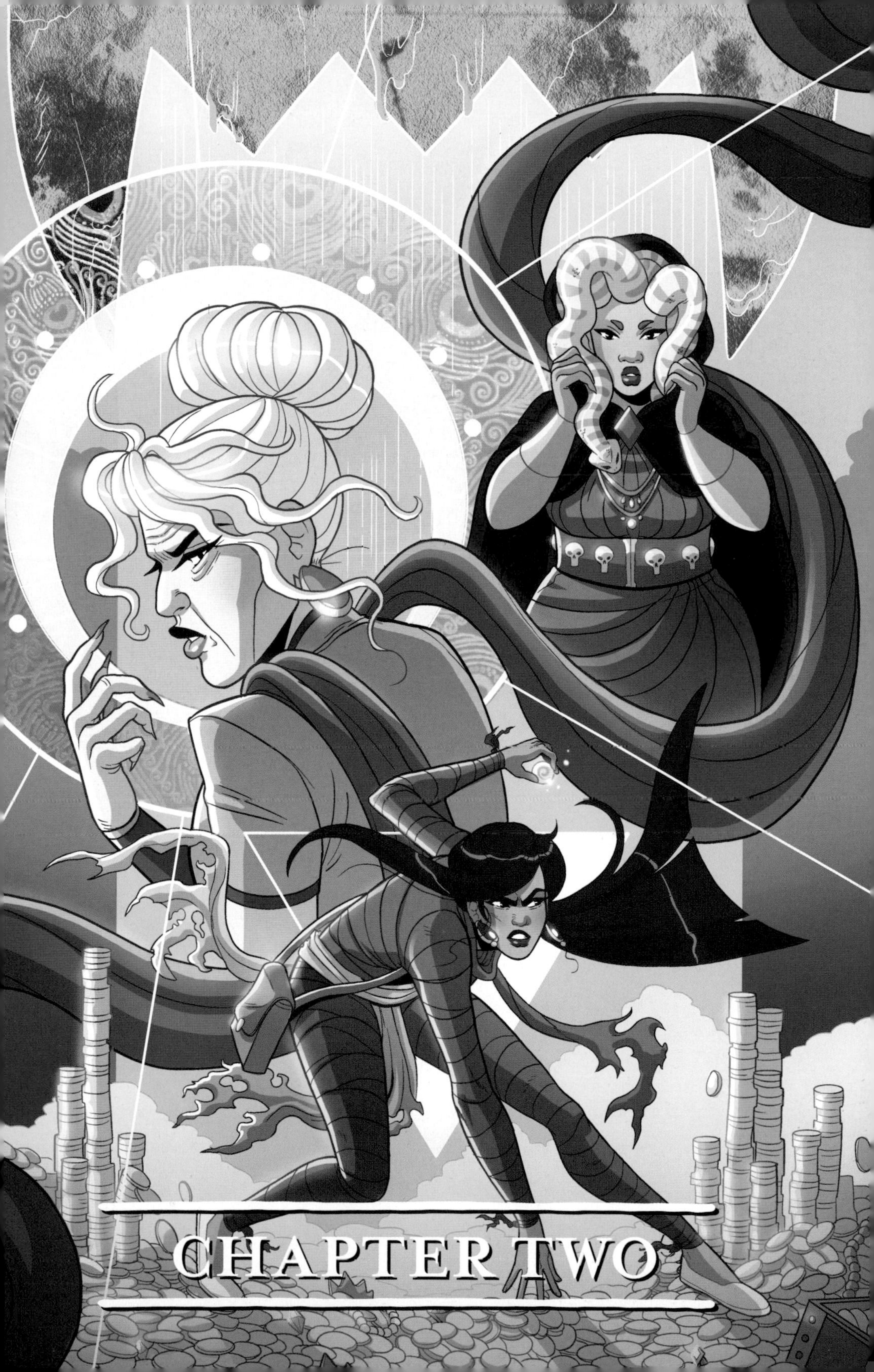
CHAPTER TWO

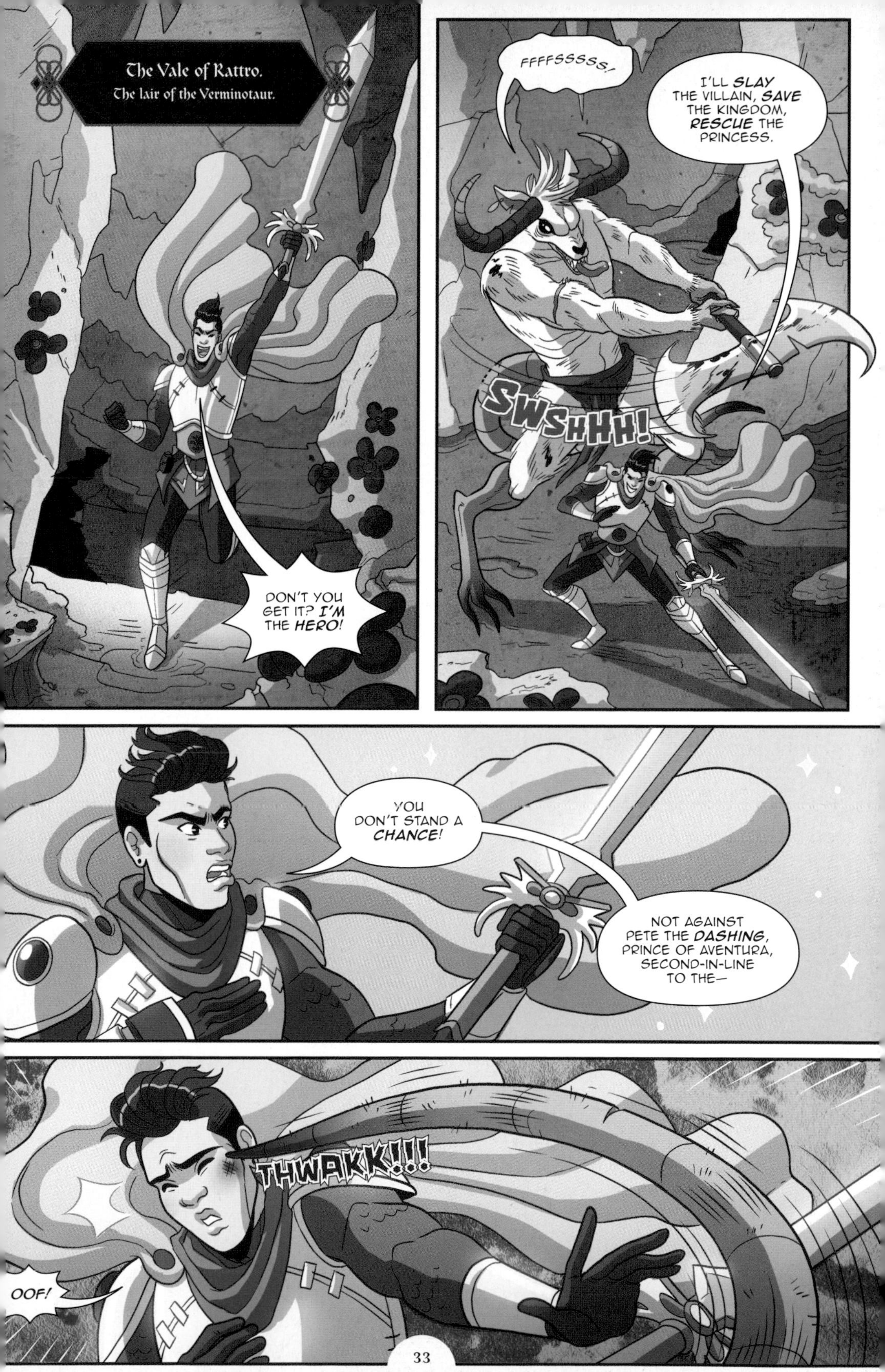
The Vale of Rattro.
The lair of the Verminotaur.
DON'T YOU GET IT? I'M THE HERO!
FFFFSSSSS!
I'LL SLAY THE VILLAIN, SAVE THE KINGDOM, RESCUE THE PRINCESS.
SWSHHH!
YOU DON'T STAND A CHANCE!
NOT AGAINST PETE THE DASHING, PRINCE OF AVENTURA, SECOND-IN-LINE TO THE—
THWAKK!!!
OOF!

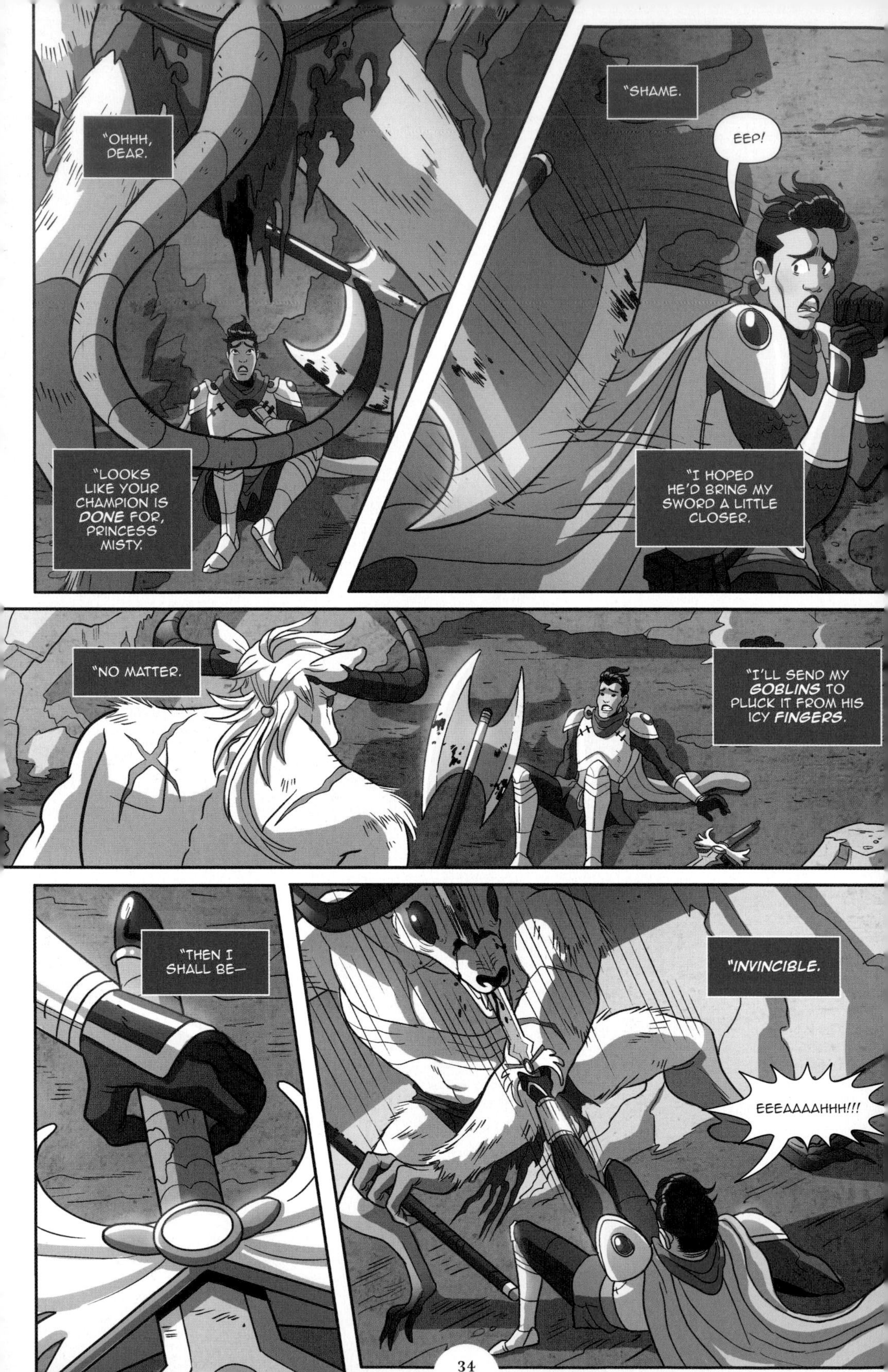
"OHHH, DEAR.
"LOOKS LIKE YOUR CHAMPION IS DONE FOR, PRINCESS MISTY.
"SHAME.
EEP!
"I HOPED HE'D BRING MY SWORD A LITTLE CLOSER.
"NO MATTER.
"I'LL SEND MY GOBLINS TO PLUCK IT FROM HIS ICY FINGERS.
"THEN I SHALL BE—
"INVINCIBLE.
EEEAAAAHHH!!!

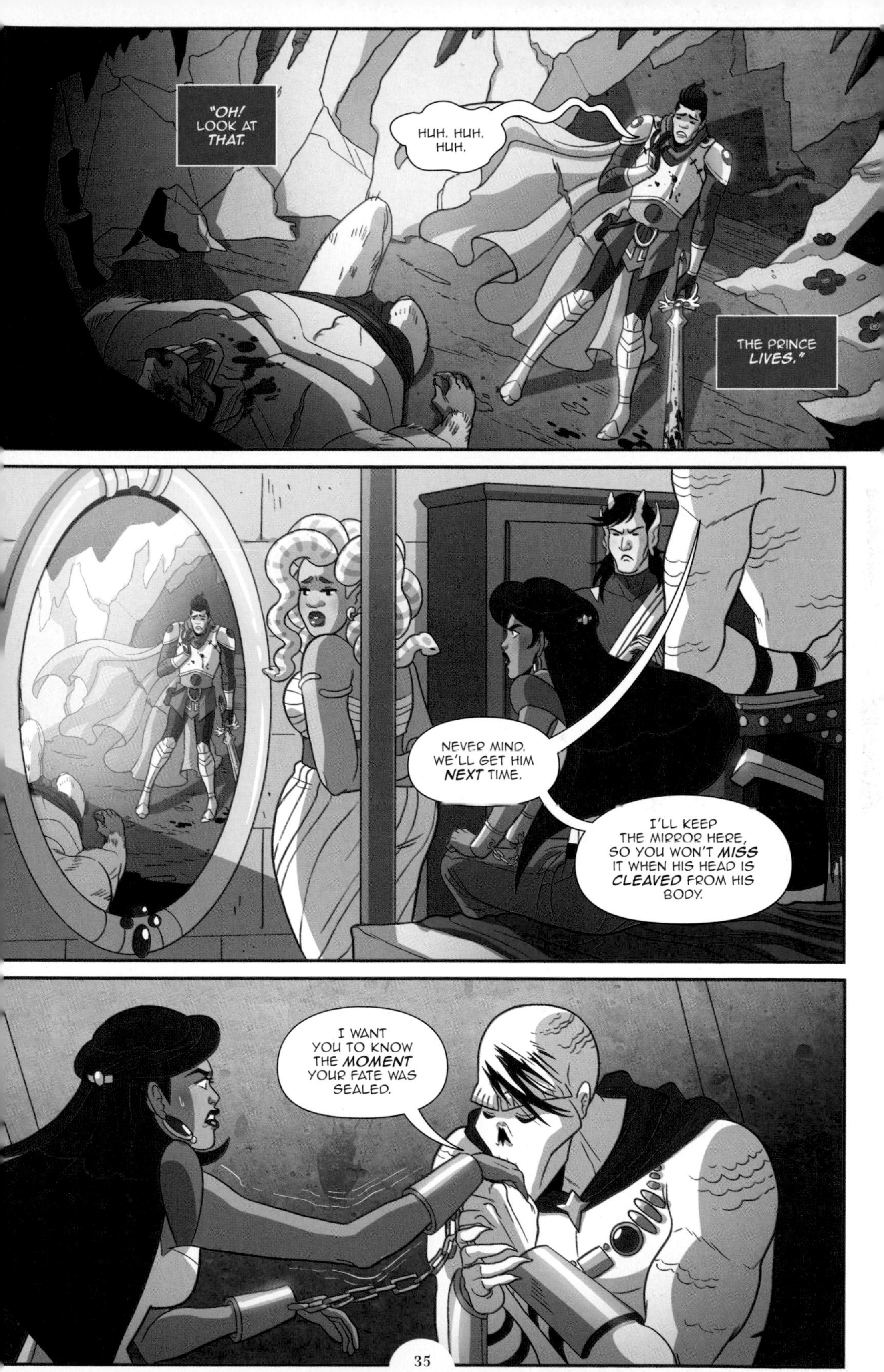
"OH! LOOK AT THAT.
HUH. HUH. HUH.
THE PRINCE LIVES."
NEVER MIND. WE'LL GET HIM NEXT TIME.
I'LL KEEP THE MIRROR HERE, SO YOU WON'T MISS IT WHEN HIS HEAD IS CLEAVED FROM HIS BODY.
I WANT YOU TO KNOW THE MOMENT YOUR FATE WAS SEALED.

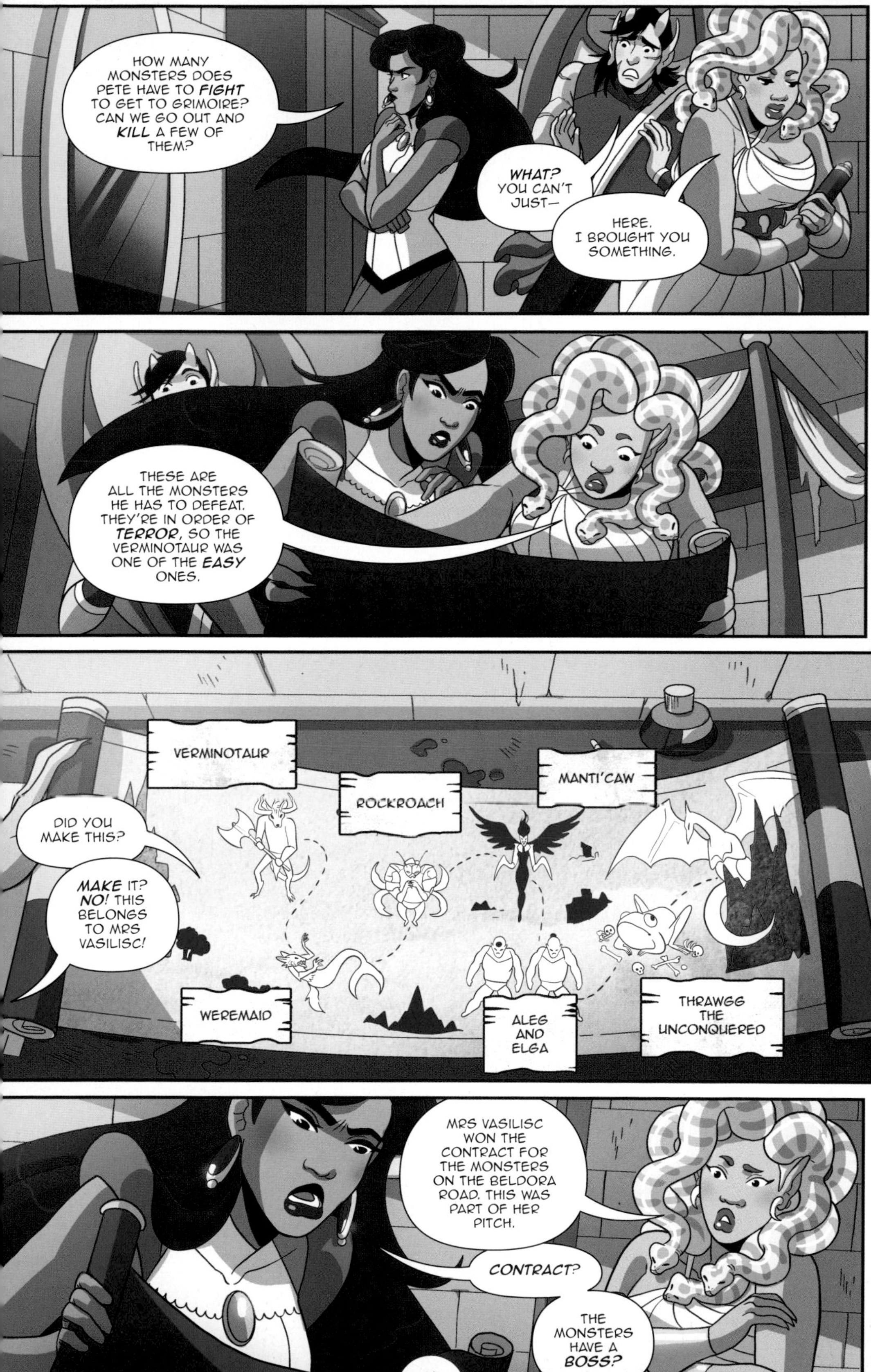

HOW MANY MONSTERS DOES PETE HAVE TO *FIGHT* TO GET TO GRIMOIRE? CAN WE GO OUT AND *KILL* A FEW OF THEM?
WHAT? YOU CAN'T JUST—
HERE. I BROUGHT YOU SOMETHING.
THESE ARE ALL THE MONSTERS HE HAS TO DEFEAT. THEY'RE IN ORDER OF *TERROR*, SO THE VERMINOTAUR WAS ONE OF THE *EASY* ONES.
VERMINOTAUR
ROCKROACH
MANTI'CAW
DID YOU MAKE THIS?
MAKE IT? *NO!* THIS BELONGS TO MRS VASILISC!
WEREMAID
ALEG AND ELGA
THRAWGG THE UNCONQUERED
MRS VASILISC WON THE CONTRACT FOR THE MONSTERS ON THE BELDORA ROAD. THIS WAS PART OF HER PITCH.
CONTRACT?
THE MONSTERS HAVE A *BOSS?*

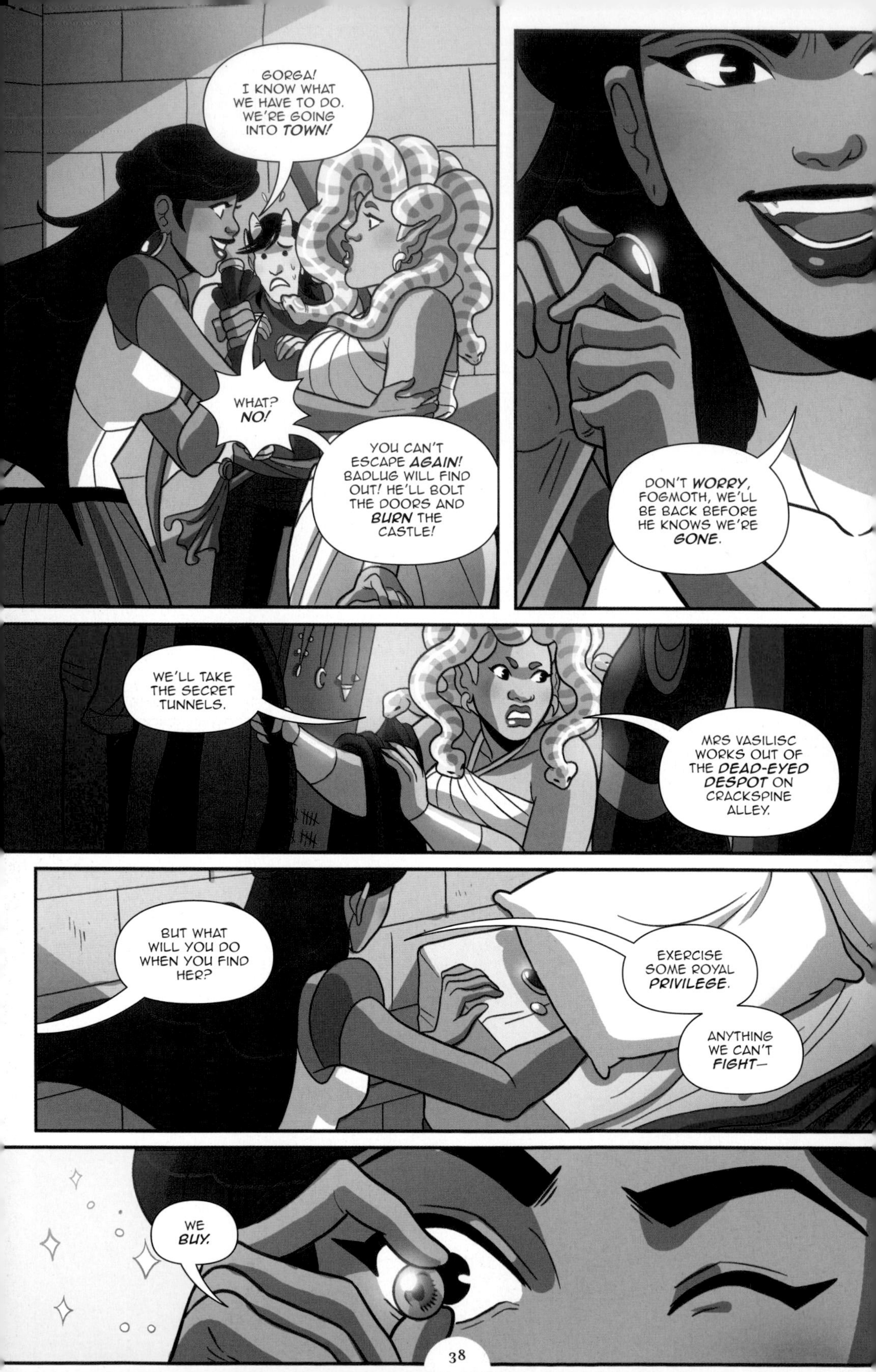
GORGA! I KNOW WHAT WE HAVE TO DO. WE'RE GOING INTO *TOWN!*
WHAT? *NO!*
YOU CAN'T ESCAPE *AGAIN!* BADLUG WILL FIND OUT! HE'LL BOLT THE DOORS AND *BURN* THE CASTLE!
DON'T *WORRY*, FOGMOTH, WE'LL BE BACK BEFORE HE KNOWS WE'RE *GONE*.
WE'LL TAKE THE SECRET TUNNELS.
MRS VASILISC WORKS OUT OF THE *DEAD-EYED DESPOT* ON CRACKSPINE ALLEY.
BUT WHAT WILL YOU DO WHEN YOU FIND HER?
EXERCISE SOME ROYAL *PRIVILEGE*.
ANYTHING WE CAN'T *FIGHT*—
WE *BUY.*

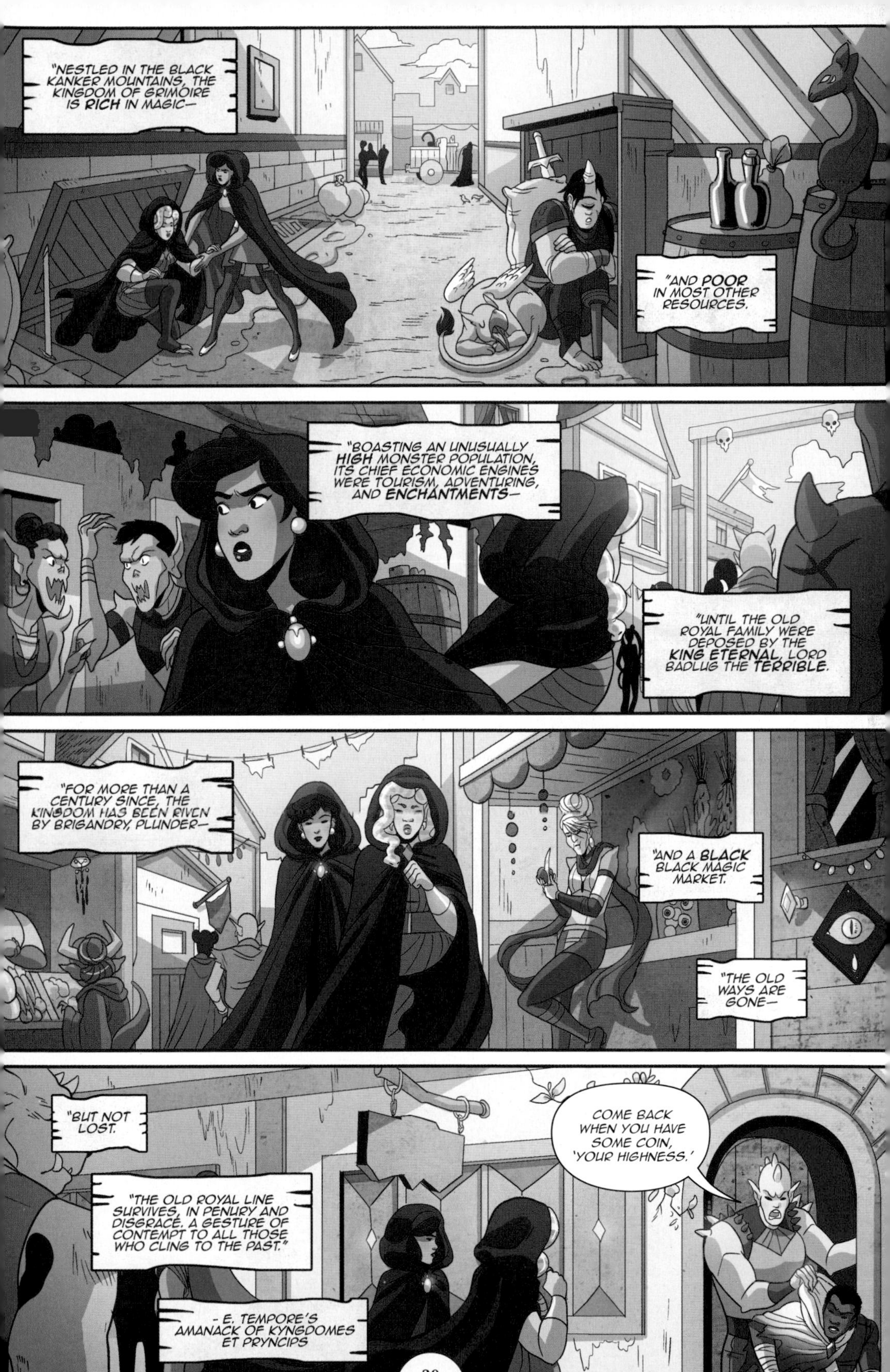

"NESTLED IN THE BLACK KANKER MOUNTAINS, THE KINGDOM OF GRIMOIRE IS RICH IN MAGIC—
"AND POOR IN MOST OTHER RESOURCES.
"BOASTING AN UNUSUALLY HIGH MONSTER POPULATION, ITS CHIEF ECONOMIC ENGINES WERE TOURISM, ADVENTURING, AND ENCHANTMENTS—
"UNTIL THE OLD ROYAL FAMILY WERE DEPOSED BY THE KING ETERNAL, LORD BADLUG THE TERRIBLE.
"FOR MORE THAN A CENTURY SINCE, THE KINGDOM HAS BEEN RIVEN BY BRIGANDRY, PLUNDER—
"AND A BLACK BLACK MAGIC MARKET.
"THE OLD WAYS ARE GONE—
"BUT NOT LOST.
"THE OLD ROYAL LINE SURVIVES, IN PENURY AND DISGRACE. A GESTURE OF CONTEMPT TO ALL THOSE WHO CLING TO THE PAST."
- E. TEMPORE'S AMANACK OF KYNGDOMES ET PRYNCIPS
COME BACK WHEN YOU HAVE SOME COIN, 'YOUR HIGHNESS.'

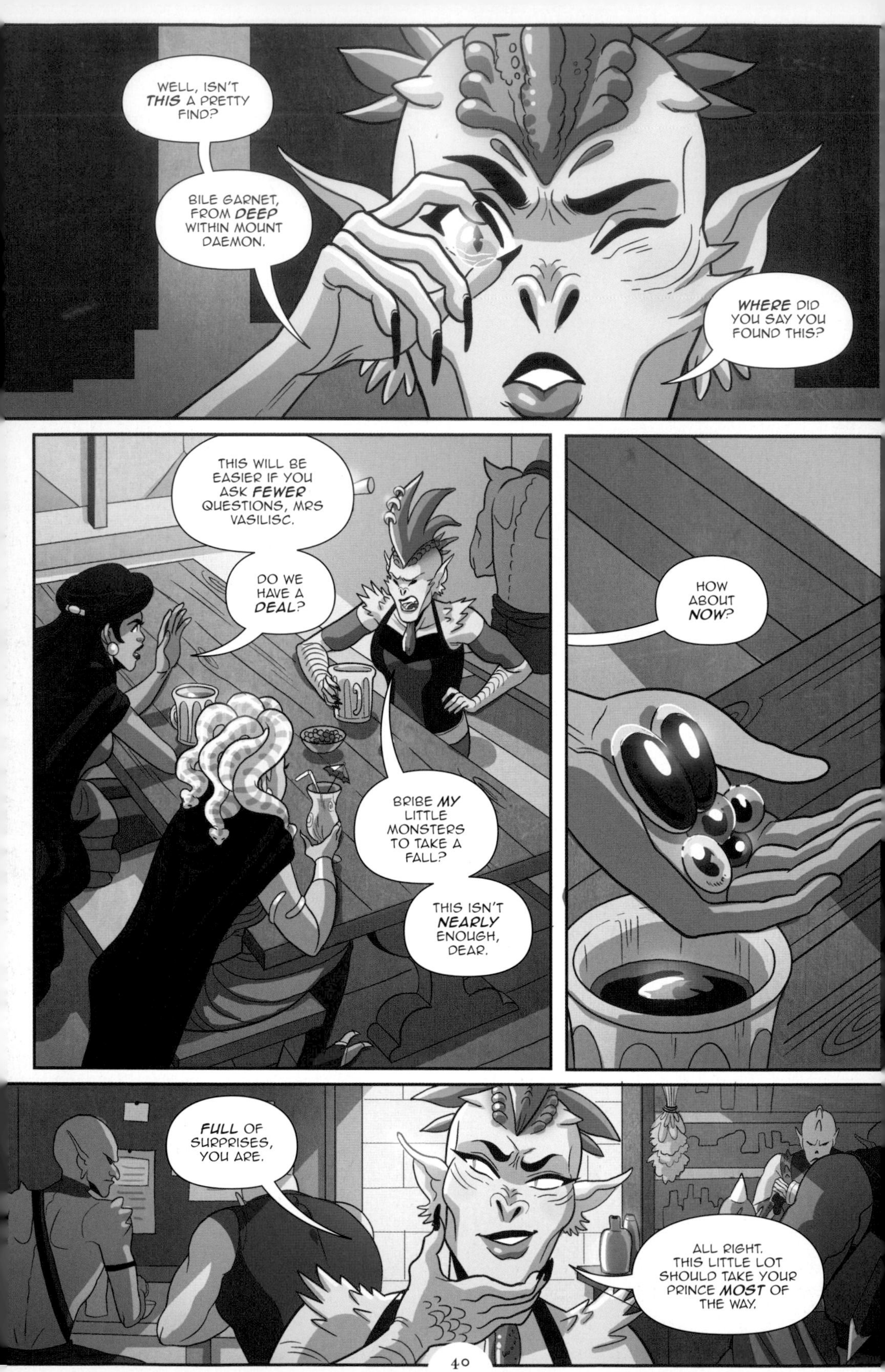
WELL, ISN'T THIS A PRETTY FIND?
BILE GARNET, FROM DEEP WITHIN MOUNT DAEMON.
WHERE DID YOU SAY YOU FOUND THIS?
THIS WILL BE EASIER IF YOU ASK FEWER QUESTIONS, MRS VASILISC.
DO WE HAVE A DEAL?
BRIBE MY LITTLE MONSTERS TO TAKE A FALL?
THIS ISN'T NEARLY ENOUGH, DEAR.
HOW ABOUT NOW?
FULL OF SURPRISES, YOU ARE.
ALL RIGHT. THIS LITTLE LOT SHOULD TAKE YOUR PRINCE MOST OF THE WAY.

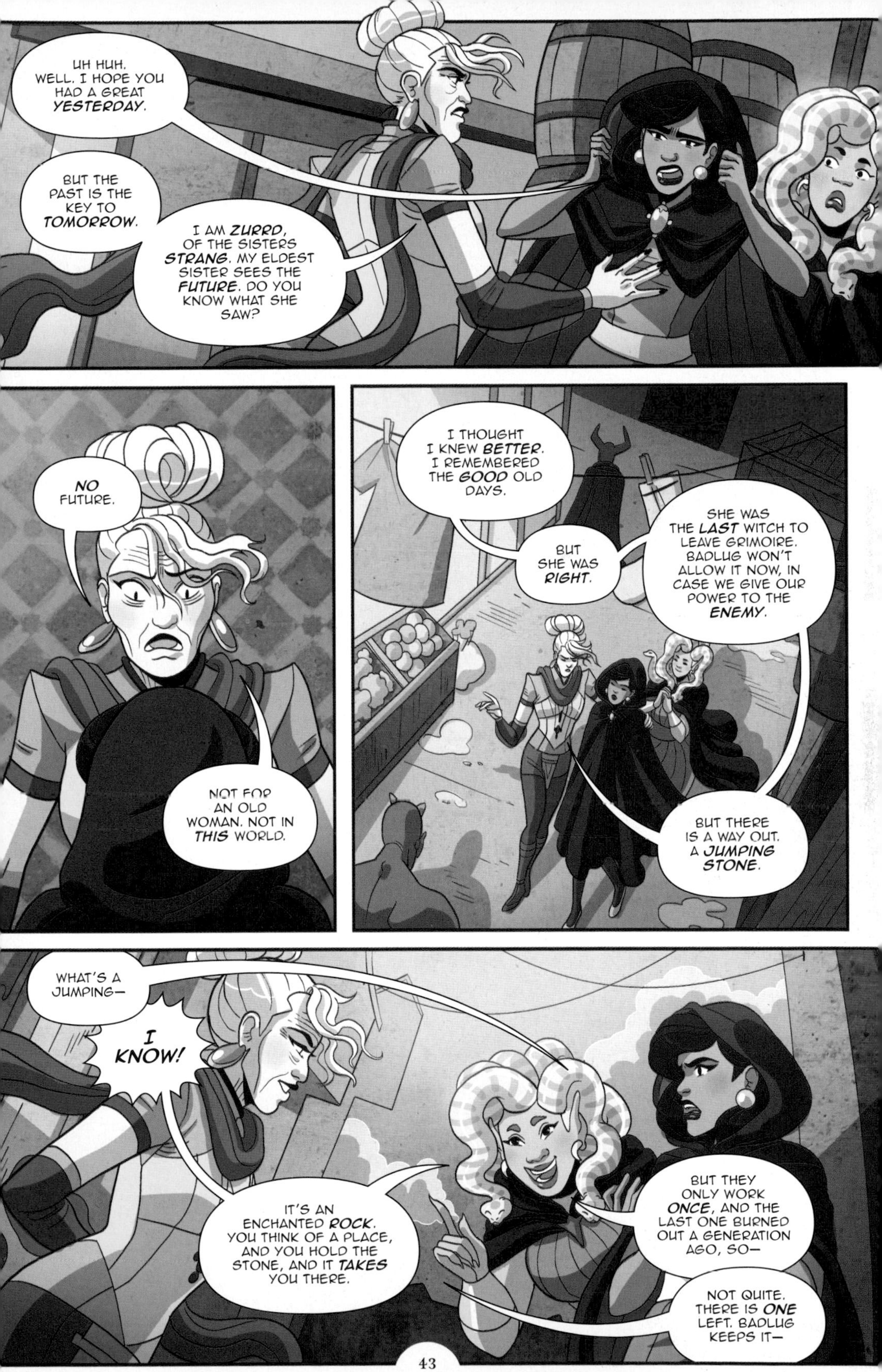
UH HUH. WELL. I HOPE YOU HAD A GREAT *YESTERDAY*.
BUT THE PAST IS THE KEY TO *TOMORROW*.
I AM *ZURRD*, OF THE SISTERS *STRANG*. MY ELDEST SISTER SEES THE *FUTURE*. DO YOU KNOW WHAT SHE SAW?
NO FUTURE.
NOT FOR AN OLD WOMAN. NOT IN *THIS* WORLD.
I THOUGHT I KNEW *BETTER*. I REMEMBERED THE *GOOD* OLD DAYS.
BUT SHE WAS *RIGHT*.
SHE WAS THE *LAST* WITCH TO LEAVE GRIMOIRE. BADLUG WON'T ALLOW IT NOW, IN CASE WE GIVE OUR POWER TO THE *ENEMY*.
BUT THERE IS A WAY OUT. A *JUMPING STONE*.
WHAT'S A JUMPING—
I KNOW!
IT'S AN ENCHANTED *ROCK*. YOU THINK OF A PLACE, AND YOU HOLD THE STONE, AND IT *TAKES* YOU THERE.
BUT THEY ONLY WORK *ONCE*, AND THE LAST ONE BURNED OUT A GENERATION AGO, SO—
NOT QUITE. THERE IS *ONE* LEFT. BADLUG KEEPS IT—

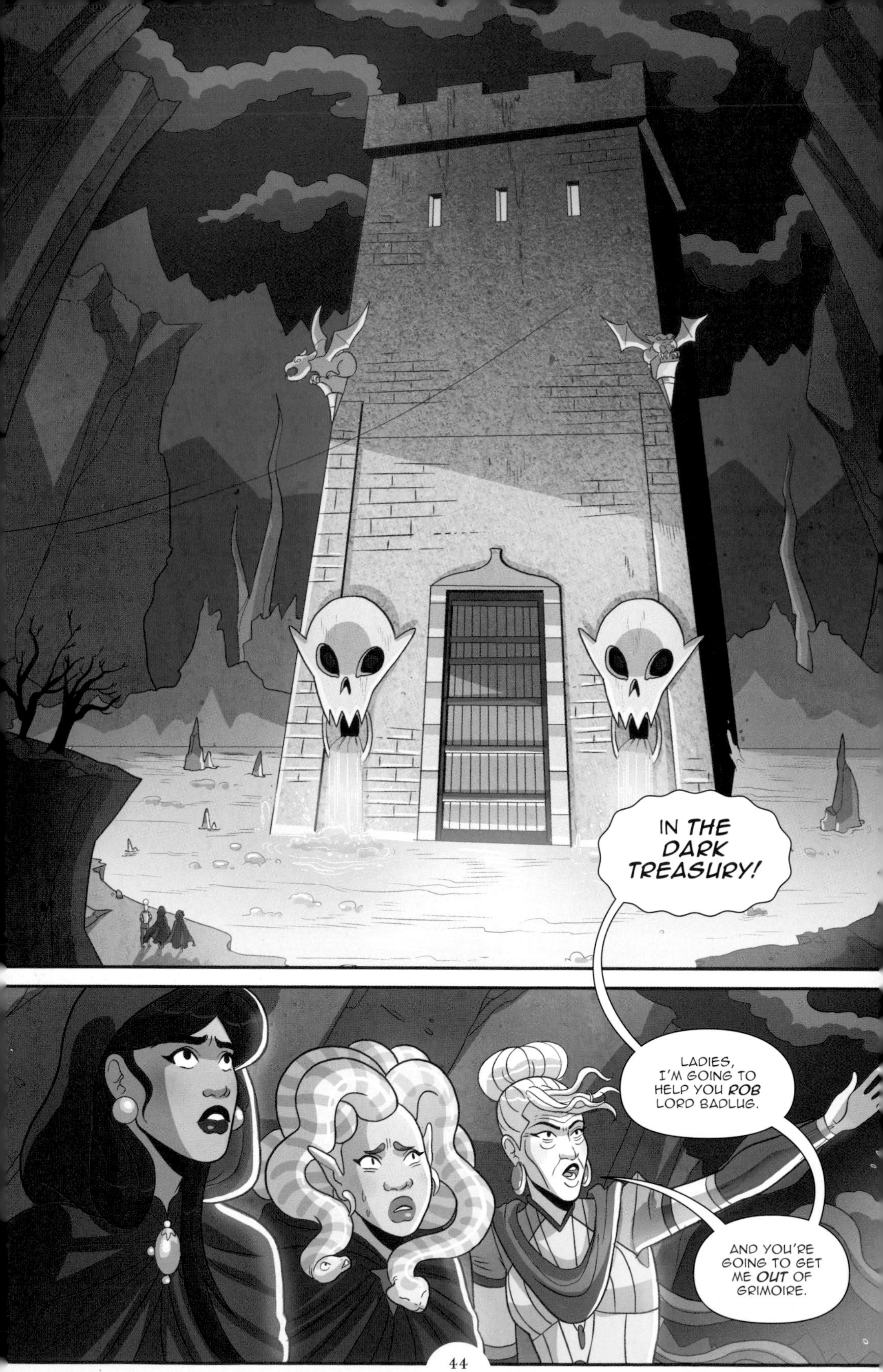
IN THE DARK TREASURY!
LADIES, I'M GOING TO HELP YOU ROB LORD BADLUG.
AND YOU'RE GOING TO GET ME OUT OF GRIMOIRE.

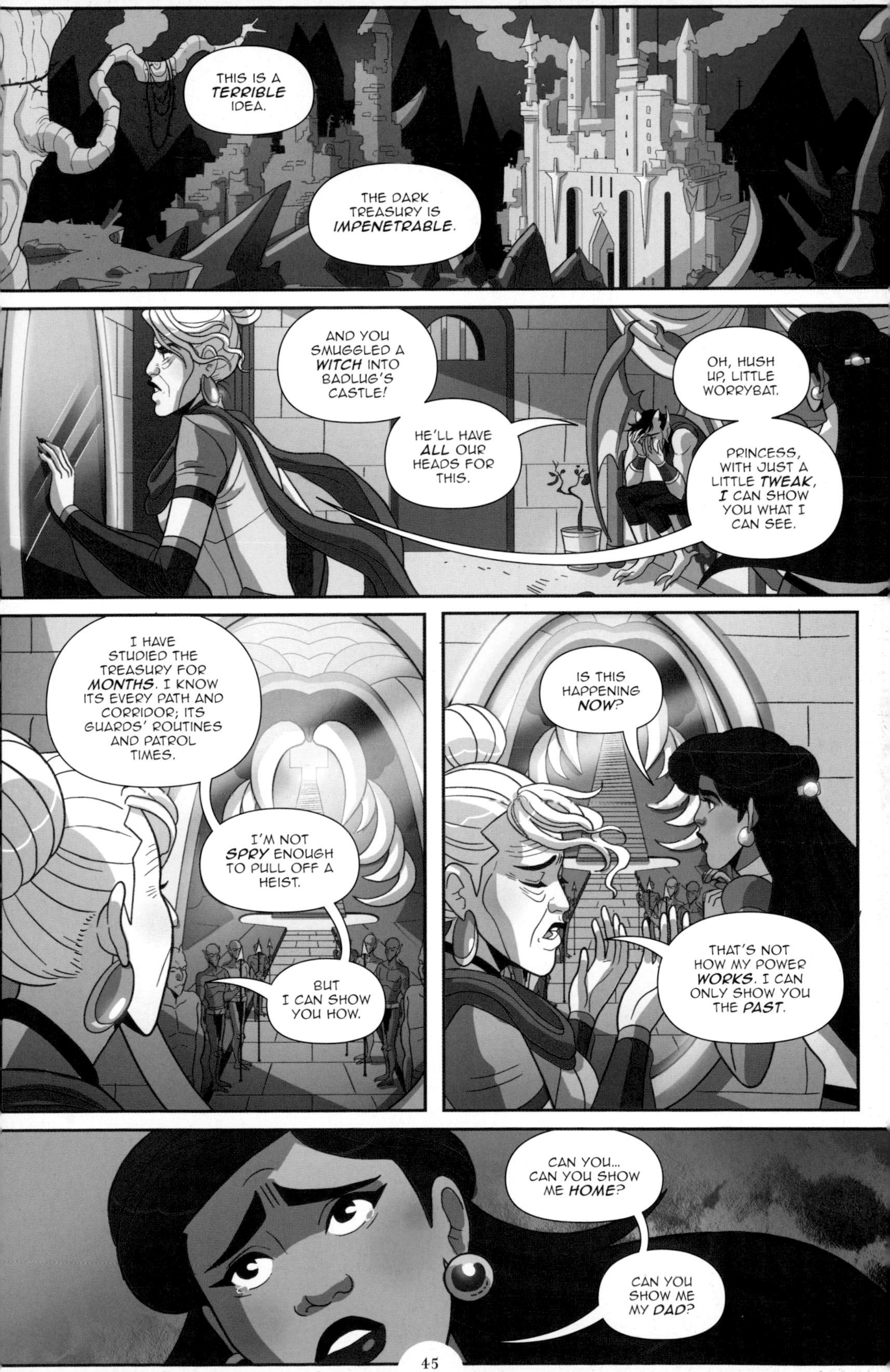
THIS IS A TERRIBLE IDEA.
THE DARK TREASURY IS IMPENETRABLE.
AND YOU SMUGGLED A WITCH INTO BADLUG'S CASTLE!
HE'LL HAVE ALL OUR HEADS FOR THIS.
OH, HUSH UP, LITTLE WORRYBAT.
PRINCESS, WITH JUST A LITTLE TWEAK, I CAN SHOW YOU WHAT I CAN SEE.
I HAVE STUDIED THE TREASURY FOR MONTHS. I KNOW ITS EVERY PATH AND CORRIDOR; ITS GUARDS' ROUTINES AND PATROL TIMES.
I'M NOT SPRY ENOUGH TO PULL OFF A HEIST.
BUT I CAN SHOW YOU HOW.
IS THIS HAPPENING NOW?
THAT'S NOT HOW MY POWER WORKS. I CAN ONLY SHOW YOU THE PAST.
CAN YOU... CAN YOU SHOW ME HOME?
CAN YOU SHOW ME MY DAD?

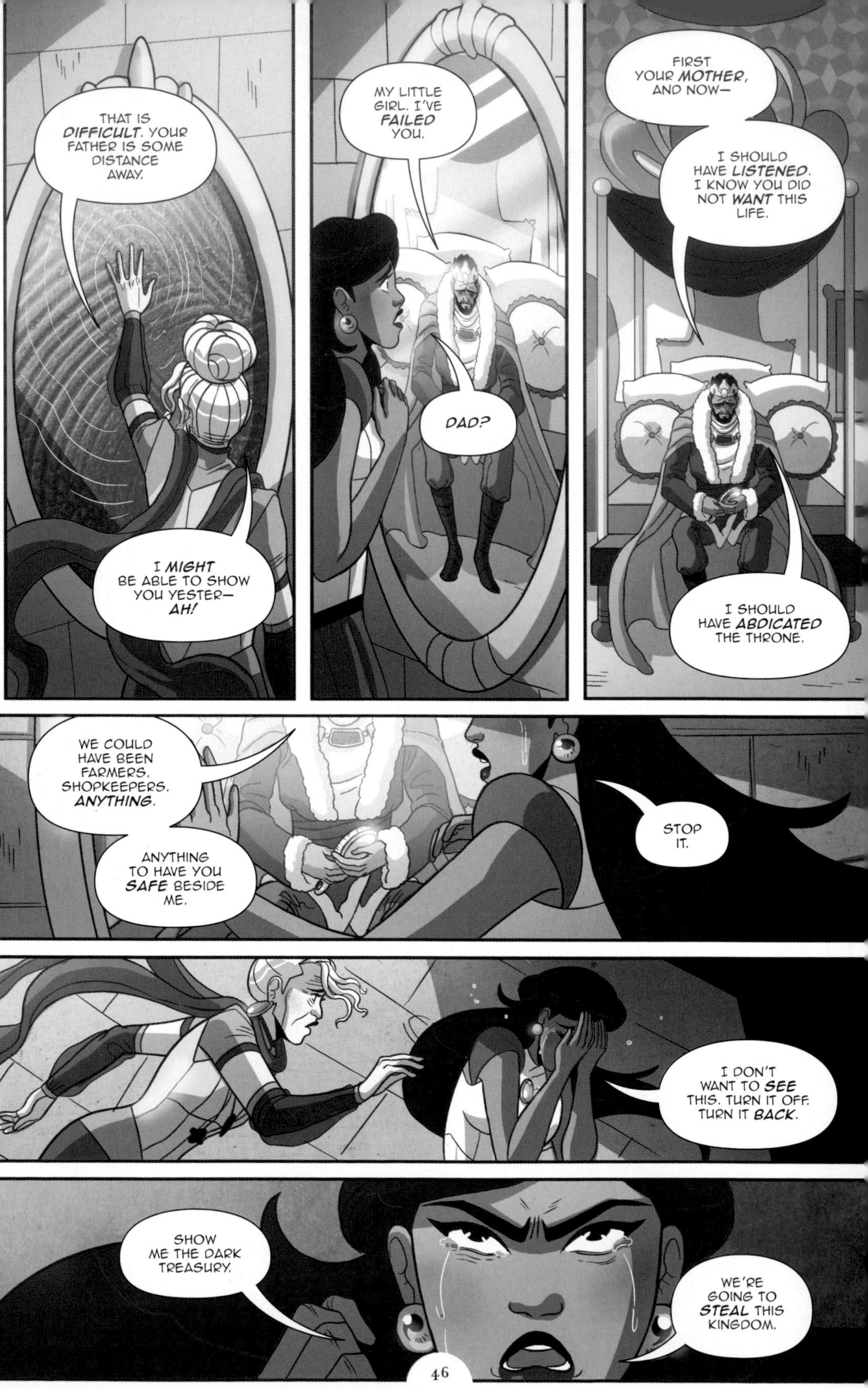
THAT IS DIFFICULT. YOUR FATHER IS SOME DISTANCE AWAY.
I MIGHT BE ABLE TO SHOW YOU YESTER— AH!
MY LITTLE GIRL. I'VE FAILED YOU.
DAD?
FIRST YOUR MOTHER, AND NOW—
I SHOULD HAVE LISTENED. I KNOW YOU DID NOT WANT THIS LIFE.
I SHOULD HAVE ABDICATED THE THRONE.
WE COULD HAVE BEEN FARMERS. SHOPKEEPERS. ANYTHING.
ANYTHING TO HAVE YOU SAFE BESIDE ME.
STOP IT.
I DON'T WANT TO SEE THIS. TURN IT OFF. TURN IT BACK.
SHOW ME THE DARK TREASURY.
WE'RE GOING TO STEAL THIS KINGDOM.

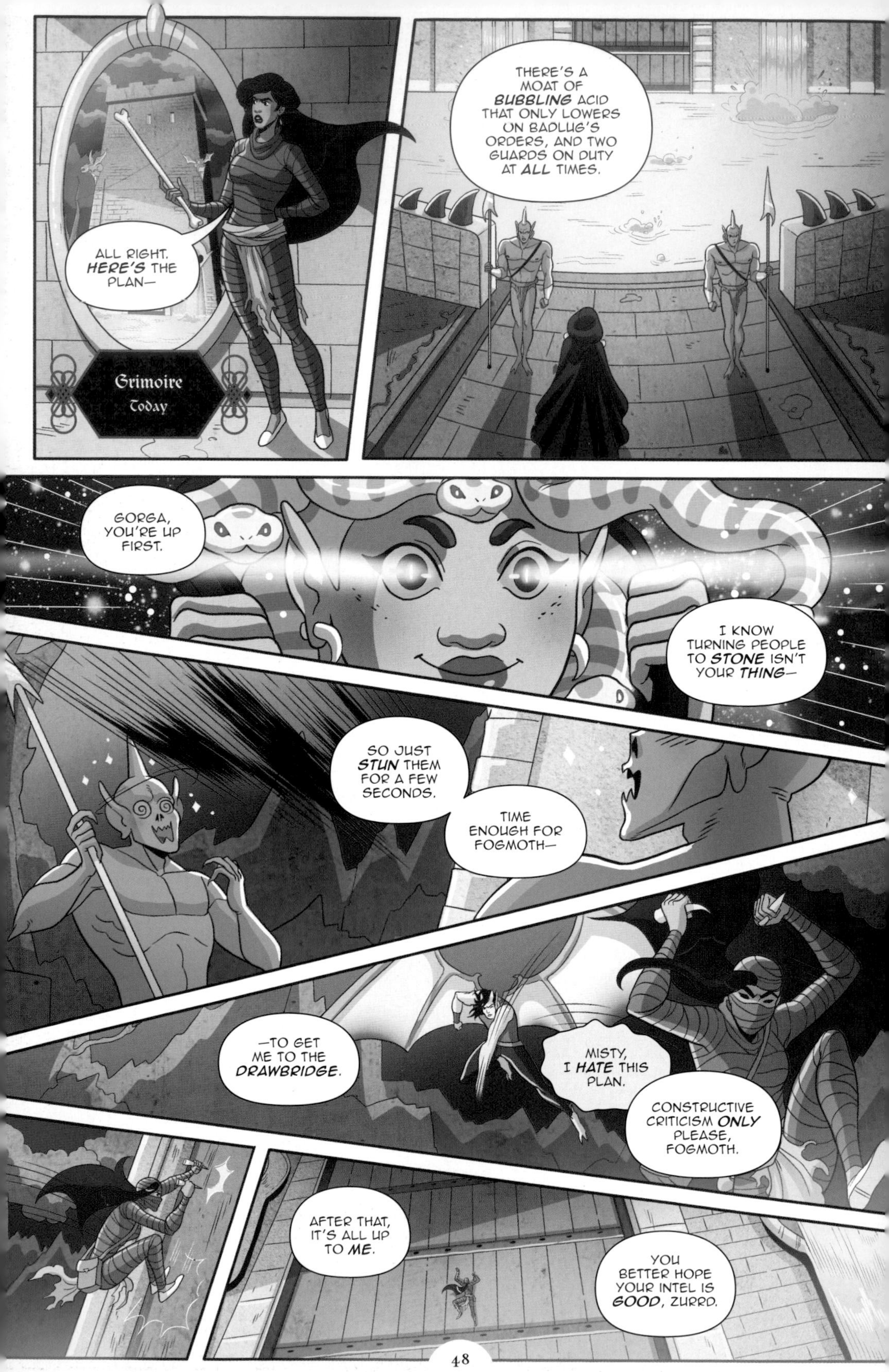
ALL RIGHT. HERE'S THE PLAN—
Grimoire
Today
THERE'S A MOAT OF BUBBLING ACID THAT ONLY LOWERS ON BADLUG'S ORDERS, AND TWO GUARDS ON DUTY AT ALL TIMES.
GORGA, YOU'RE UP FIRST.
I KNOW TURNING PEOPLE TO STONE ISN'T YOUR THING—
SO JUST STUN THEM FOR A FEW SECONDS.
TIME ENOUGH FOR FOGMOTH—
—TO GET ME TO THE DRAWBRIDGE.
MISTY, I HATE THIS PLAN.
CONSTRUCTIVE CRITICISM ONLY PLEASE, FOGMOTH.
AFTER THAT, IT'S ALL UP TO ME.
YOU BETTER HOPE YOUR INTEL IS GOOD, ZURRD.

ALL I CAN TELL YOU IS WHAT'S HAPPENED *EVERY* NIGHT BEFORE.

YOU JUST HAVE TO *TIME* IT RIGHT.

THE ACID RESERVOIRS TURN OVER EVERY *TWENTY-THREE* HOURS AND *FORTY-ONE* MINUTES.

TONIGHT, THAT MEANS *THIRTEEN MINUTES* AFTER MIDNIGHT.

PLINK
PLINK
PLINK
PLINK

zzzWIP!!!

PLINK

SHLONK!

WHEN THE LAST GRAIN OF SAND *FALLS—*

YOU HAVE *SEVEN SECONDS* TO GET INSIDE.

GET IT WRONG BY *ONE SECOND—*

AND YOU'RE *DEAD.*

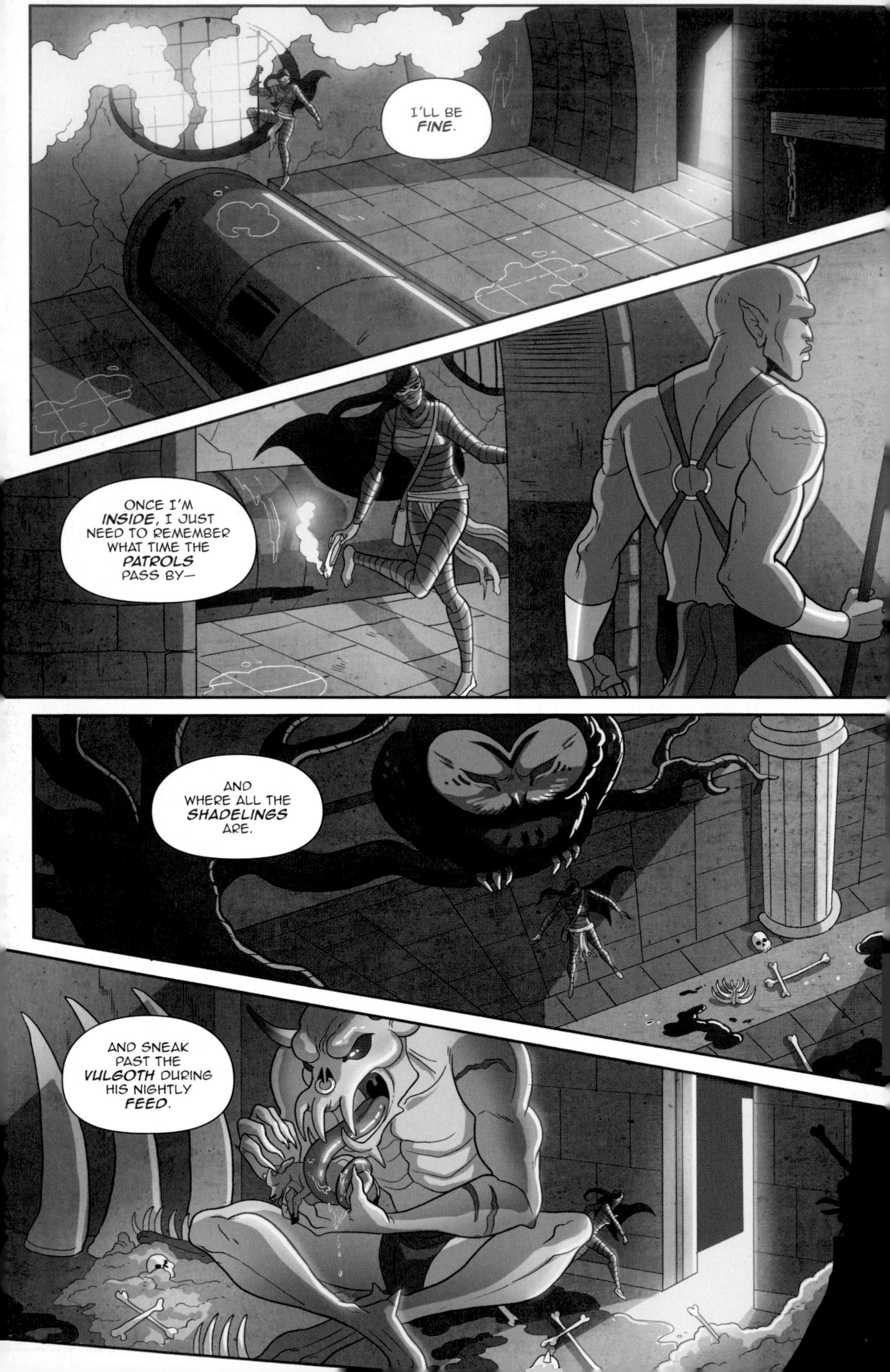
I'LL BE *FINE*.
ONCE I'M *INSIDE*, I JUST NEED TO REMEMBER WHAT TIME THE *PATROLS* PASS BY—
AND WHERE ALL THE *SHADELINGS* ARE.
AND SNEAK PAST THE *VULGOTH* DURING HIS NIGHTLY *FEED*.

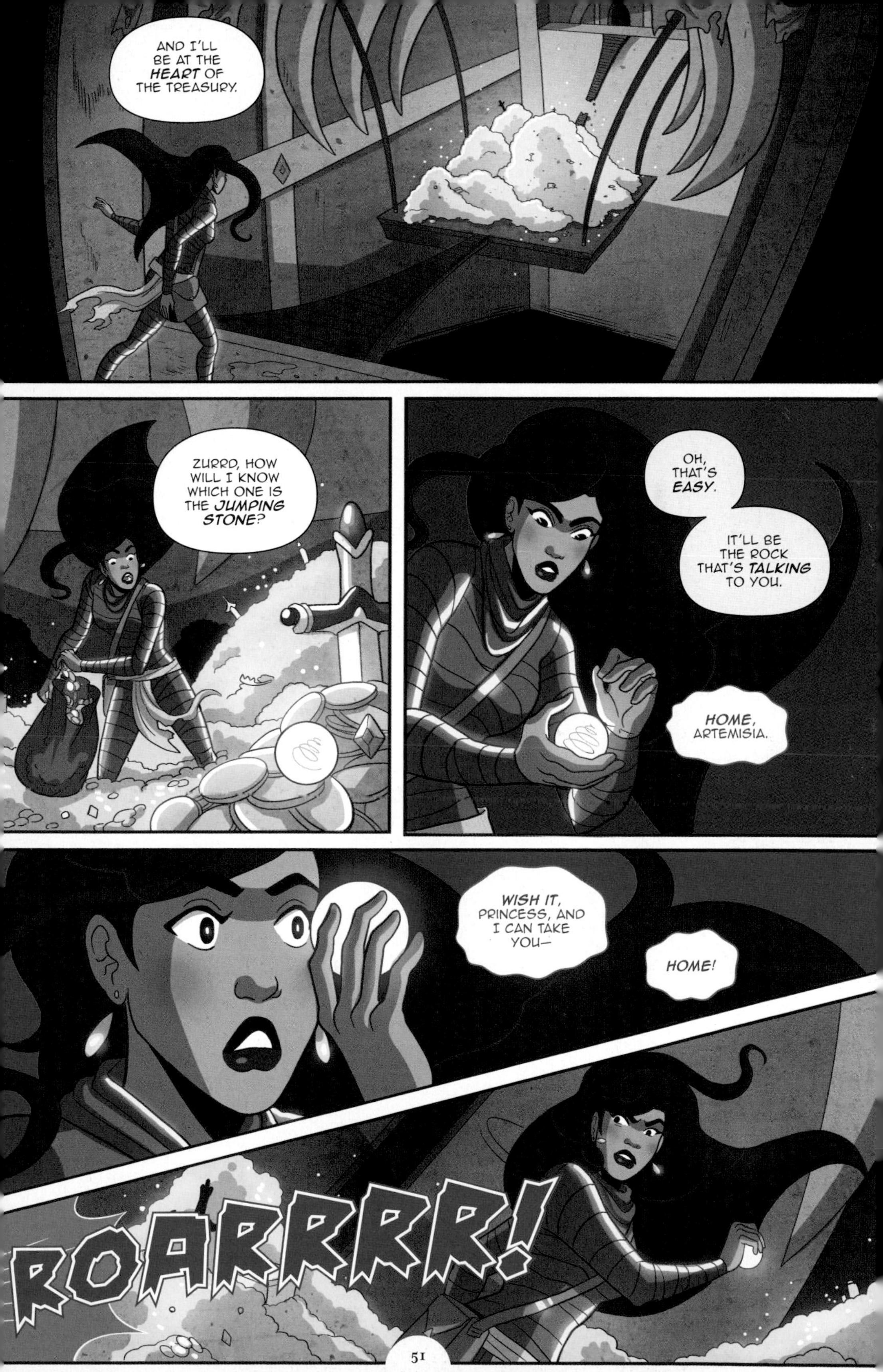
AND I'LL BE AT THE HEART OF THE TREASURY.
ZURRD, HOW WILL I KNOW WHICH ONE IS THE JUMPING STONE?
OH, THAT'S EASY.
IT'LL BE THE ROCK THAT'S TALKING TO YOU.
HOME, ARTEMISIA.
WISH IT, PRINCESS, AND I CAN TAKE YOU—
HOME!
ROARRRR!

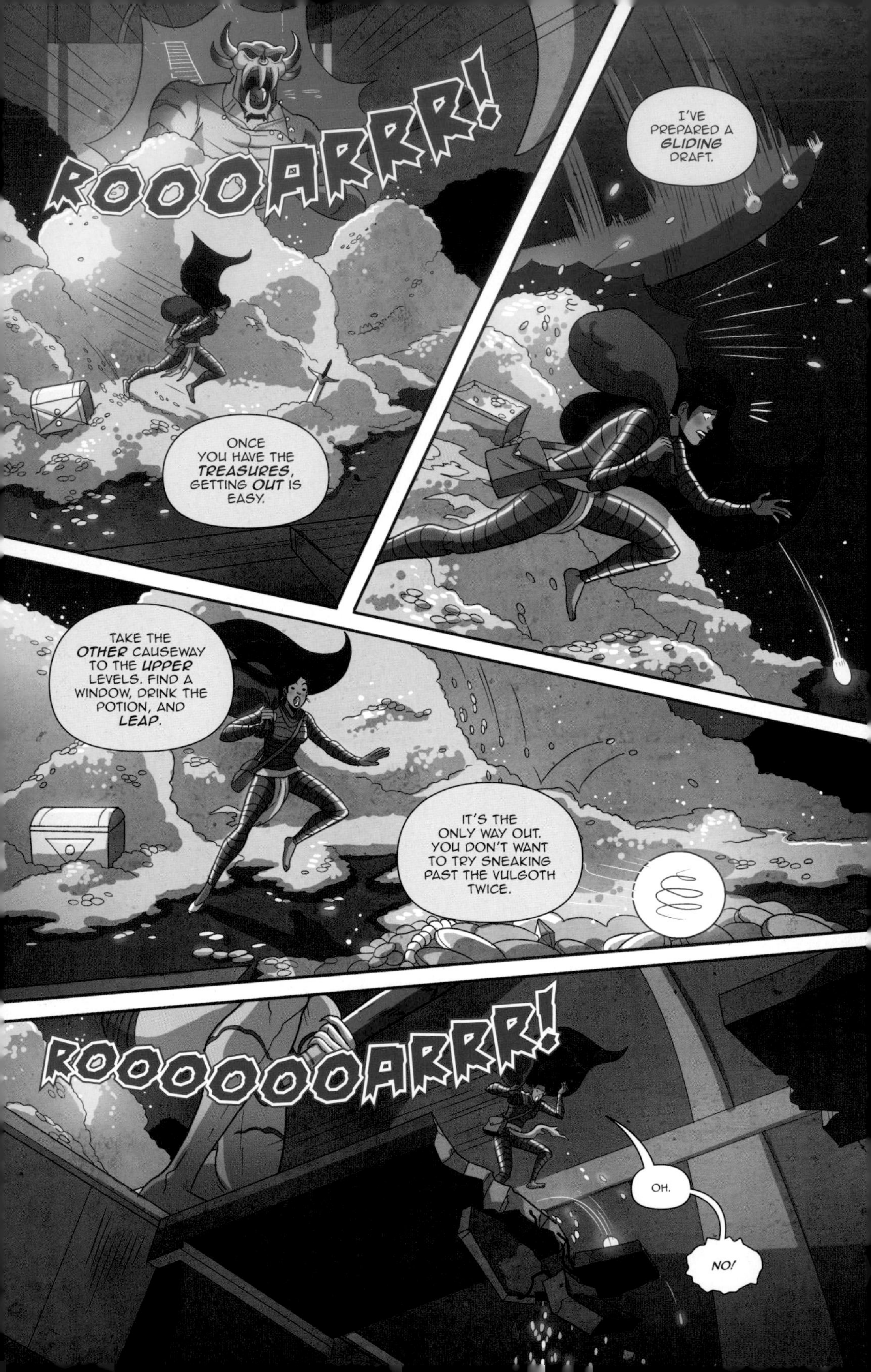
ROOOARRR!
ONCE YOU HAVE THE TREASURES, GETTING OUT IS EASY.
I'VE PREPARED A GLIDING DRAFT.
TAKE THE OTHER CAUSEWAY TO THE UPPER LEVELS. FIND A WINDOW, DRINK THE POTION, AND LEAP.
IT'S THE ONLY WAY OUT. YOU DON'T WANT TO TRY SNEAKING PAST THE VULGOTH TWICE.
ROOOOOOOARRR!
OH.
NO!

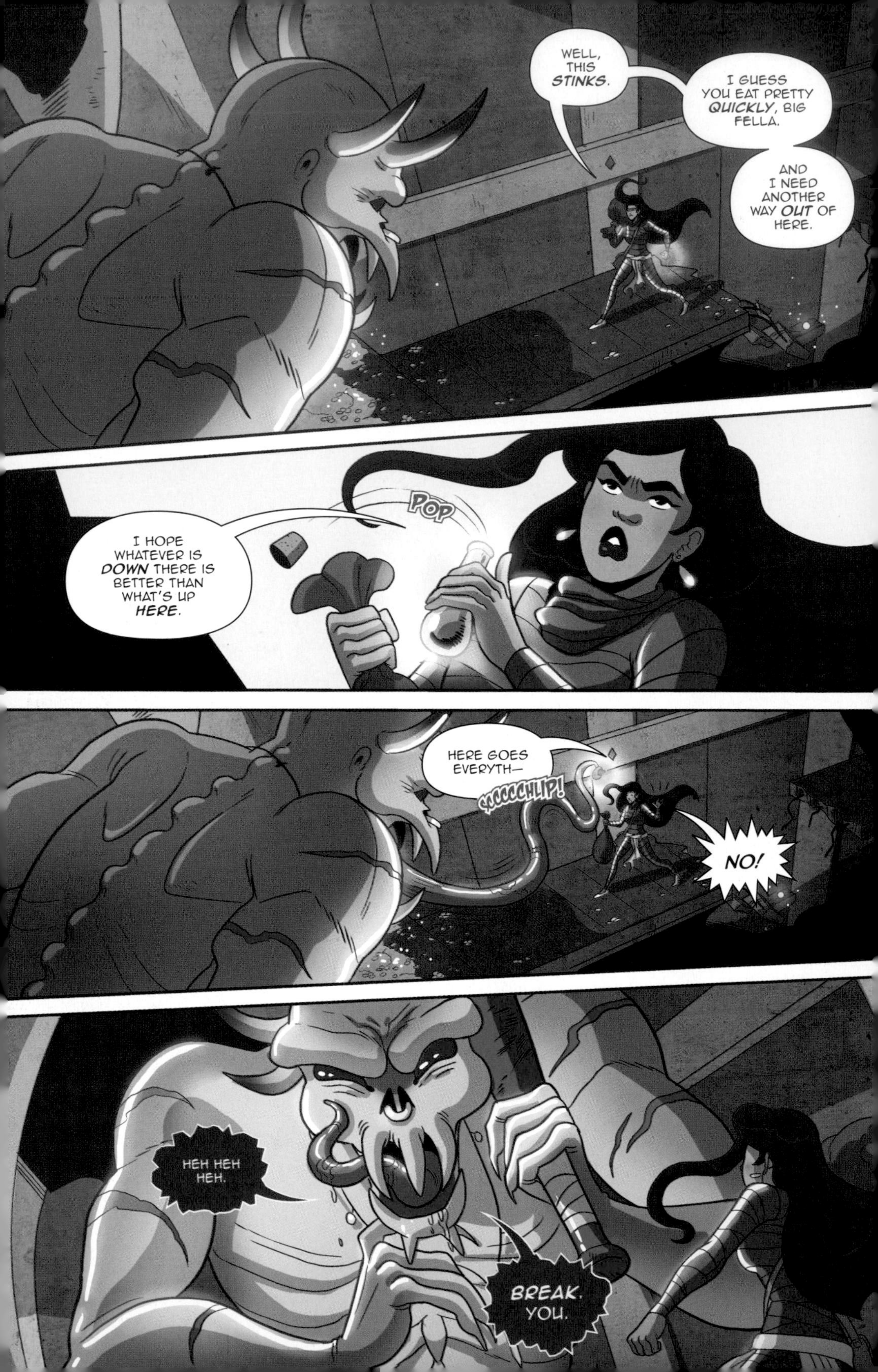

WELL, THIS STINKS.
I GUESS YOU EAT PRETTY QUICKLY, BIG FELLA.
AND I NEED ANOTHER WAY OUT OF HERE.
POP
I HOPE WHATEVER IS DOWN THERE IS BETTER THAN WHAT'S UP HERE.
HERE GOES EVERYTH—
SCCCCCHLIP!
NO!
HEH HEH HEH.
BREAK. YOU.

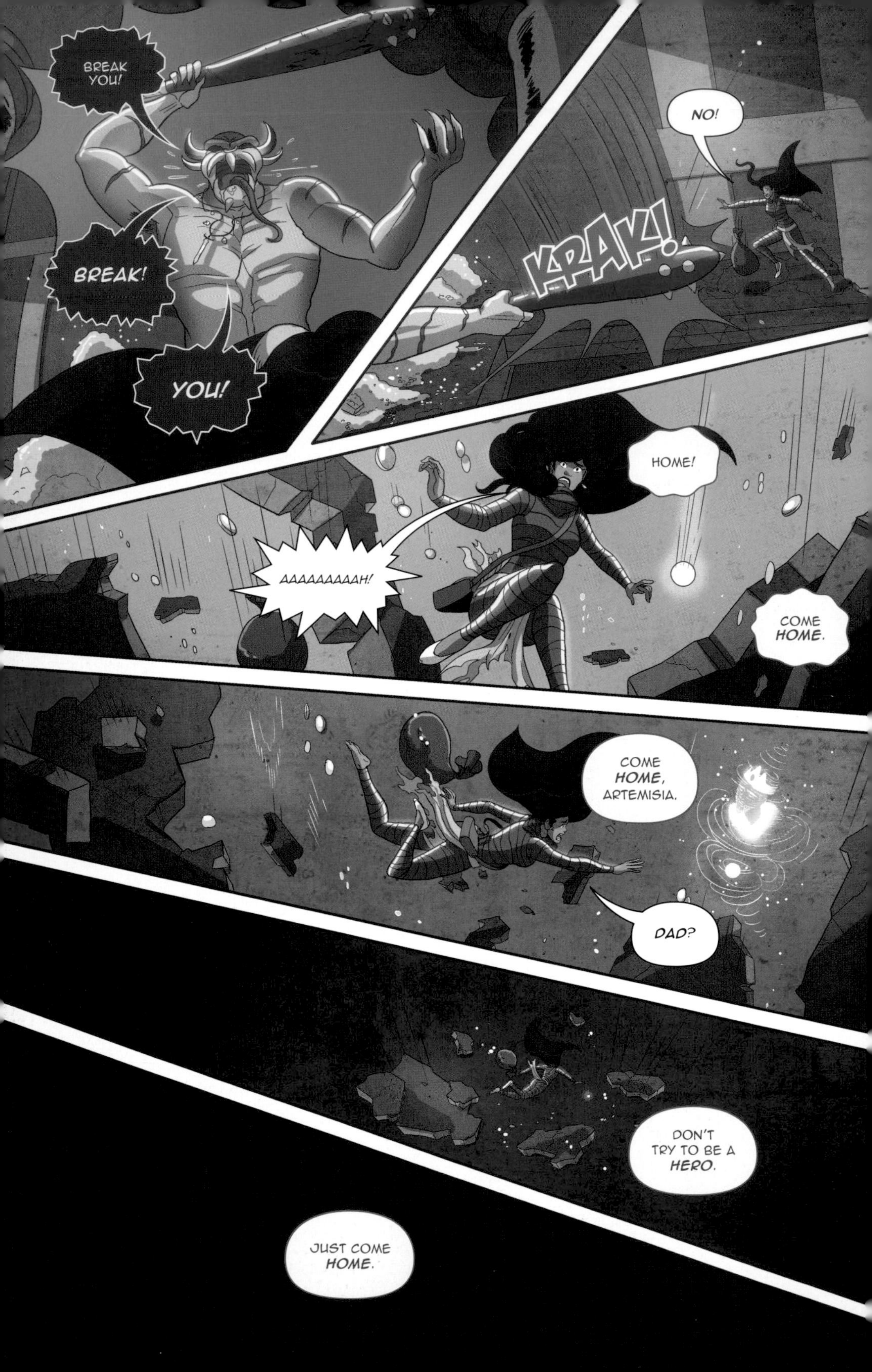
BREAK YOU!
BREAK!
YOU!
NO!
KRAK!
HOME!
AAAAAAAAAAH!
COME HOME.
COME HOME, ARTEMISIA.
DAD?
DON'T TRY TO BE A HERO.
JUST COME HOME.

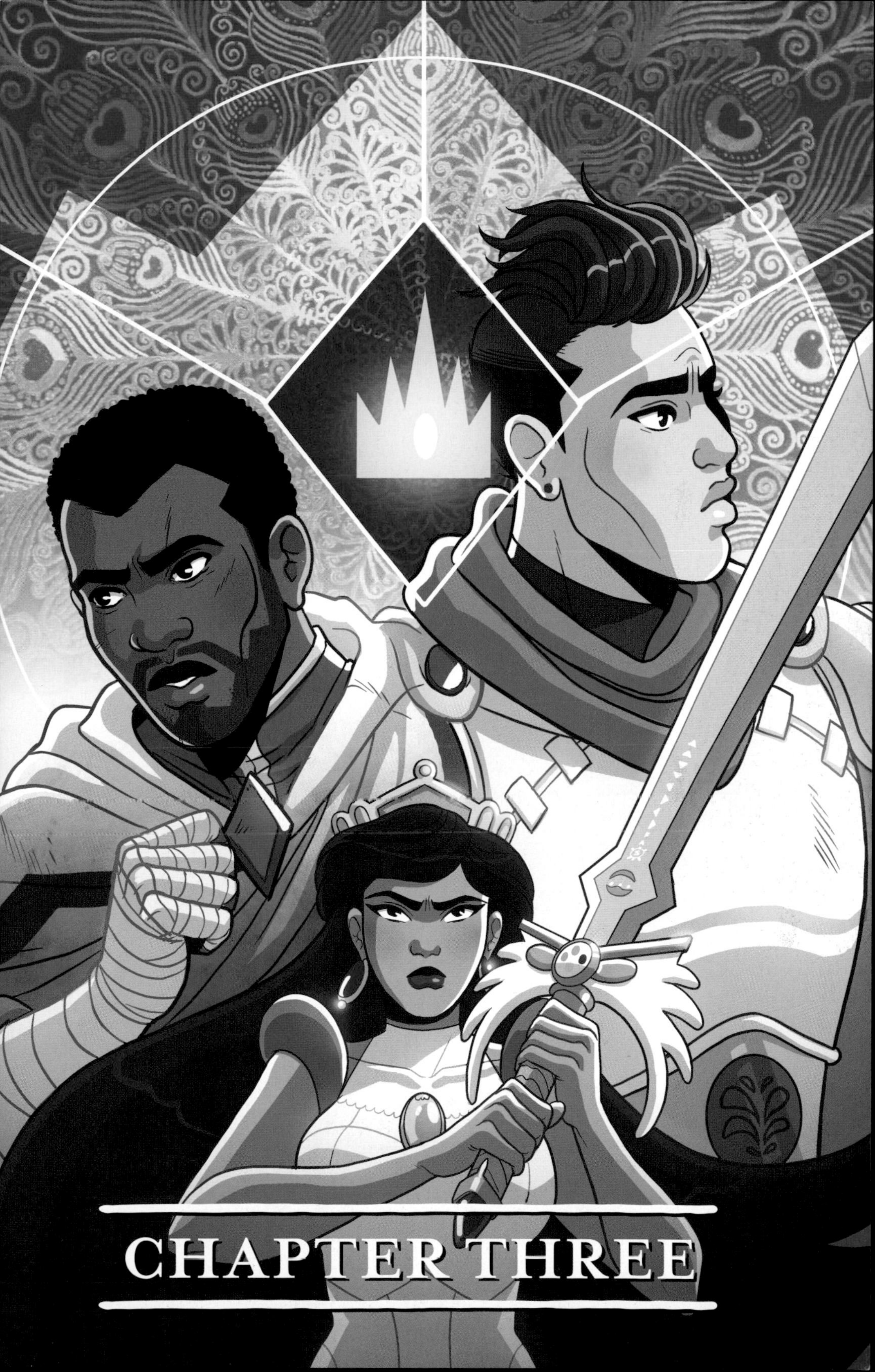

CHAPTER THREE

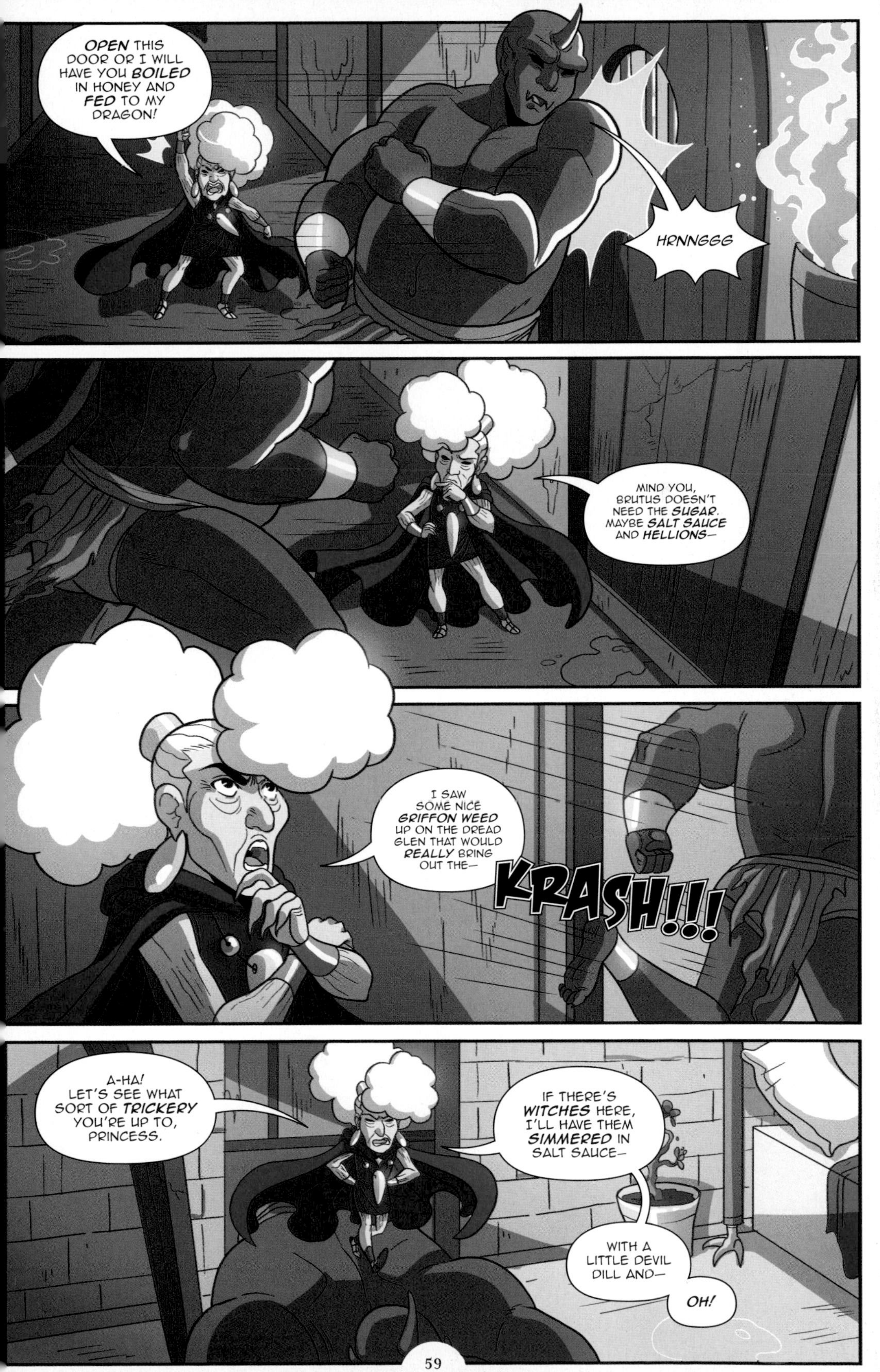
OPEN THIS DOOR OR I WILL HAVE YOU BOILED IN HONEY AND FED TO MY DRAGON!
HRNNGGG
MIND YOU, BRUTUS DOESN'T NEED THE SUGAR. MAYBE SALT SAUCE AND HELLIONS—
I SAW SOME NICE GRIFFON WEED UP ON THE DREAD GLEN THAT WOULD REALLY BRING OUT THE—
KRASH!!!
A-HA! LET'S SEE WHAT SORT OF TRICKERY YOU'RE UP TO, PRINCESS.
IF THERE'S WITCHES HERE, I'LL HAVE THEM SIMMERED IN SALT SAUCE—
WITH A LITTLE DEVIL DILL AND—
OH!

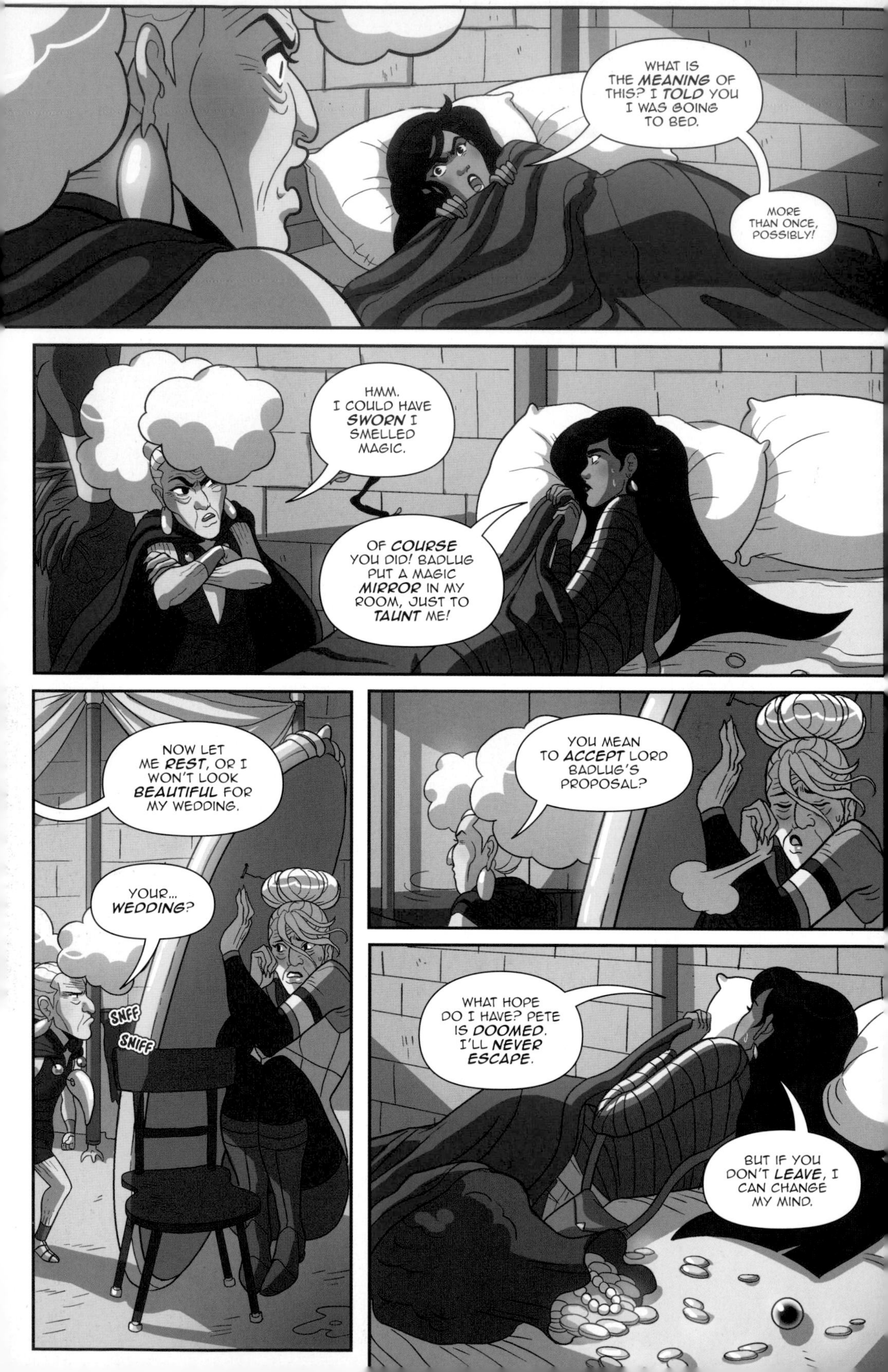
WHAT IS THE MEANING OF THIS? I TOLD YOU I WAS GOING TO BED.
MORE THAN ONCE, POSSIBLY!
HMM. I COULD HAVE SWORN I SMELLED MAGIC.
OF COURSE YOU DID! BADLUG PUT A MAGIC MIRROR IN MY ROOM, JUST TO TAUNT ME!
NOW LET ME REST, OR I WON'T LOOK BEAUTIFUL FOR MY WEDDING.
YOUR... WEDDING?
SNFF
SNIFF
YOU MEAN TO ACCEPT LORD BADLUG'S PROPOSAL?
WHAT HOPE DO I HAVE? PETE IS DOOMED. I'LL NEVER ESCAPE.
BUT IF YOU DON'T LEAVE, I CAN CHANGE MY MIND.

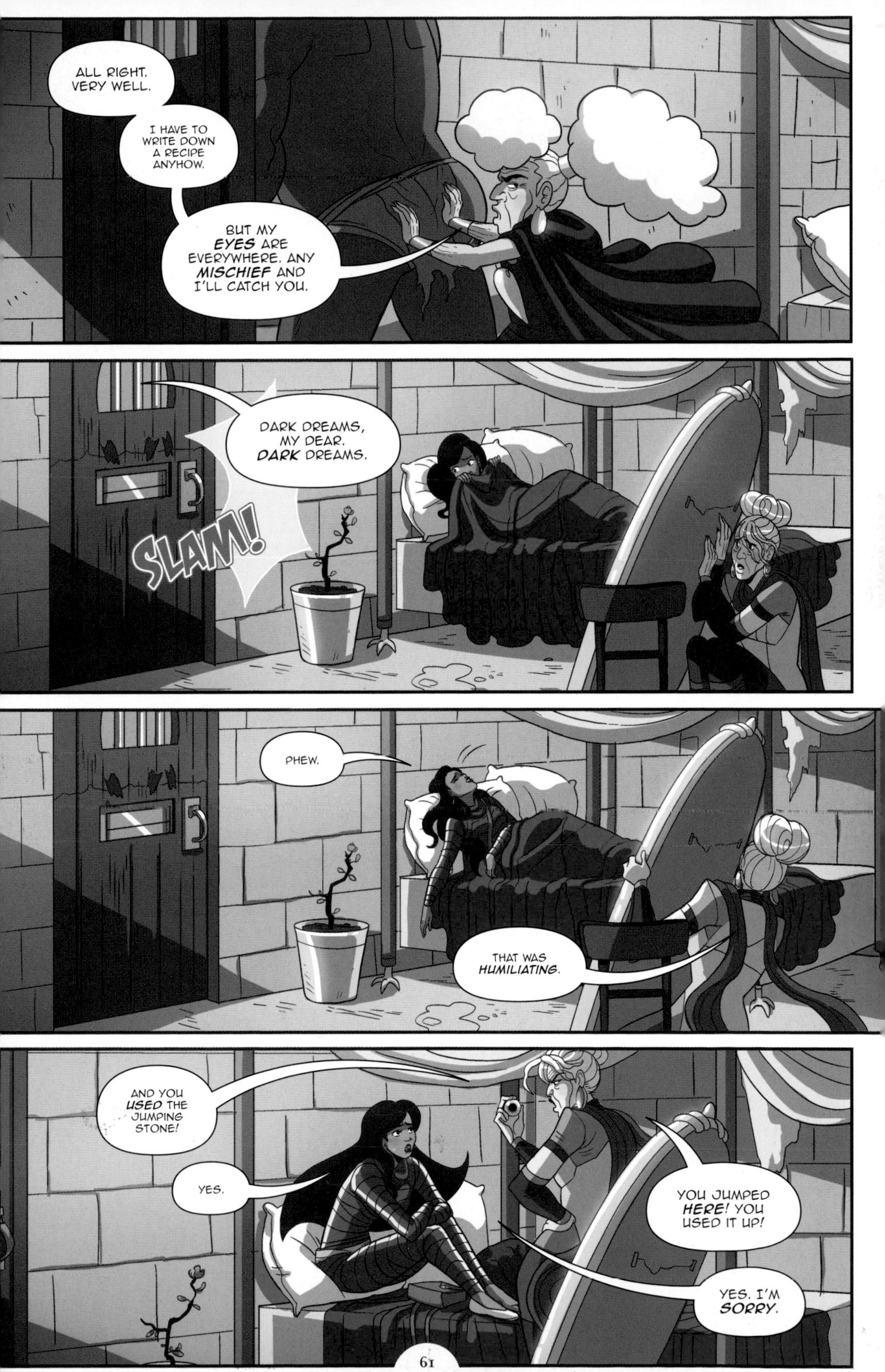
ALL RIGHT. VERY WELL.
I HAVE TO WRITE DOWN A RECIPE ANYHOW.
BUT MY **EYES** ARE EVERYWHERE. ANY **MISCHIEF** AND I'LL CATCH YOU.
DARK DREAMS, MY DEAR. **DARK** DREAMS.
SLAM!
PHEW.
THAT WAS **HUMILIATING**.
AND YOU **USED** THE JUMPING STONE!
YES.
YOU JUMPED **HERE**! YOU USED IT UP!
YES. I'M **SORRY**.

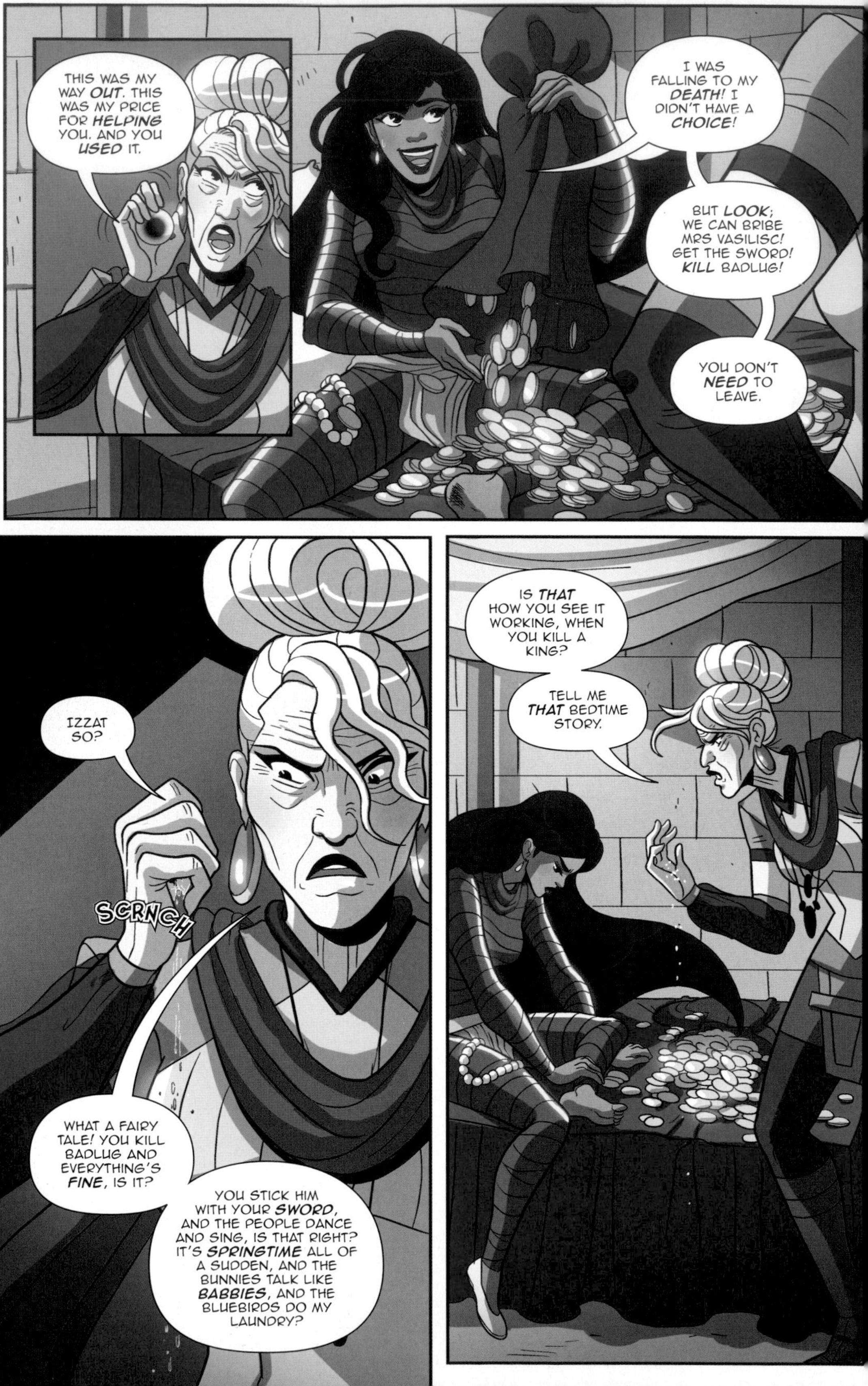
THIS WAS MY WAY OUT. THIS WAS MY PRICE FOR HELPING YOU. AND YOU USED IT.
I WAS FALLING TO MY DEATH! I DIDN'T HAVE A CHOICE!
BUT LOOK; WE CAN BRIBE MRS VASILISC! GET THE SWORD! KILL BADLUG!
YOU DON'T NEED TO LEAVE.
IZZAT SO?
SCRNCH
WHAT A FAIRY TALE! YOU KILL BADLUG AND EVERYTHING'S FINE, IS IT?
YOU STICK HIM WITH YOUR SWORD, AND THE PEOPLE DANCE AND SING, IS THAT RIGHT? IT'S SPRINGTIME ALL OF A SUDDEN, AND THE BUNNIES TALK LIKE BABBIES, AND THE BLUEBIRDS DO MY LAUNDRY?
IS THAT HOW YOU SEE IT WORKING, WHEN YOU KILL A KING?
TELL ME THAT BEDTIME STORY.

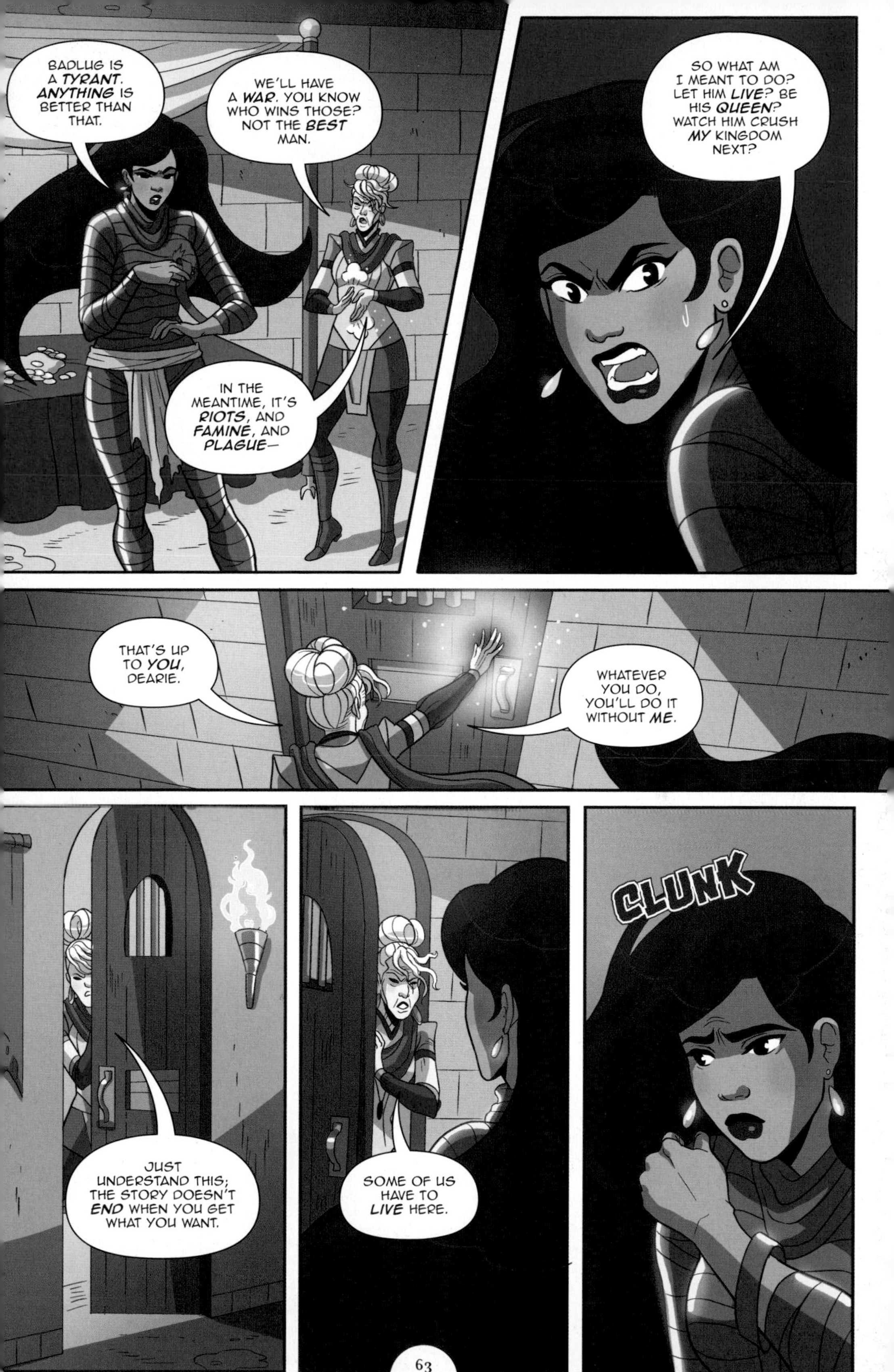
BADLUG IS A *TYRANT*. *ANYTHING* IS BETTER THAN THAT.
WE'LL HAVE A *WAR*. YOU KNOW WHO WINS THOSE? NOT THE *BEST* MAN.
IN THE MEANTIME, IT'S *RIOTS*, AND *FAMINE*, AND *PLAGUE*—
SO WHAT AM I MEANT TO DO? LET HIM *LIVE*? BE HIS *QUEEN*? WATCH HIM CRUSH *MY* KINGDOM NEXT?
THAT'S UP TO *YOU*, DEARIE.
WHATEVER YOU DO, YOU'LL DO IT WITHOUT *ME*.
JUST UNDERSTAND THIS; THE STORY DOESN'T *END* WHEN YOU GET WHAT YOU WANT.
SOME OF US HAVE TO *LIVE* HERE.
CLUNK

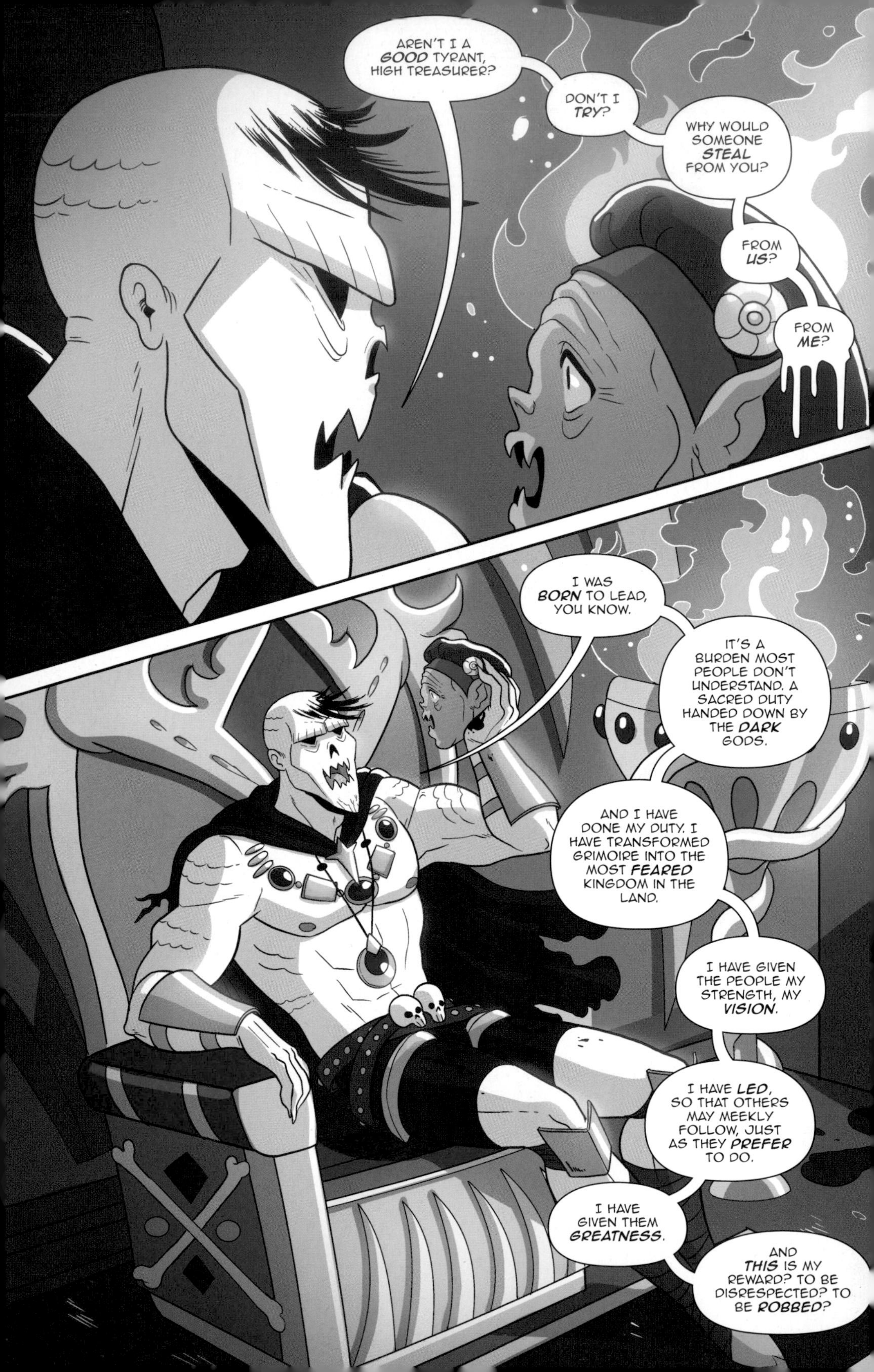
AREN'T I A GOOD TYRANT, HIGH TREASURER?
DON'T I TRY?
WHY WOULD SOMEONE STEAL FROM YOU?
FROM US?
FROM ME?
I WAS BORN TO LEAD, YOU KNOW.
IT'S A BURDEN MOST PEOPLE DON'T UNDERSTAND. A SACRED DUTY HANDED DOWN BY THE DARK GODS.
AND I HAVE DONE MY DUTY. I HAVE TRANSFORMED GRIMOIRE INTO THE MOST FEARED KINGDOM IN THE LAND.
I HAVE GIVEN THE PEOPLE MY STRENGTH, MY VISION.
I HAVE LED, SO THAT OTHERS MAY MEEKLY FOLLOW, JUST AS THEY PREFER TO DO.
I HAVE GIVEN THEM GREATNESS.
AND THIS IS MY REWARD? TO BE DISRESPECTED? TO BE ROBBED?

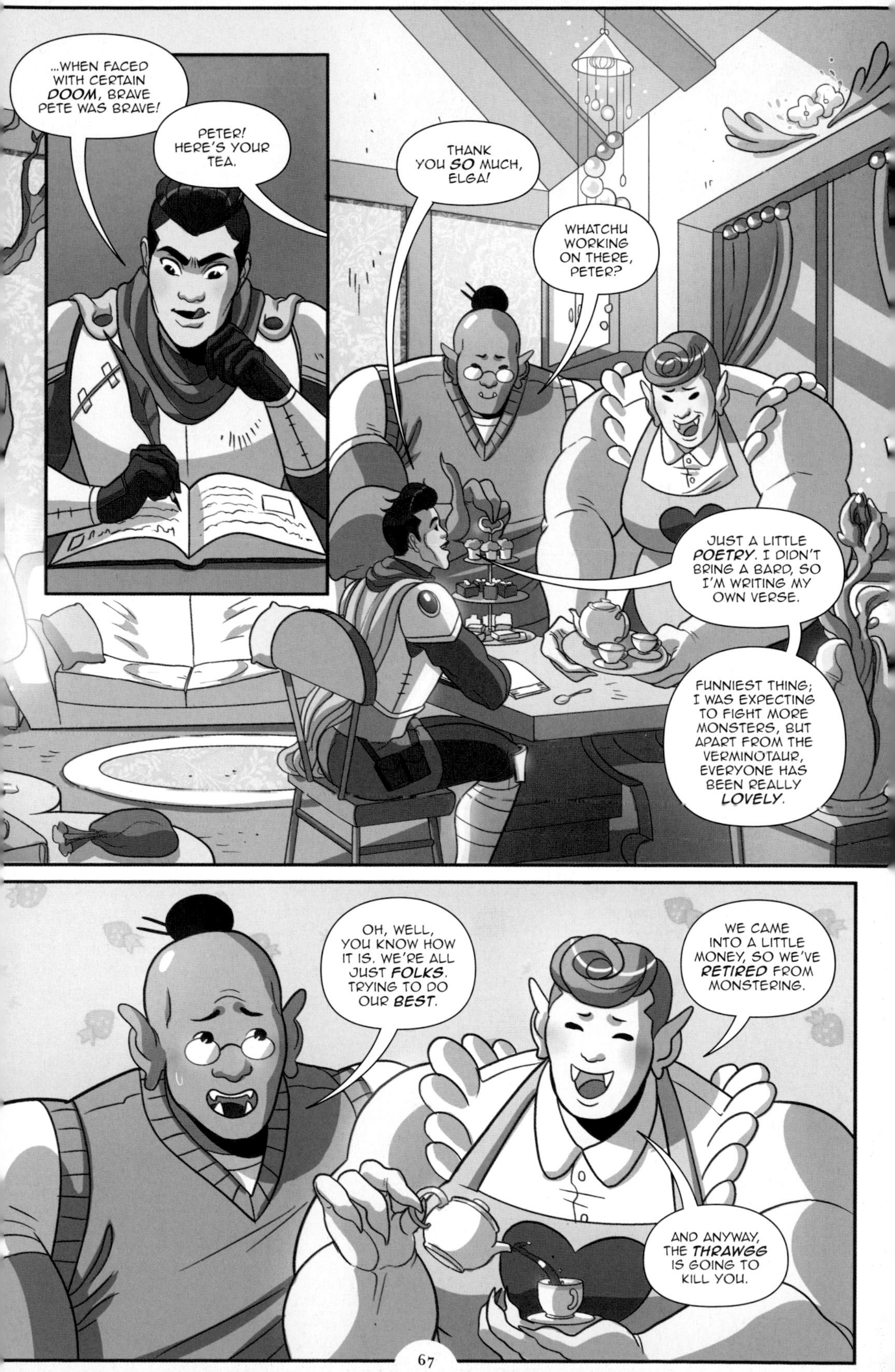
...WHEN FACED WITH CERTAIN DOOM, BRAVE PETE WAS BRAVE!
PETER! HERE'S YOUR TEA.
THANK YOU SO MUCH, ELGA!
WHATCHU WORKING ON THERE, PETER?
JUST A LITTLE POETRY. I DIDN'T BRING A BARD, SO I'M WRITING MY OWN VERSE.
FUNNIEST THING; I WAS EXPECTING TO FIGHT MORE MONSTERS, BUT APART FROM THE VERMINOTAUR, EVERYONE HAS BEEN REALLY LOVELY.
OH, WELL, YOU KNOW HOW IT IS. WE'RE ALL JUST FOLKS. TRYING TO DO OUR BEST.
WE CAME INTO A LITTLE MONEY, SO WE'VE RETIRED FROM MONSTERING.
AND ANYWAY, THE THRAWGG IS GOING TO KILL YOU.

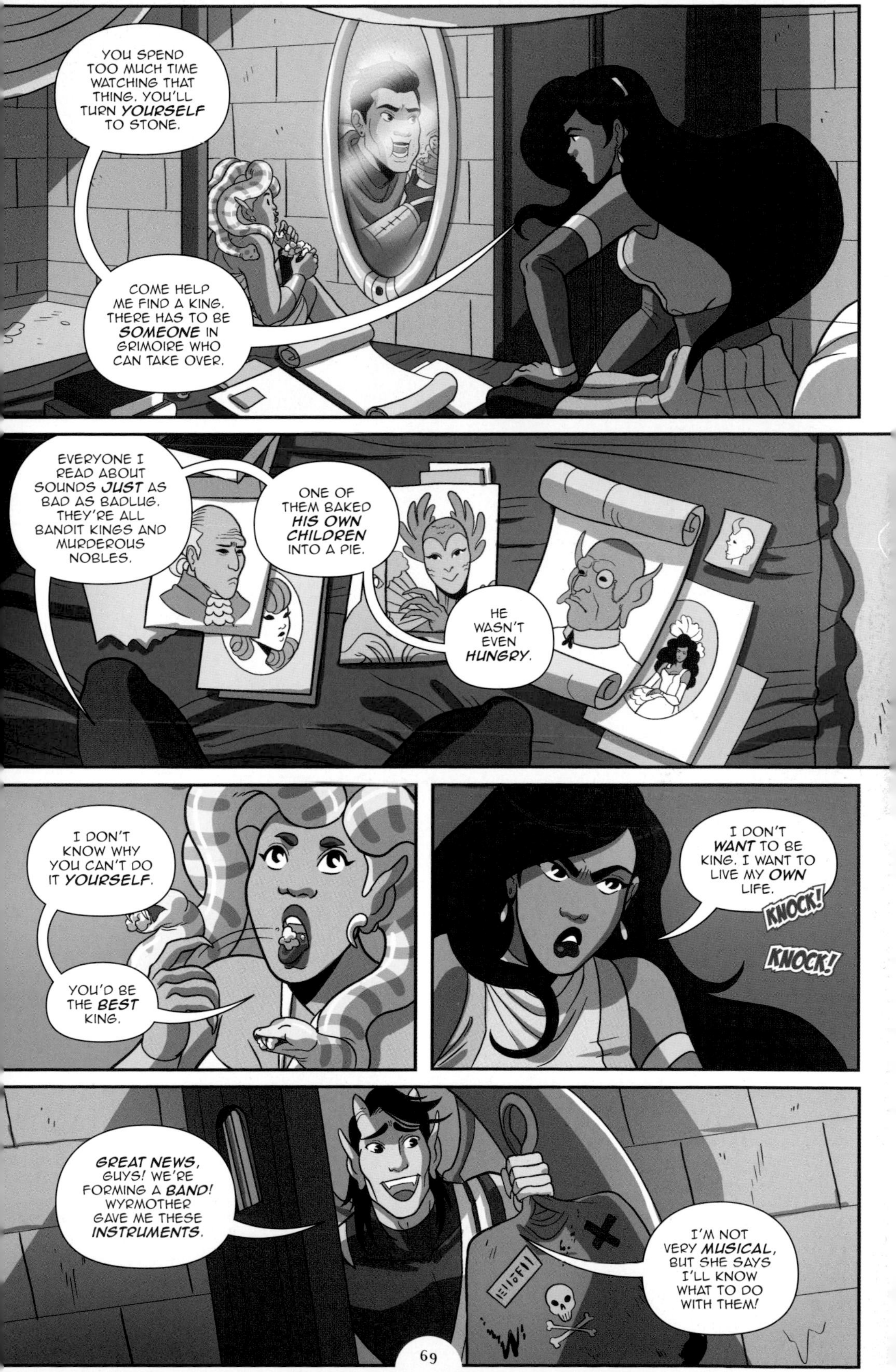
YOU SPEND TOO MUCH TIME WATCHING THAT THING. YOU'LL TURN *YOURSELF* TO STONE.
COME HELP ME FIND A KING. THERE HAS TO BE *SOMEONE* IN GRIMOIRE WHO CAN TAKE OVER.
EVERYONE I READ ABOUT SOUNDS *JUST* AS BAD AS BADLUG. THEY'RE ALL BANDIT KINGS AND MURDEROUS NOBLES.
ONE OF THEM BAKED *HIS OWN CHILDREN* INTO A PIE.
HE WASN'T EVEN *HUNGRY*.
I DON'T KNOW WHY YOU CAN'T DO IT *YOURSELF*.
YOU'D BE THE *BEST* KING.
I DON'T *WANT* TO BE KING. I WANT TO LIVE MY *OWN* LIFE.
KNOCK!
KNOCK!
GREAT NEWS, GUYS! WE'RE FORMING A *BAND*! WYRMOTHER GAVE ME THESE *INSTRUMENTS*.
I'M NOT VERY *MUSICAL*, BUT SHE SAYS I'LL KNOW WHAT TO DO WITH THEM!

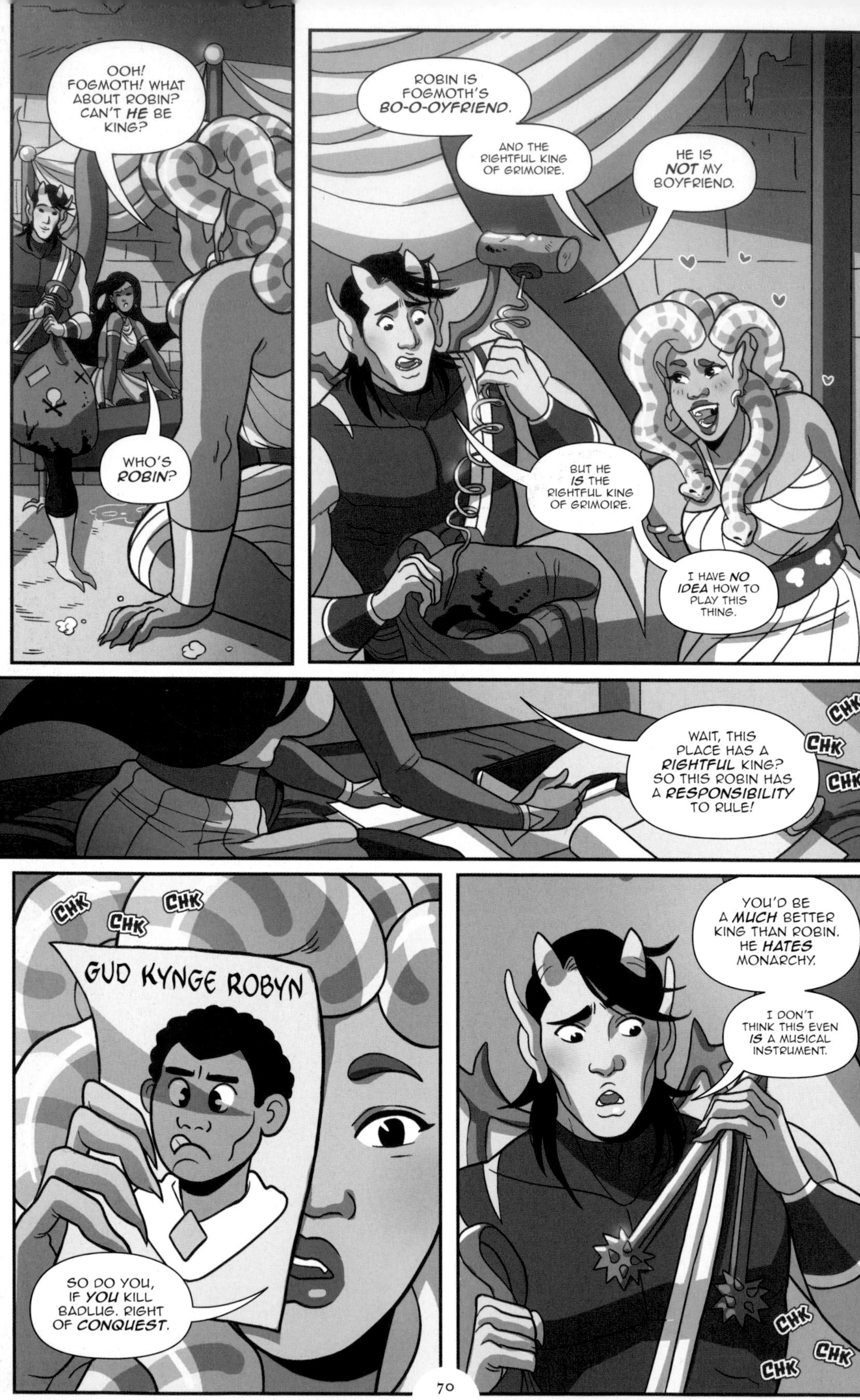
OOH! FOGMOTH! WHAT ABOUT ROBIN? CAN'T *HE* BE KING?
WHO'S *ROBIN*?
ROBIN IS FOGMOTH'S *BO-O-OYFRIEND*.
AND THE RIGHTFUL KING OF GRIMOIRE.
HE IS *NOT* MY BOYFRIEND.
BUT HE *IS* THE RIGHTFUL KING OF GRIMOIRE.
I HAVE *NO IDEA* HOW TO PLAY THIS THING.
WAIT, THIS PLACE HAS A *RIGHTFUL* KING? SO THIS ROBIN HAS A *RESPONSIBILITY* TO RULE!
CHK
CHK
CHK
CHK
CHK
CHK
GUD KYNGE ROBYN
SO DO YOU, IF *YOU* KILL BADLUG. RIGHT OF *CONQUEST*.
YOU'D BE A *MUCH* BETTER KING THAN ROBIN. HE *HATES* MONARCHY.
I DON'T THINK THIS EVEN *IS* A MUSICAL INSTRUMENT.
CHK
CHK
CHK

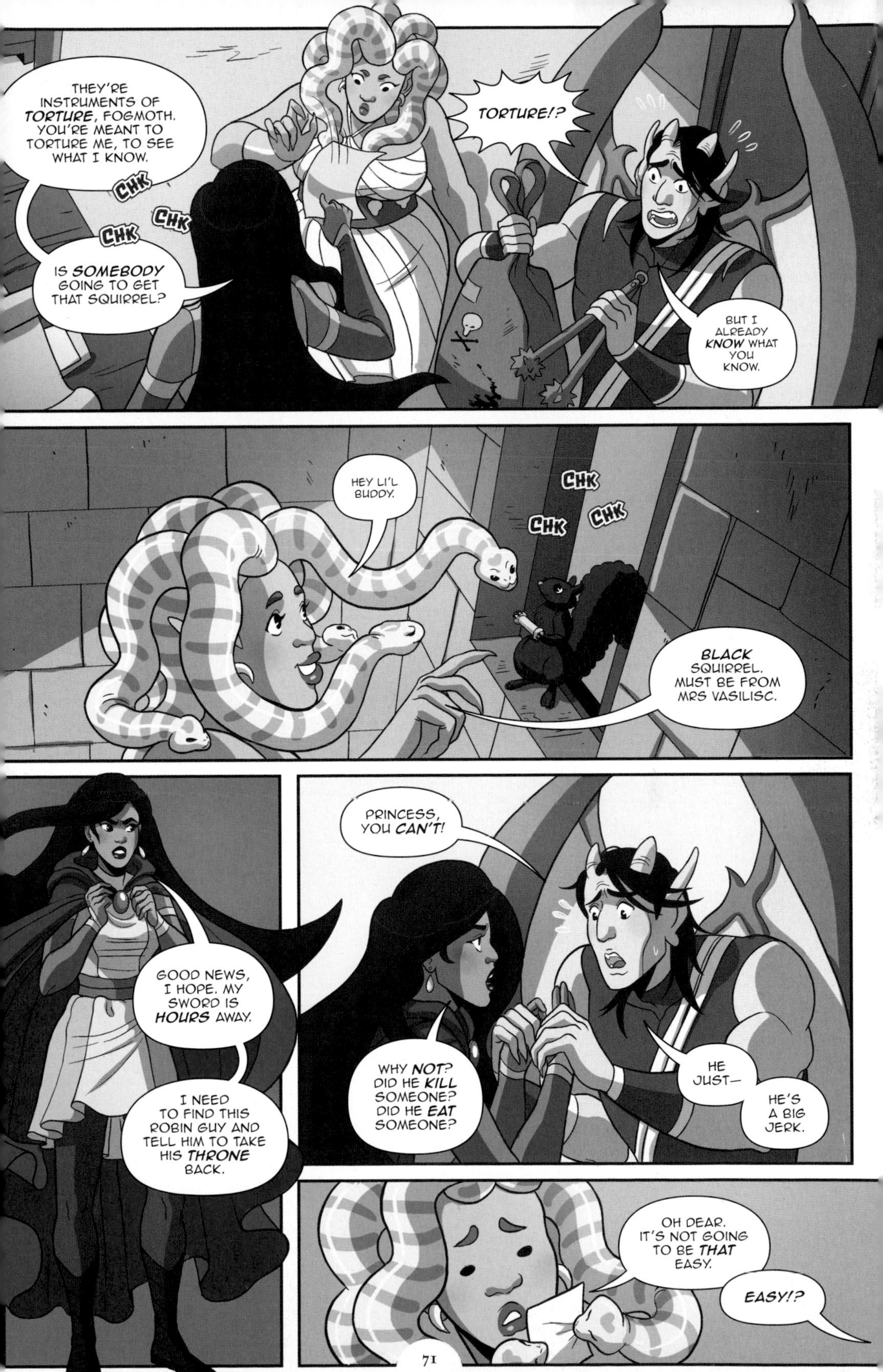
THEY'RE INSTRUMENTS OF TORTURE, FOGMOTH. YOU'RE MEANT TO TORTURE ME, TO SEE WHAT I KNOW.
CHK
CHK
CHK
IS SOMEBODY GOING TO GET THAT SQUIRREL?
TORTURE!?
BUT I ALREADY KNOW WHAT YOU KNOW.
HEY LI'L BUDDY.
CHK
CHK
CHK
BLACK SQUIRREL. MUST BE FROM MRS VASILISC.
GOOD NEWS, I HOPE. MY SWORD IS HOURS AWAY.
I NEED TO FIND THIS ROBIN GUY AND TELL HIM TO TAKE HIS THRONE BACK.
PRINCESS, YOU CAN'T!
WHY NOT? DID HE KILL SOMEONE? DID HE EAT SOMEONE?
HE JUST—
HE'S A BIG JERK.
OH DEAR. IT'S NOT GOING TO BE THAT EASY.
EASY!?

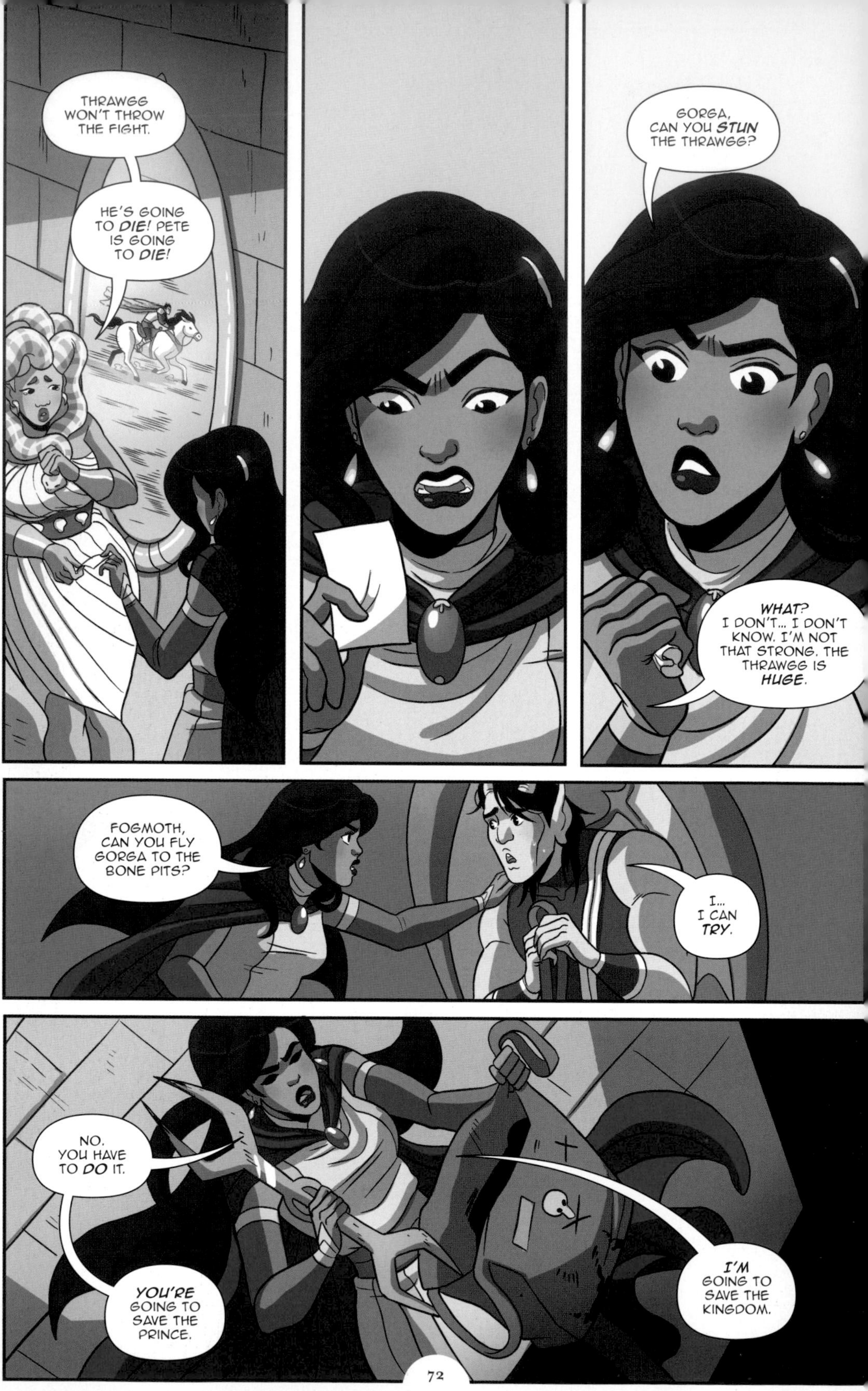
THRAWGG WON'T THROW THE FIGHT.
HE'S GOING TO *DIE*! PETE IS GOING TO *DIE*!
GORGA, CAN YOU ***STUN*** THE THRAWGG?
WHAT? I DON'T... I DON'T KNOW. I'M NOT THAT STRONG. THE THRAWGG IS ***HUGE***.
FOGMOTH, CAN YOU FLY GORGA TO THE BONE PITS?
I... I CAN *TRY*.
NO. YOU HAVE TO *DO* IT.
YOU'RE GOING TO SAVE THE PRINCE.
I'M GOING TO SAVE THE KINGDOM.

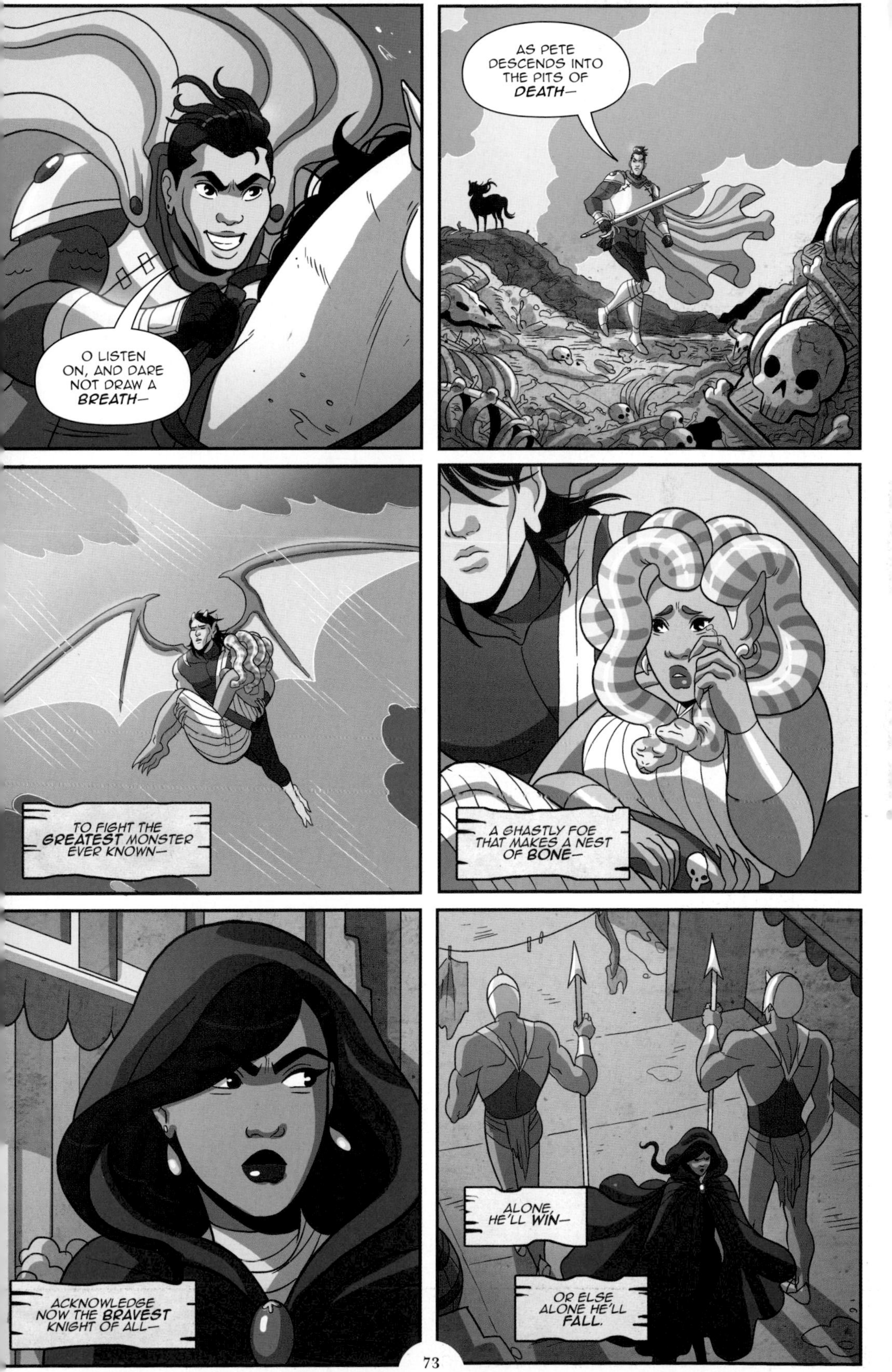
O LISTEN ON, AND DARE NOT DRAW A BREATH—
AS PETE DESCENDS INTO THE PITS OF DEATH—
TO FIGHT THE GREATEST MONSTER EVER KNOWN—
A GHASTLY FOE THAT MAKES A NEST OF BONE—
ACKNOWLEDGE NOW THE BRAVEST KNIGHT OF ALL—
ALONE, HE'LL WIN—
OR ELSE ALONE HE'LL FALL.

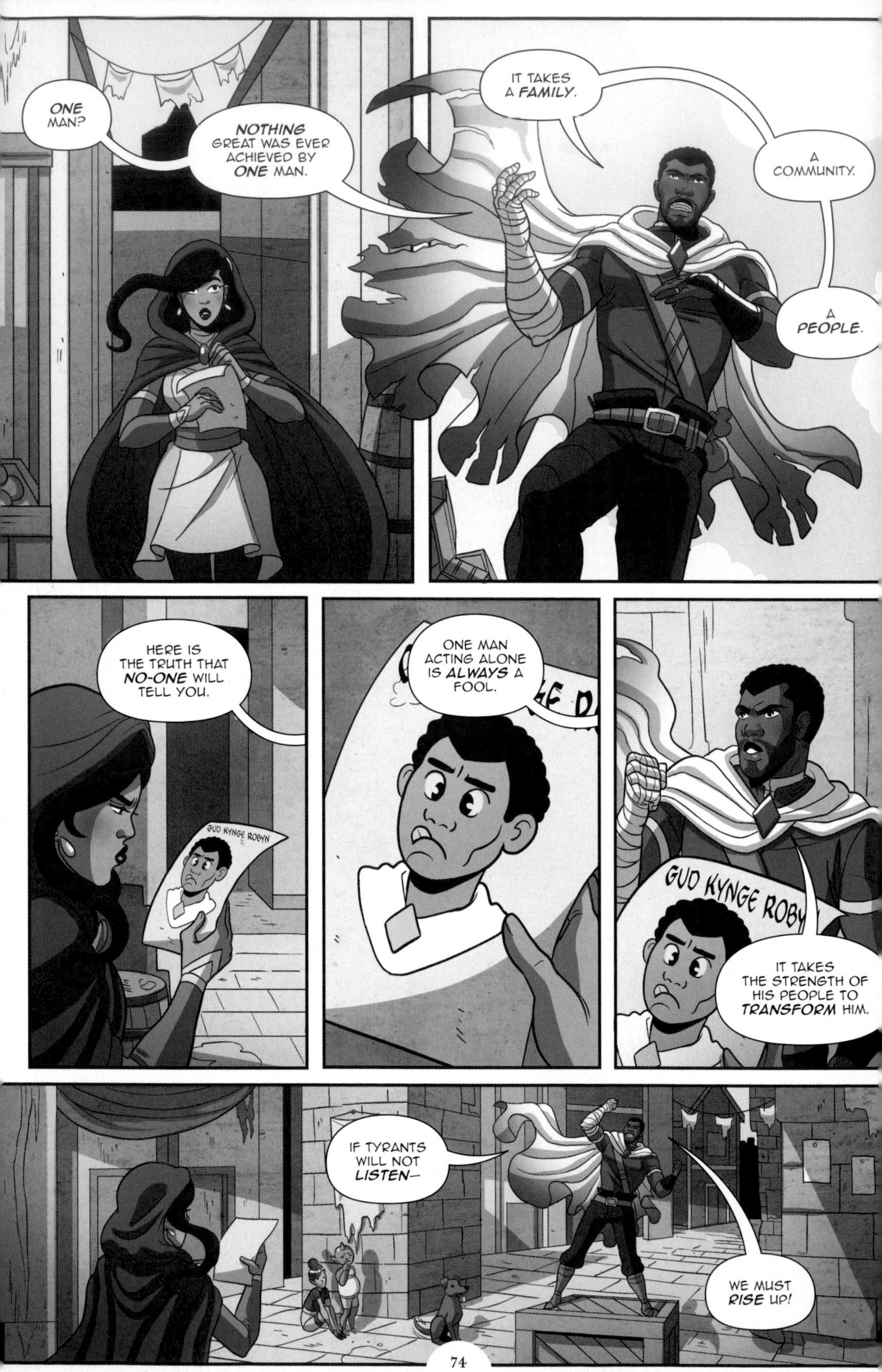
ONE MAN?
NOTHING GREAT WAS EVER ACHIEVED BY ONE MAN.
IT TAKES A FAMILY.
A COMMUNITY.
A PEOPLE.
HERE IS THE TRUTH THAT NO-ONE WILL TELL YOU.
GUD KYNGE ROBYN
ONE MAN ACTING ALONE IS ALWAYS A FOOL.
GUD KYNGE ROBY
IT TAKES THE STRENGTH OF HIS PEOPLE TO TRANSFORM HIM.
IF TYRANTS WILL NOT LISTEN—
WE MUST RISE UP!

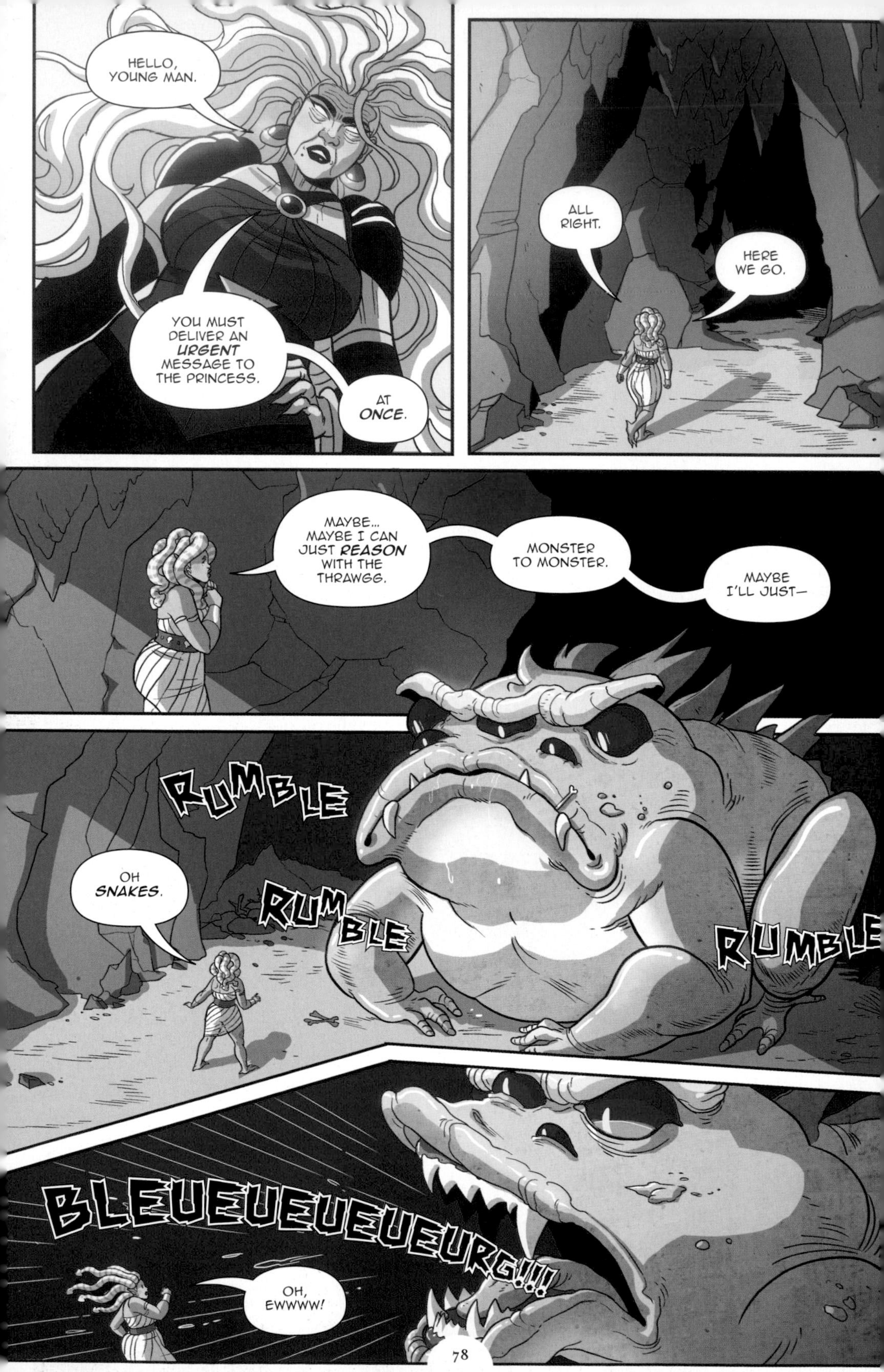
HELLO, YOUNG MAN.
YOU MUST DELIVER AN URGENT MESSAGE TO THE PRINCESS.
AT ONCE.
ALL RIGHT.
HERE WE GO.
MAYBE... MAYBE I CAN JUST REASON WITH THE THRAWGG.
MONSTER TO MONSTER.
MAYBE I'LL JUST—
RUMBLE
OH SNAKES.
RUMBLE
RUMBLE
BLEUEUEUEUEUEURG!!!
OH, EWWWW!

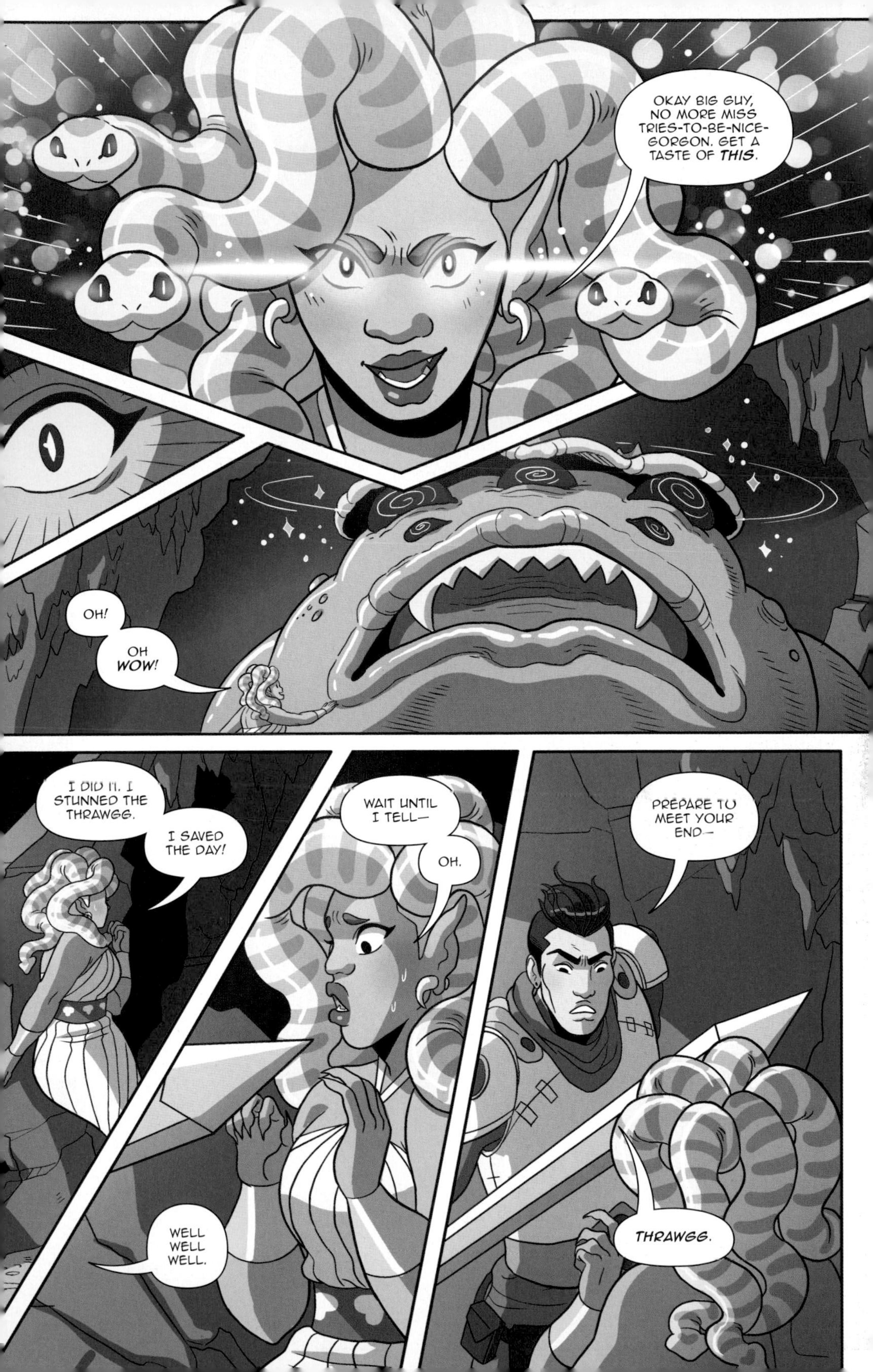
OKAY BIG GUY, NO MORE MISS TRIES-TO-BE-NICE-GORGON. GET A TASTE OF *THIS*.
OH!
OH *WOW!*
I DID IT. I STUNNED THE THRAWGG.
I SAVED THE DAY!
WAIT UNTIL I TELL—
OH.
WELL WELL WELL.
PREPARE TO MEET YOUR END—
THRAWGG.

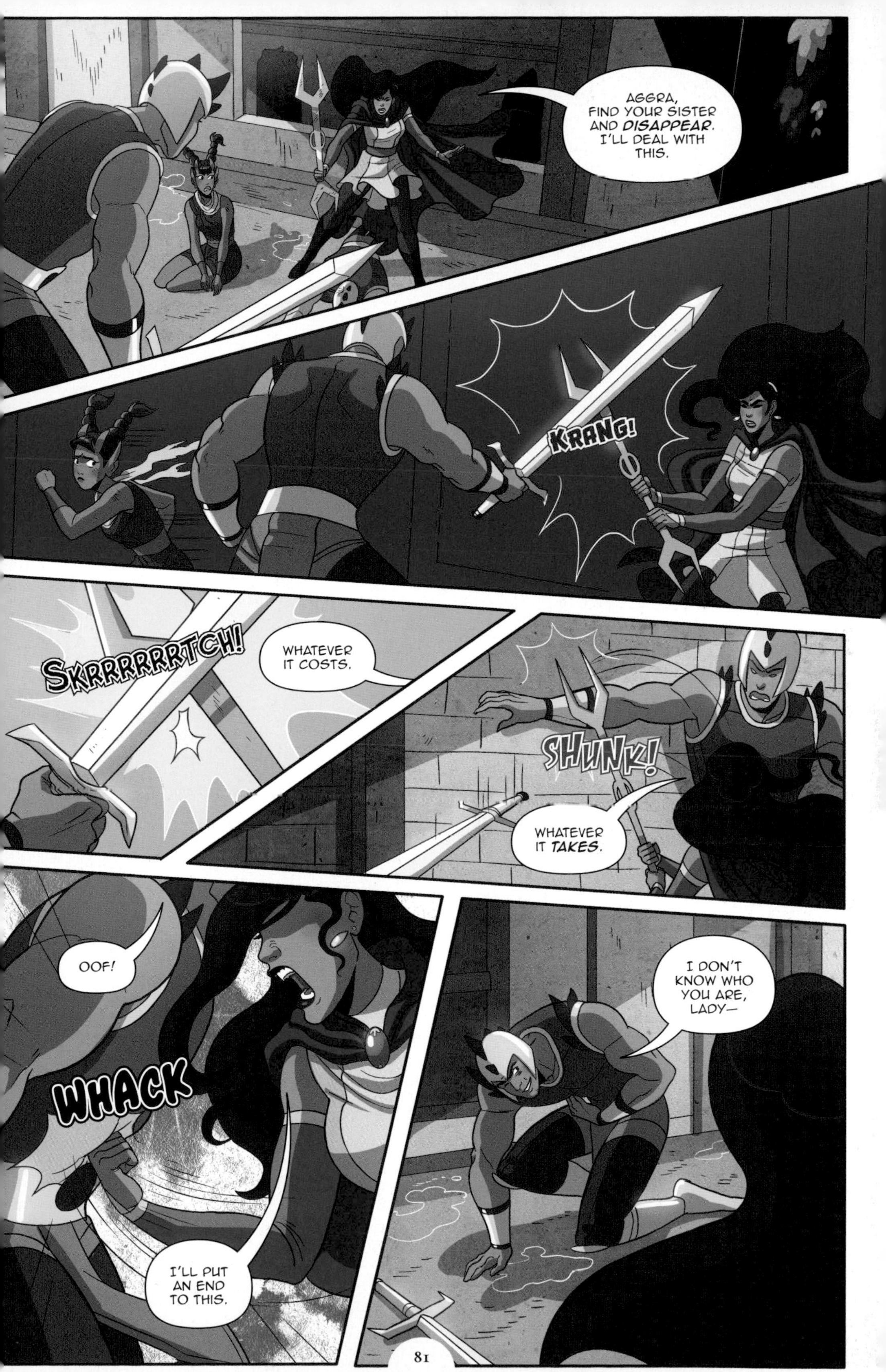
AGGRA, FIND YOUR SISTER AND DISAPPEAR. I'LL DEAL WITH THIS.
KRANG!
SKRRRRRRTCH!
WHATEVER IT COSTS.
SHUNK!
WHATEVER IT TAKES.
OOF!
WHACK
I'LL PUT AN END TO THIS.
I DON'T KNOW WHO YOU ARE, LADY—

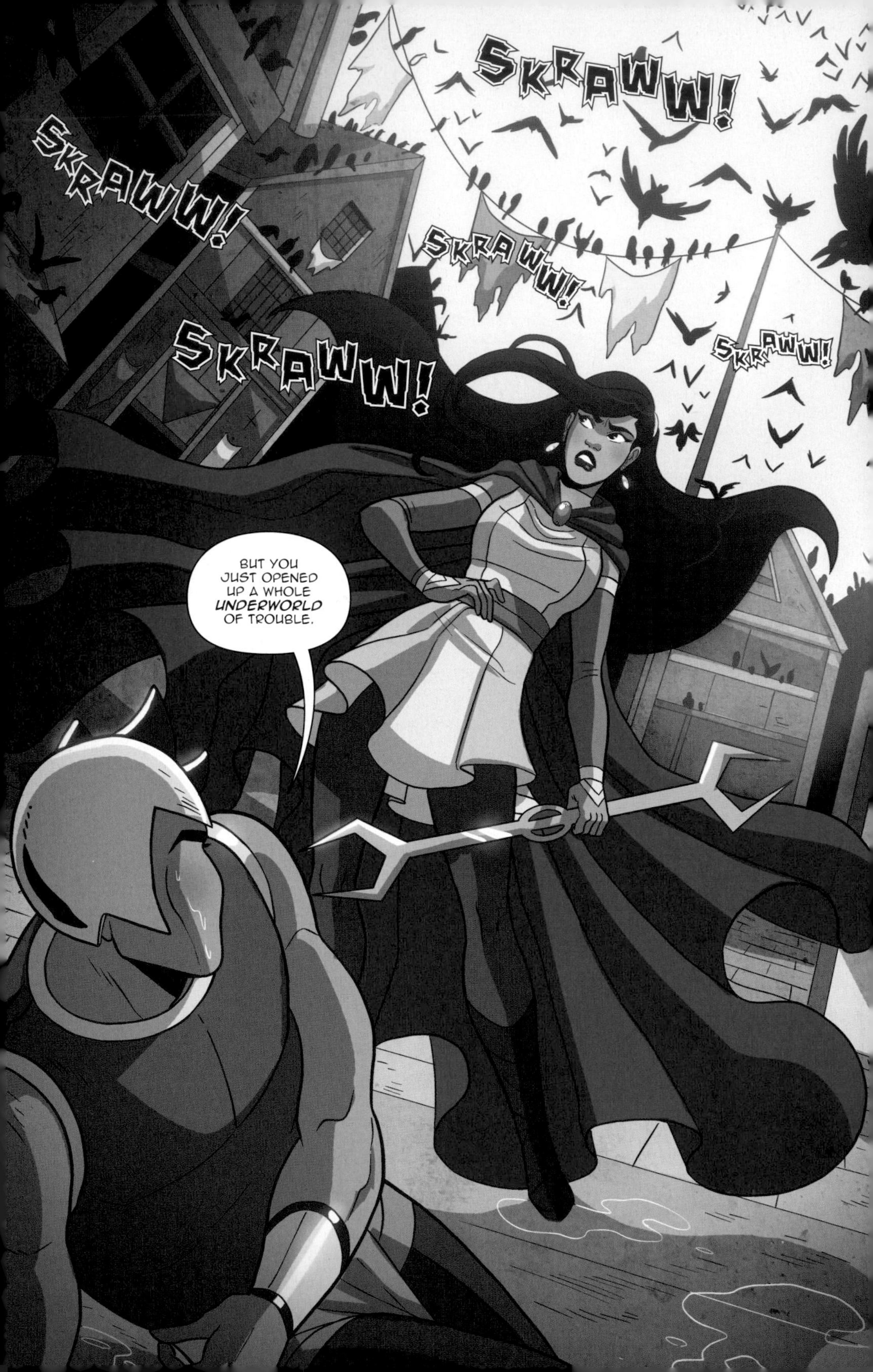
SKRAWW!
SKRAWW!
SKRAWW!
SKRAWW!
SKRAWW!
BUT YOU JUST OPENED UP A WHOLE *UNDERWORLD* OF TROUBLE.

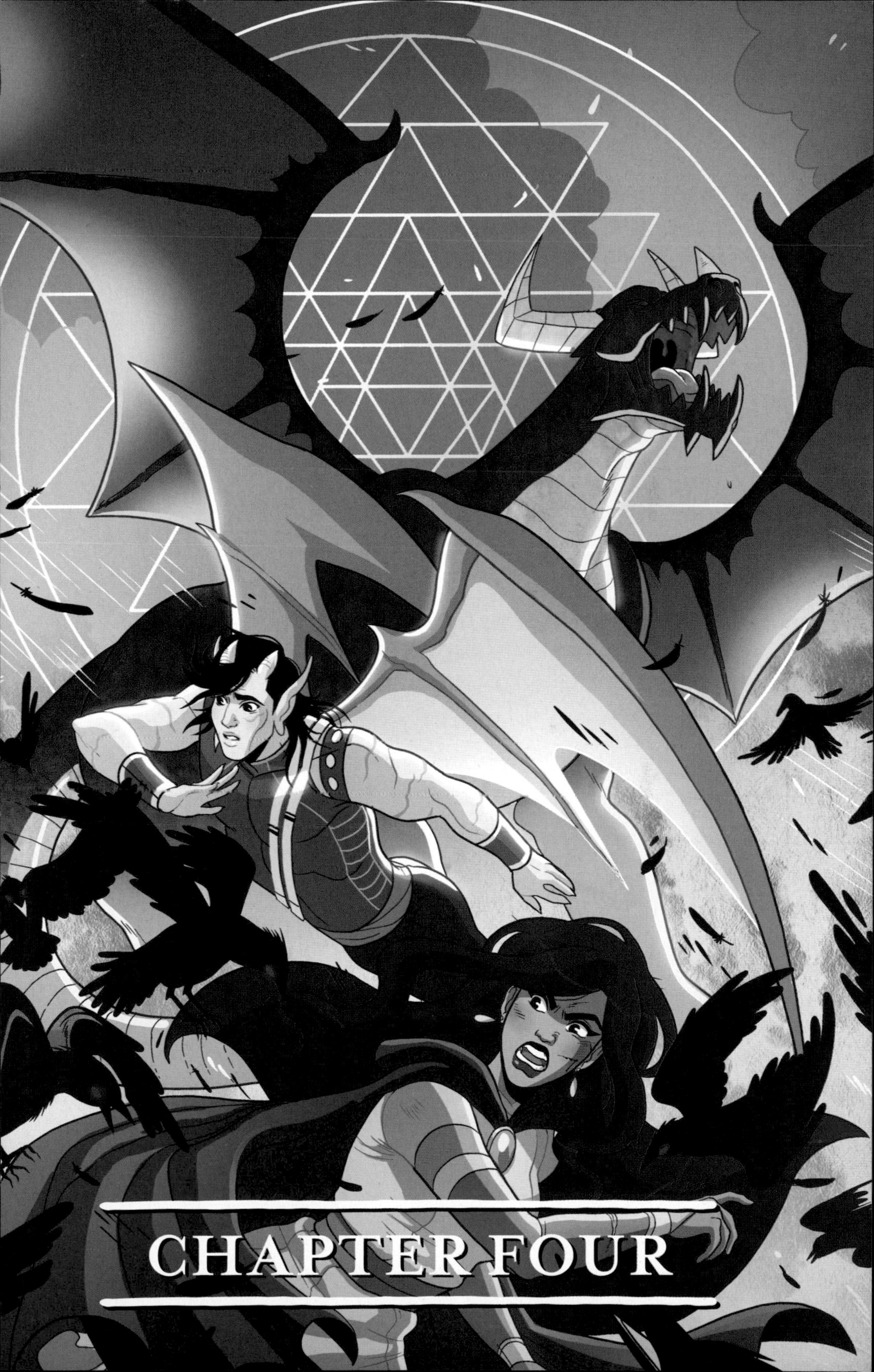

CHAPTER FOUR

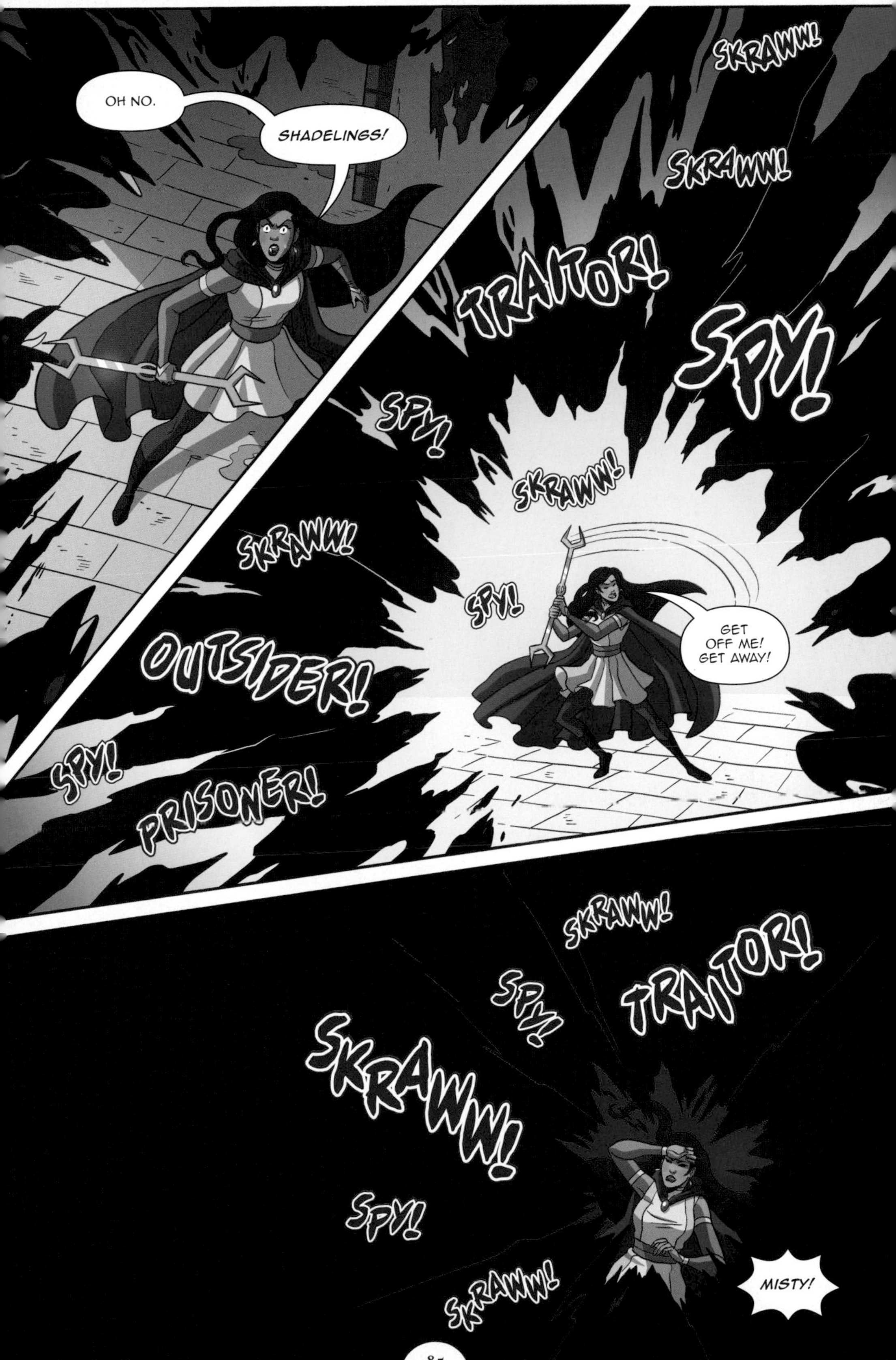
OH NO.
SHADELINGS!
SKRAWW!
SKRAWW!
TRAITOR!
SPY!
SPY!
SKRAWW!
SKRAWW!
SPY!
GET OFF ME! GET AWAY!
OUTSIDER!
SPY!
PRISONER!
SKRAWW!
SPY!
TRAITOR!
SKRAWW!
SPY!
SKRAWW!
MISTY!

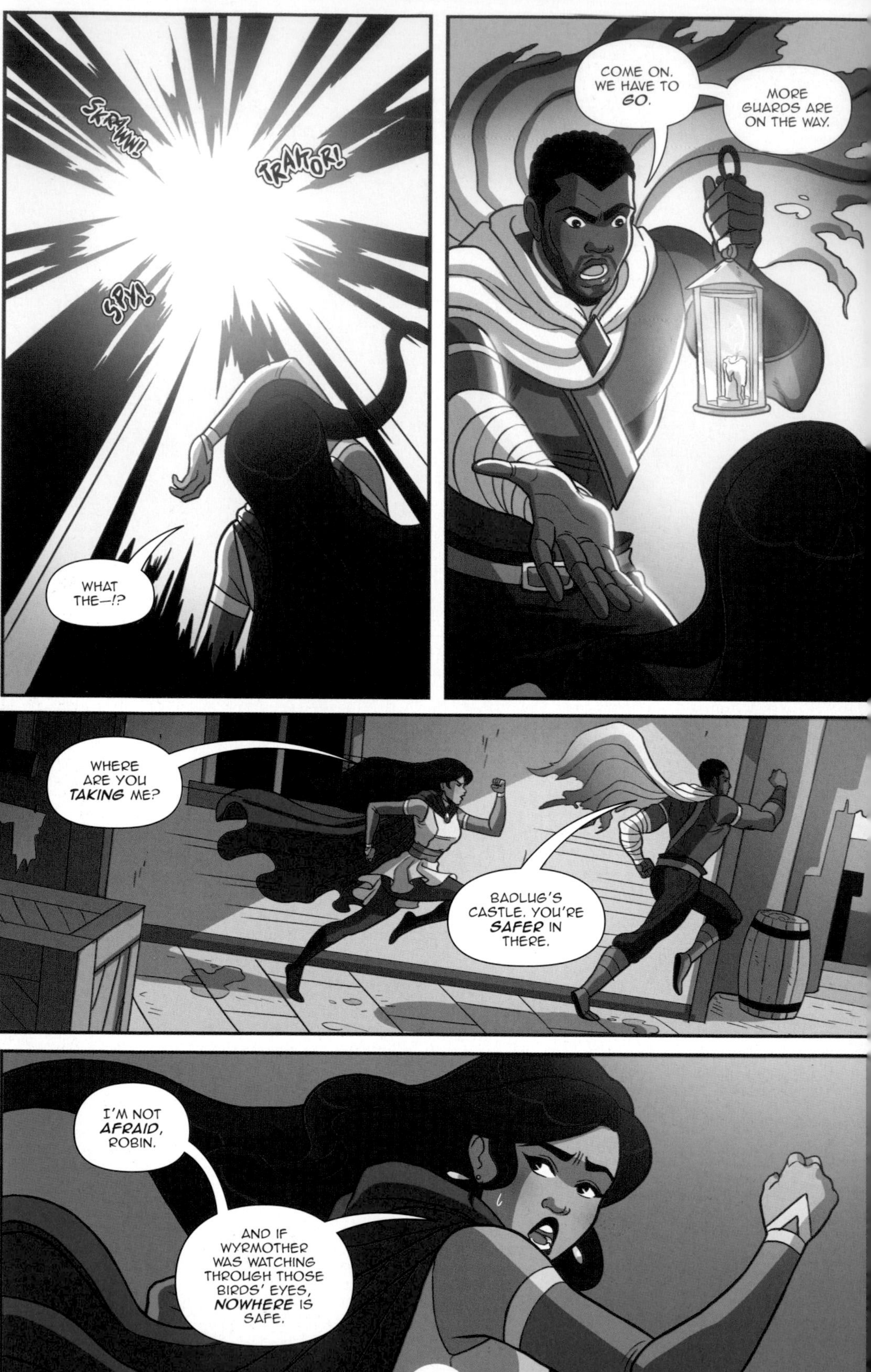
SKRAWW!
TRAITOR!
SPY!
WHAT THE—!?
COME ON. WE HAVE TO *GO*.
MORE GUARDS ARE ON THE WAY.
WHERE ARE YOU *TAKING* ME?
BADLUG'S CASTLE. YOU'RE *SAFER* IN THERE.
I'M NOT *AFRAID*, ROBIN.
AND IF WYRMOTHER WAS WATCHING THROUGH THOSE BIRDS' EYES, *NOWHERE* IS SAFE.

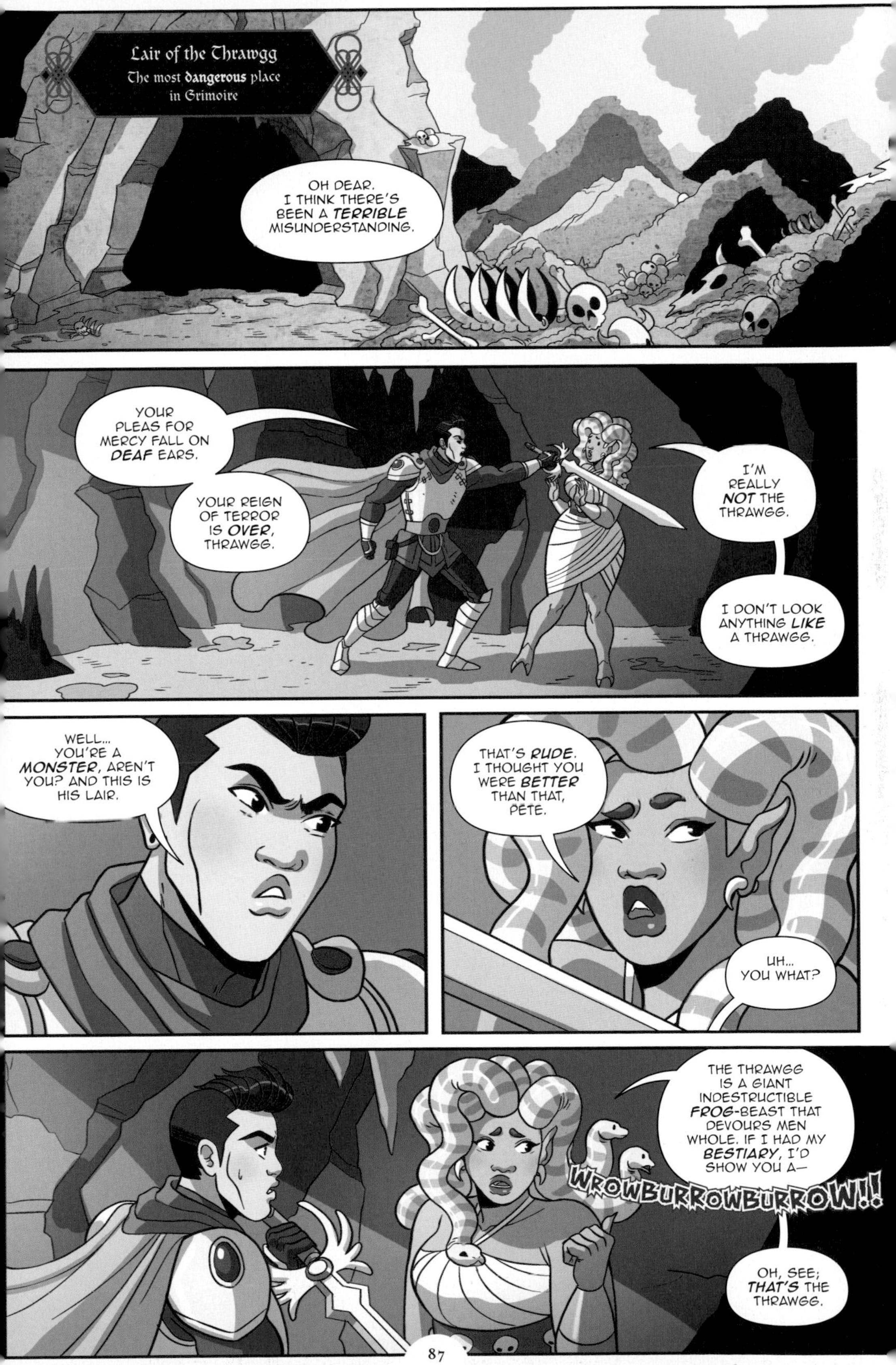
Lair of the Thrawgg
The most **dangerous** place in Grimoire
OH DEAR. I THINK THERE'S BEEN A *TERRIBLE* MISUNDERSTANDING.
YOUR PLEAS FOR MERCY FALL ON *DEAF* EARS.
YOUR REIGN OF TERROR IS *OVER*, THRAWGG.
I'M REALLY *NOT* THE THRAWGG.
I DON'T LOOK ANYTHING *LIKE* A THRAWGG.
WELL... YOU'RE A *MONSTER*, AREN'T YOU? AND THIS IS HIS LAIR.
THAT'S *RUDE*. I THOUGHT YOU WERE *BETTER* THAN THAT, PETE.
UH... YOU WHAT?
THE THRAWGG IS A GIANT INDESTRUCTIBLE *FROG*-BEAST THAT DEVOURS MEN WHOLE. IF I HAD MY *BESTIARY*, I'D SHOW YOU A—
WROWBURROWBURROW!!
OH, SEE; *THAT'S* THE THRAWGG.

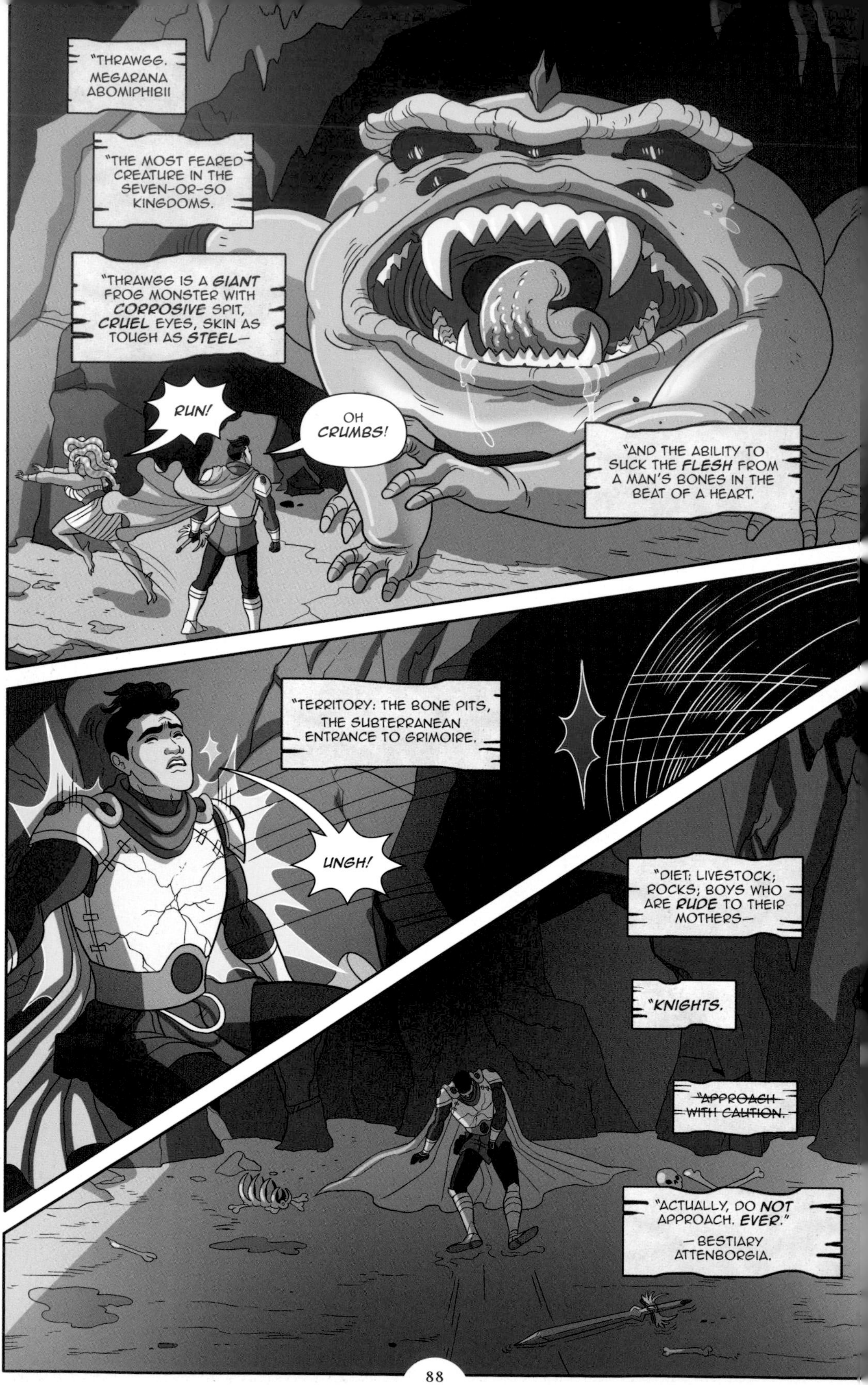

"THRAWGG. MEGARANA ABOMIPHIBII
"THE MOST FEARED CREATURE IN THE SEVEN-OR-SO KINGDOMS.
"THRAWGG IS A GIANT FROG MONSTER WITH CORROSIVE SPIT, CRUEL EYES, SKIN AS TOUGH AS STEEL—
RUN!
OH CRUMBS!
"AND THE ABILITY TO SUCK THE FLESH FROM A MAN'S BONES IN THE BEAT OF A HEART.
"TERRITORY: THE BONE PITS, THE SUBTERRANEAN ENTRANCE TO GRIMOIRE.
UNGH!
"DIET: LIVESTOCK; ROCKS; BOYS WHO ARE RUDE TO THEIR MOTHERS—
"KNIGHTS.
~~"APPROACH WITH CAUTION.~~
"ACTUALLY, DO NOT APPROACH. EVER."
—BESTIARY ATTENBORGIA.

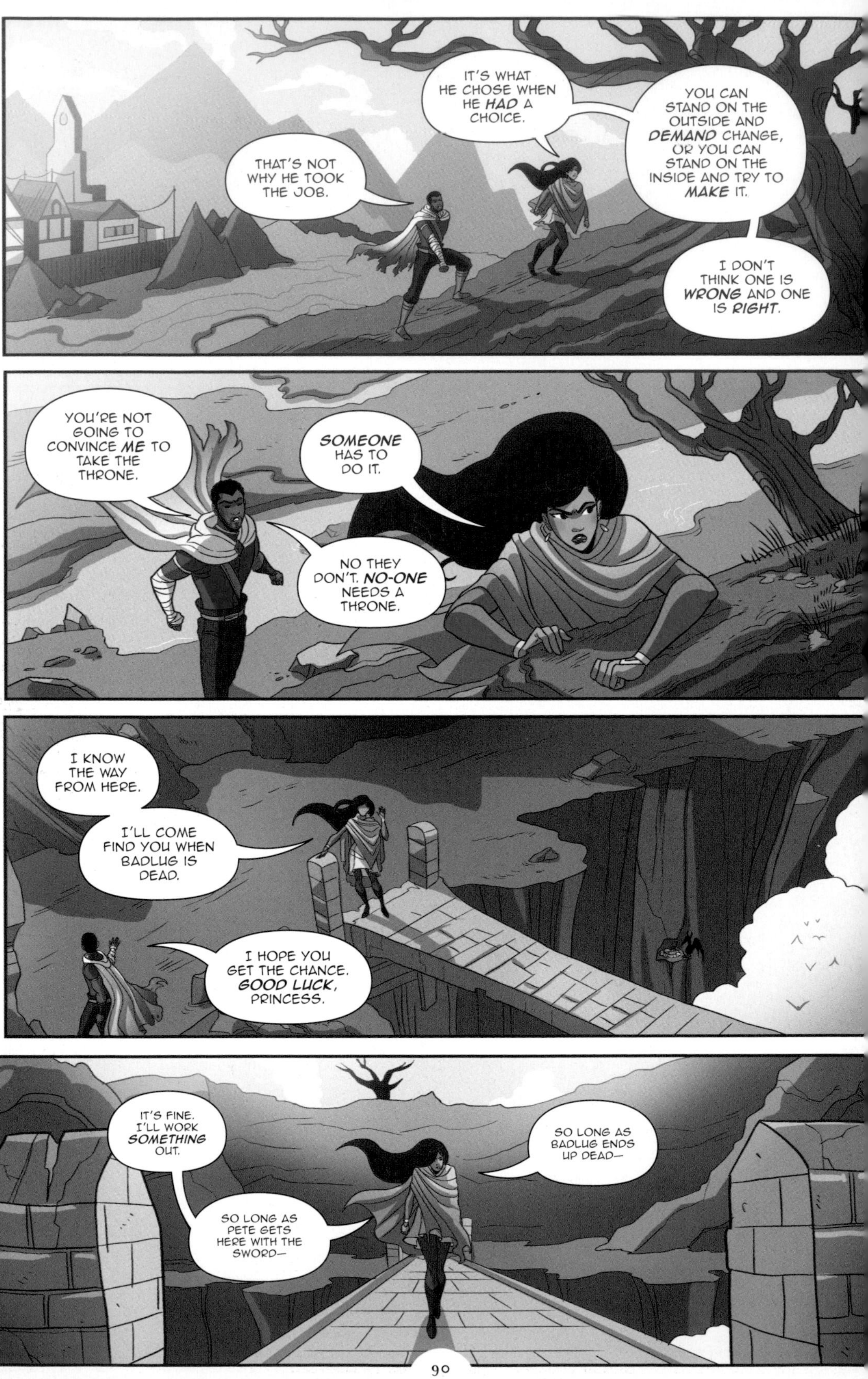
THAT'S NOT WHY HE TOOK THE JOB.
IT'S WHAT HE CHOSE WHEN HE *HAD* A CHOICE.
YOU CAN STAND ON THE OUTSIDE AND *DEMAND* CHANGE, OR YOU CAN STAND ON THE INSIDE AND TRY TO *MAKE* IT.
I DON'T THINK ONE IS *WRONG* AND ONE IS *RIGHT*.
YOU'RE NOT GOING TO CONVINCE *ME* TO TAKE THE THRONE.
SOMEONE HAS TO DO IT.
NO THEY DON'T. *NO-ONE* NEEDS A THRONE.
I KNOW THE WAY FROM HERE.
I'LL COME FIND YOU WHEN BADLUG IS DEAD.
I HOPE YOU GET THE CHANCE. *GOOD LUCK*, PRINCESS.
IT'S FINE. I'LL WORK *SOMETHING* OUT.
SO LONG AS PETE GETS HERE WITH THE SWORD—
SO LONG AS BADLUG ENDS UP DEAD—

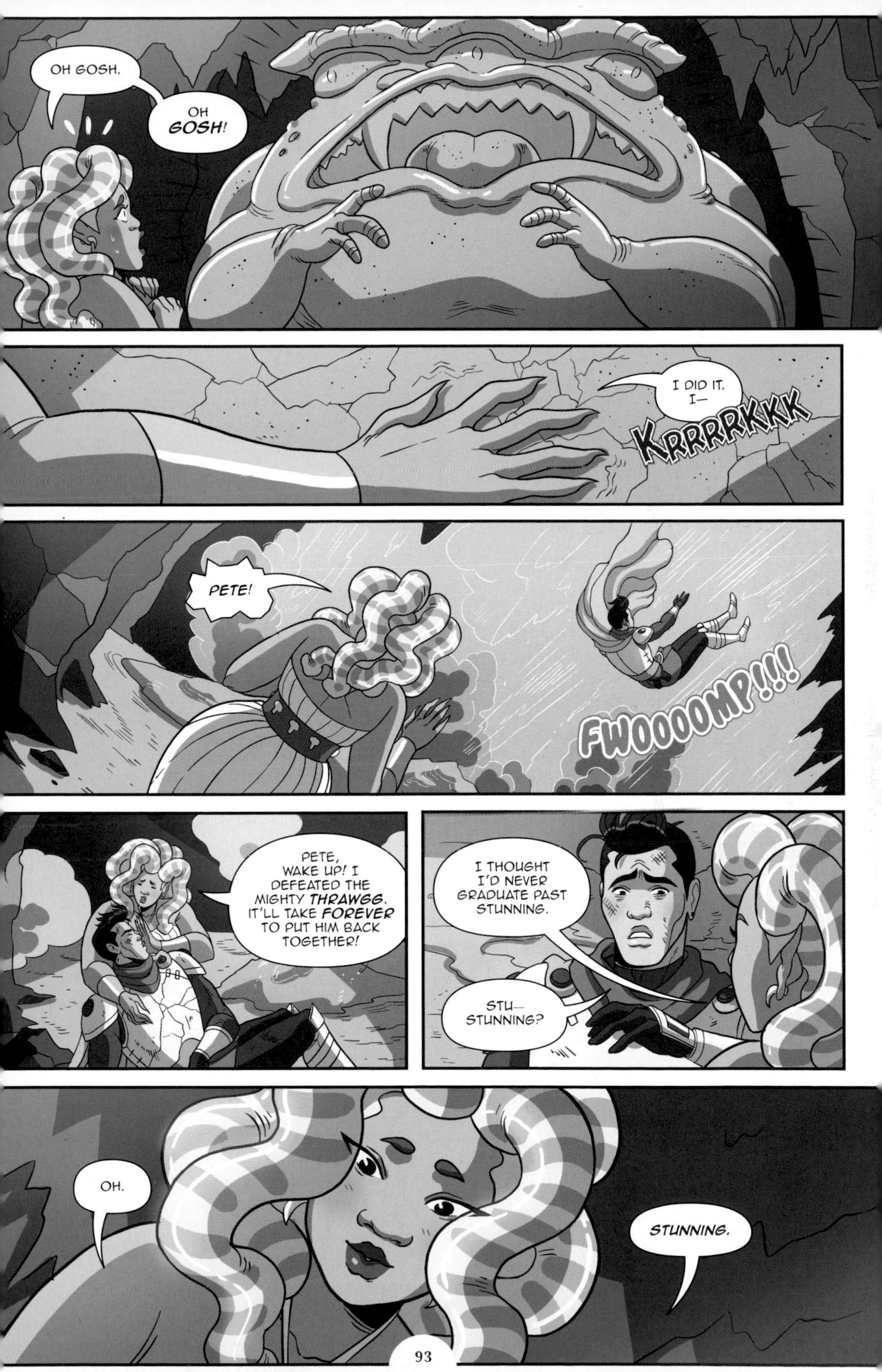
OH GOSH.
OH *GOSH!*
I DID IT. I—
KRRRRKKK
PETE!
FWOOOOMP!!!
PETE, WAKE UP! I DEFEATED THE MIGHTY *THRAWGG.* IT'LL TAKE *FOREVER* TO PUT HIM BACK TOGETHER!
I THOUGHT I'D NEVER GRADUATE PAST STUNNING.
STU— STUNNING?
OH.
STUNNING.

95

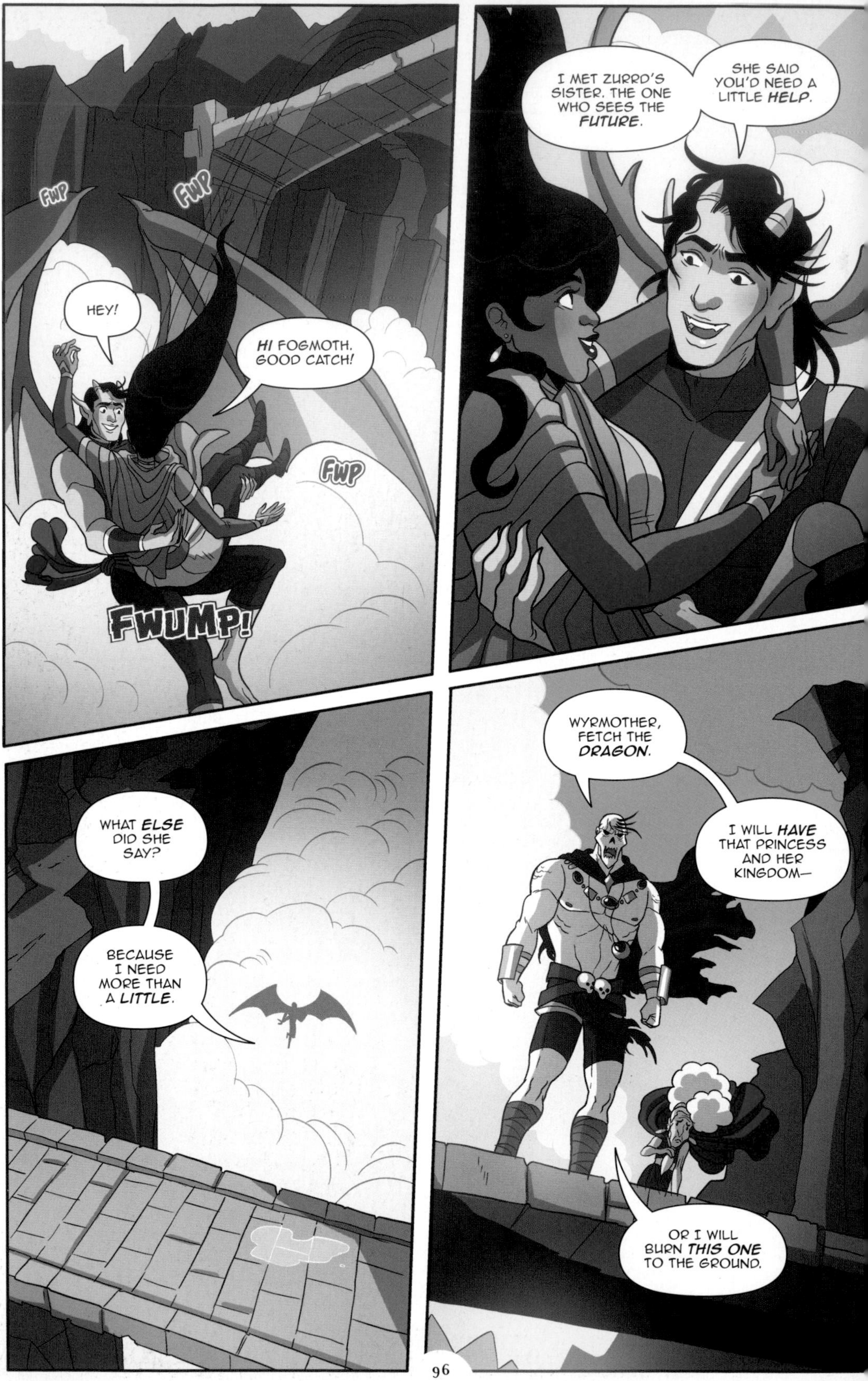
FWP
FWP
HEY!
HI FOGMOTH. GOOD CATCH!
FWP
FWUMP!
I MET ZURRD'S SISTER. THE ONE WHO SEES THE FUTURE.
SHE SAID YOU'D NEED A LITTLE HELP.
WHAT ELSE DID SHE SAY?
BECAUSE I NEED MORE THAN A LITTLE.
WYRMOTHER, FETCH THE DRAGON.
I WILL HAVE THAT PRINCESS AND HER KINGDOM—
OR I WILL BURN THIS ONE TO THE GROUND.

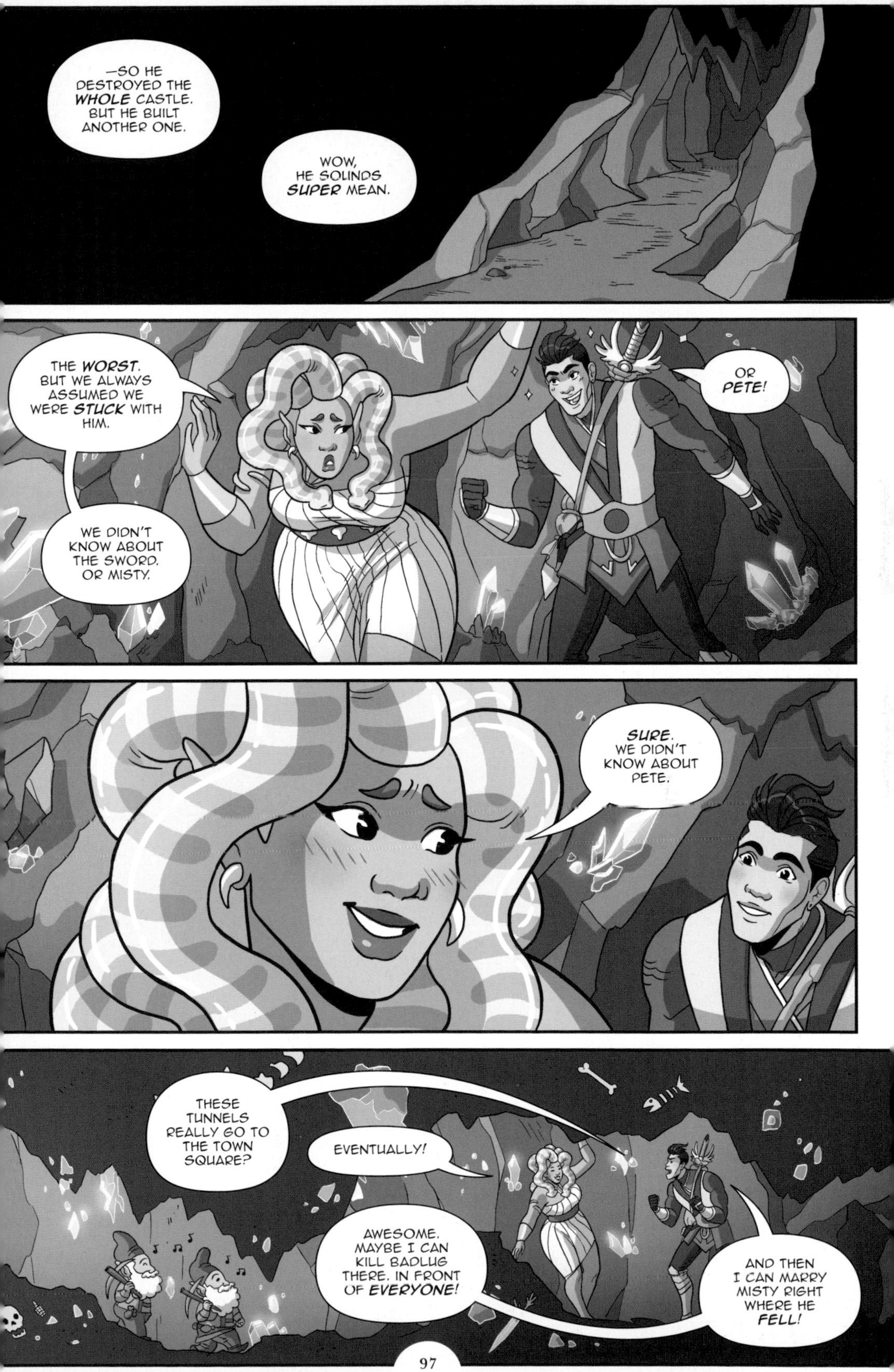
—SO HE DESTROYED THE *WHOLE* CASTLE. BUT HE BUILT ANOTHER ONE.
WOW, HE SOUNDS *SUPER* MEAN.
THE *WORST*. BUT WE ALWAYS ASSUMED WE WERE *STUCK* WITH HIM.
WE DIDN'T KNOW ABOUT THE SWORD. OR MISTY.
OR *PETE!*
SURE. WE DIDN'T KNOW ABOUT PETE.
THESE TUNNELS REALLY GO TO THE TOWN SQUARE?
EVENTUALLY!
AWESOME. MAYBE I CAN KILL BADLUG THERE. IN FRONT OF *EVERYONE!*
AND THEN I CAN MARRY MISTY RIGHT WHERE HE *FELL!*

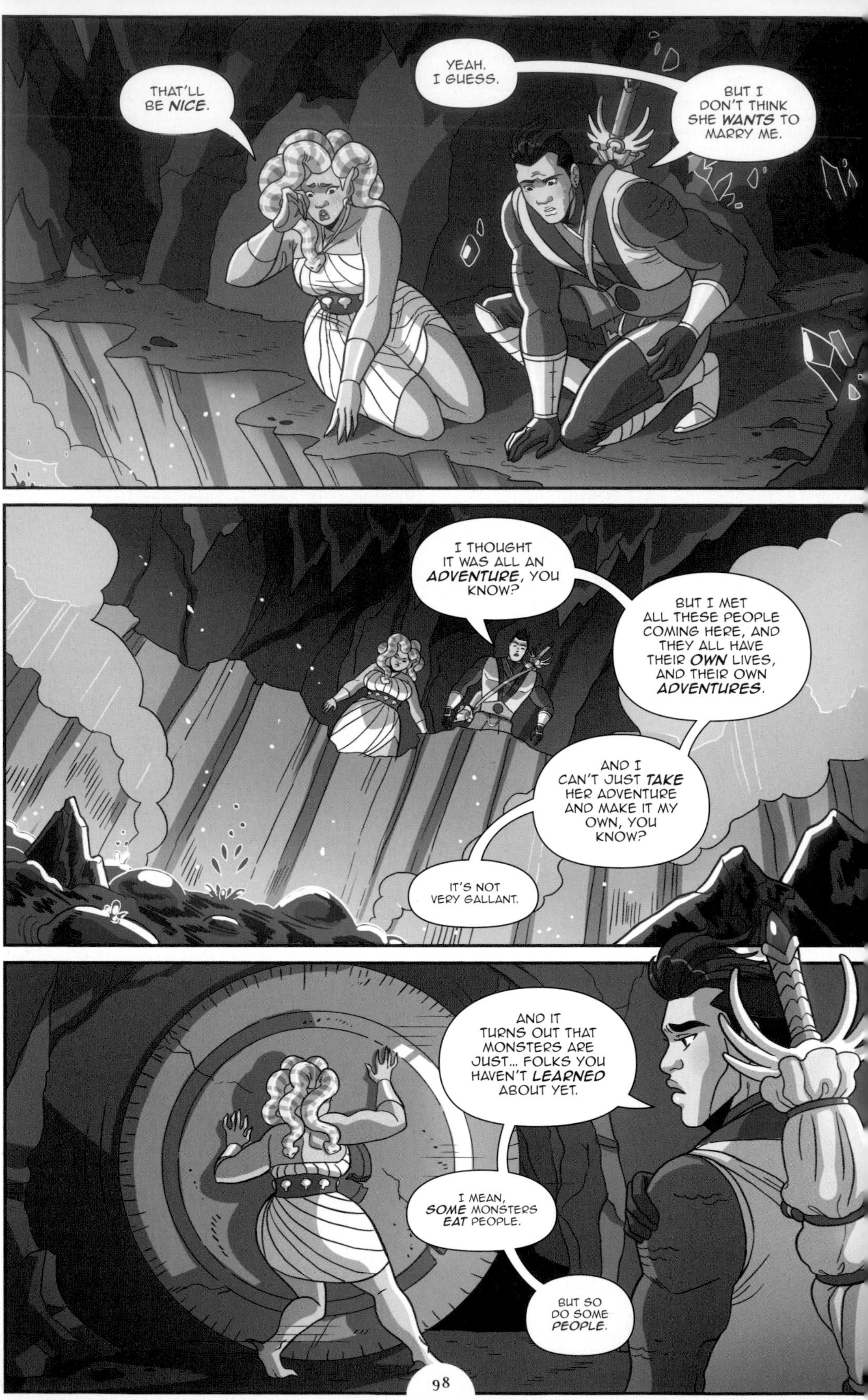
THAT'LL BE *NICE*.
YEAH. I GUESS.
BUT I DON'T THINK SHE *WANTS* TO MARRY ME.
I THOUGHT IT WAS ALL AN *ADVENTURE*, YOU KNOW?
BUT I MET ALL THESE PEOPLE COMING HERE, AND THEY ALL HAVE THEIR *OWN* LIVES, AND THEIR OWN *ADVENTURES*.
AND I CAN'T JUST *TAKE* HER ADVENTURE AND MAKE IT MY OWN, YOU KNOW?
IT'S NOT VERY GALLANT.
AND IT TURNS OUT THAT MONSTERS ARE JUST... FOLKS YOU HAVEN'T *LEARNED* ABOUT YET.
I MEAN, *SOME* MONSTERS *EAT* PEOPLE.
BUT SO DO SOME *PEOPLE*.

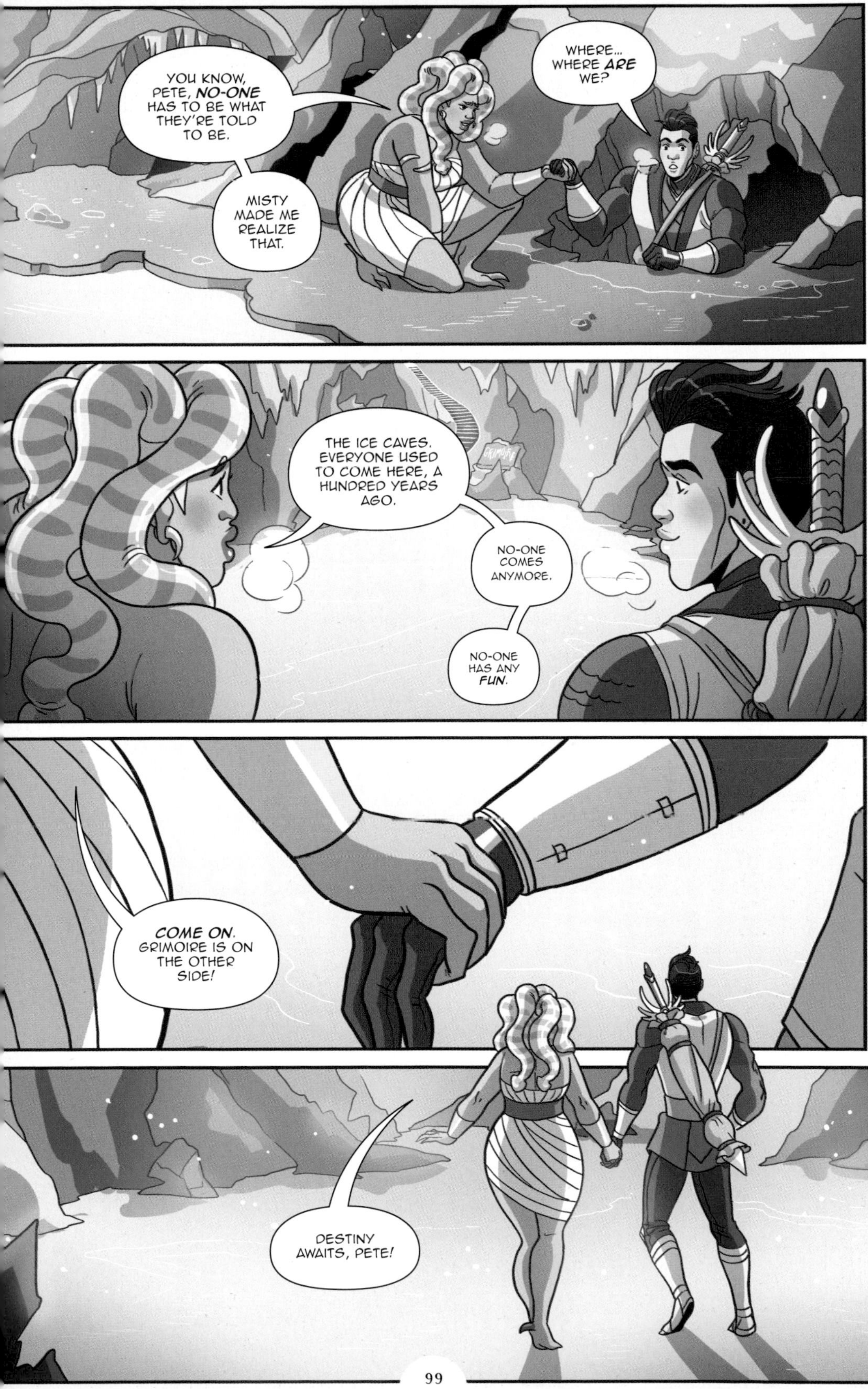
YOU KNOW, PETE, NO-ONE HAS TO BE WHAT THEY'RE TOLD TO BE.
MISTY MADE ME REALIZE THAT.
WHERE... WHERE ARE WE?
THE ICE CAVES. EVERYONE USED TO COME HERE, A HUNDRED YEARS AGO.
NO-ONE COMES ANYMORE.
NO-ONE HAS ANY FUN.
COME ON. GRIMOIRE IS ON THE OTHER SIDE!
DESTINY AWAITS, PETE!

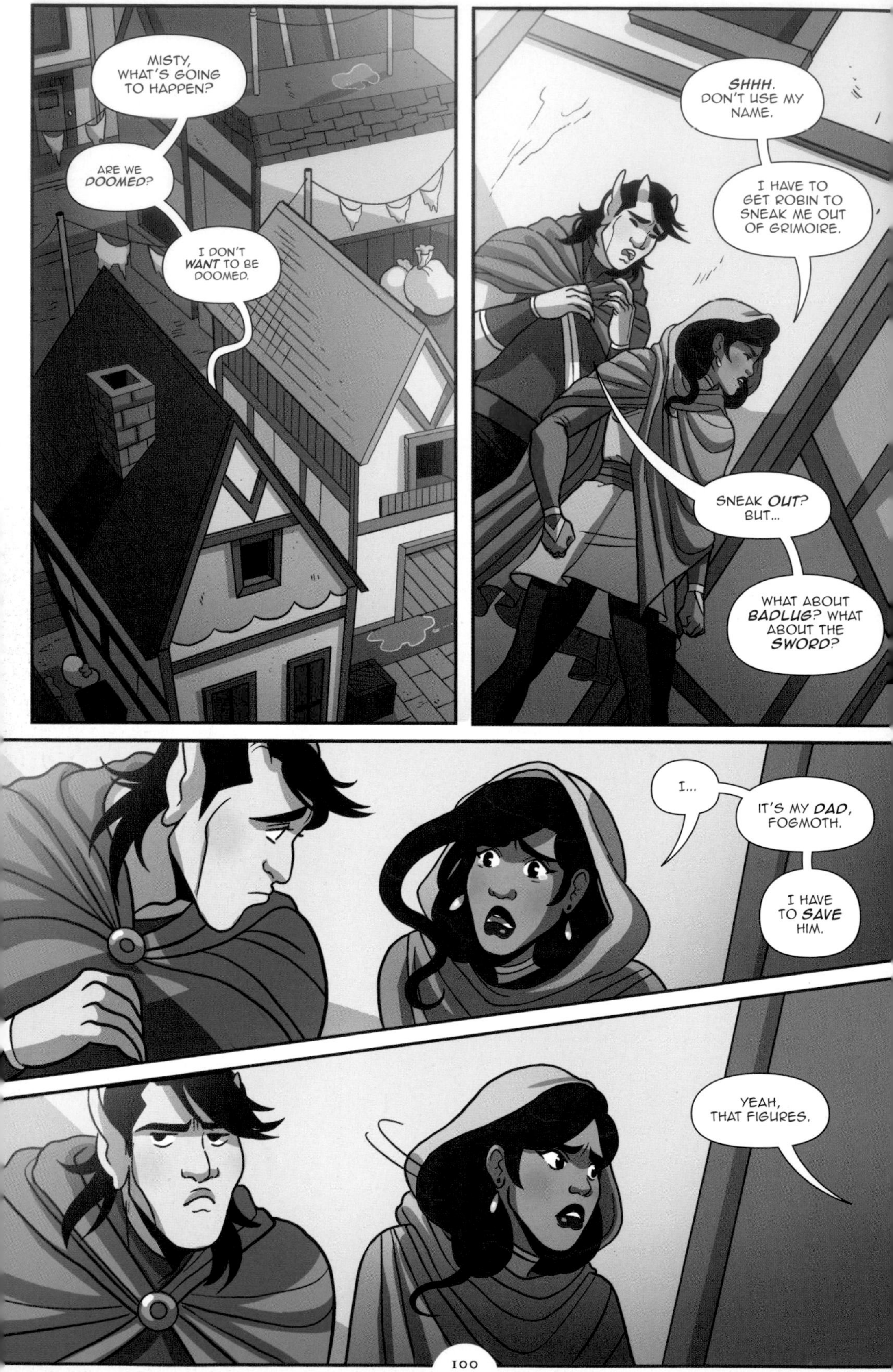
MISTY, WHAT'S GOING TO HAPPEN?
ARE WE *DOOMED*?
I DON'T *WANT* TO BE DOOMED.
SHHH. DON'T USE MY NAME.
I HAVE TO GET ROBIN TO SNEAK ME OUT OF GRIMOIRE.
SNEAK *OUT*? BUT...
WHAT ABOUT *BADLUG*? WHAT ABOUT THE *SWORD*?
I...
IT'S MY *DAD*, FOGMOTH.
I HAVE TO *SAVE* HIM.
YEAH, THAT FIGURES.

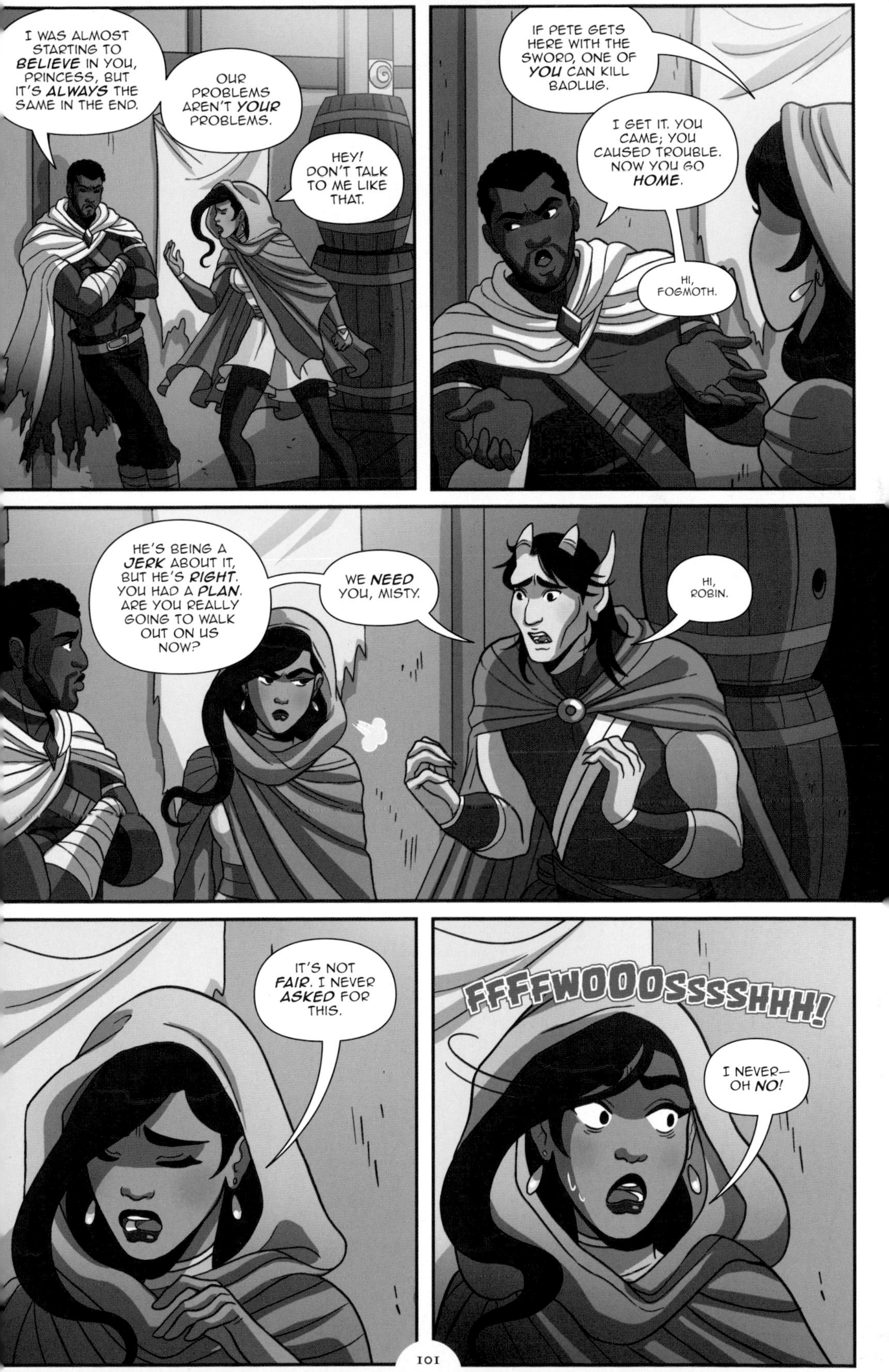
I WAS ALMOST STARTING TO **BELIEVE** IN YOU, PRINCESS, BUT IT'S **ALWAYS** THE SAME IN THE END.
OUR PROBLEMS AREN'T **YOUR** PROBLEMS.
HEY! DON'T TALK TO ME LIKE THAT.
IF PETE GETS HERE WITH THE SWORD, ONE OF **YOU** CAN KILL BADLUG.
I GET IT. YOU CAME; YOU CAUSED TROUBLE. NOW YOU GO **HOME**.
HI, FOGMOTH.
HE'S BEING A **JERK** ABOUT IT, BUT HE'S **RIGHT**. YOU HAD A **PLAN**. ARE YOU REALLY GOING TO WALK OUT ON US NOW?
WE **NEED** YOU, MISTY.
HI, ROBIN.
IT'S NOT **FAIR**. I NEVER **ASKED** FOR THIS.
FFFFWOOOOSSSSSHHH!
I NEVER— OH **NO**!

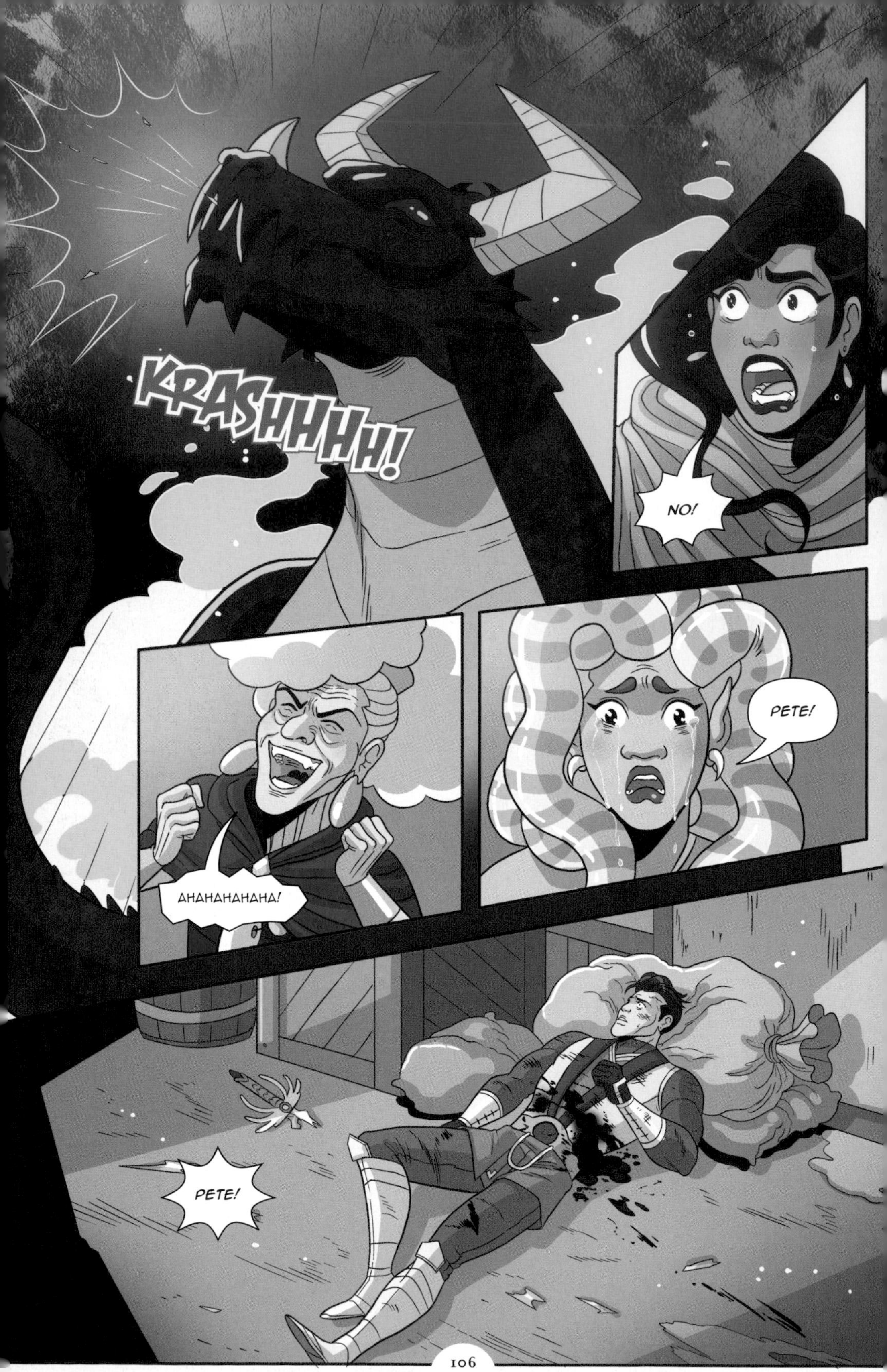
KRASHHHH!
NO!
AHAHAHAHAHA!
PETE!
PETE!

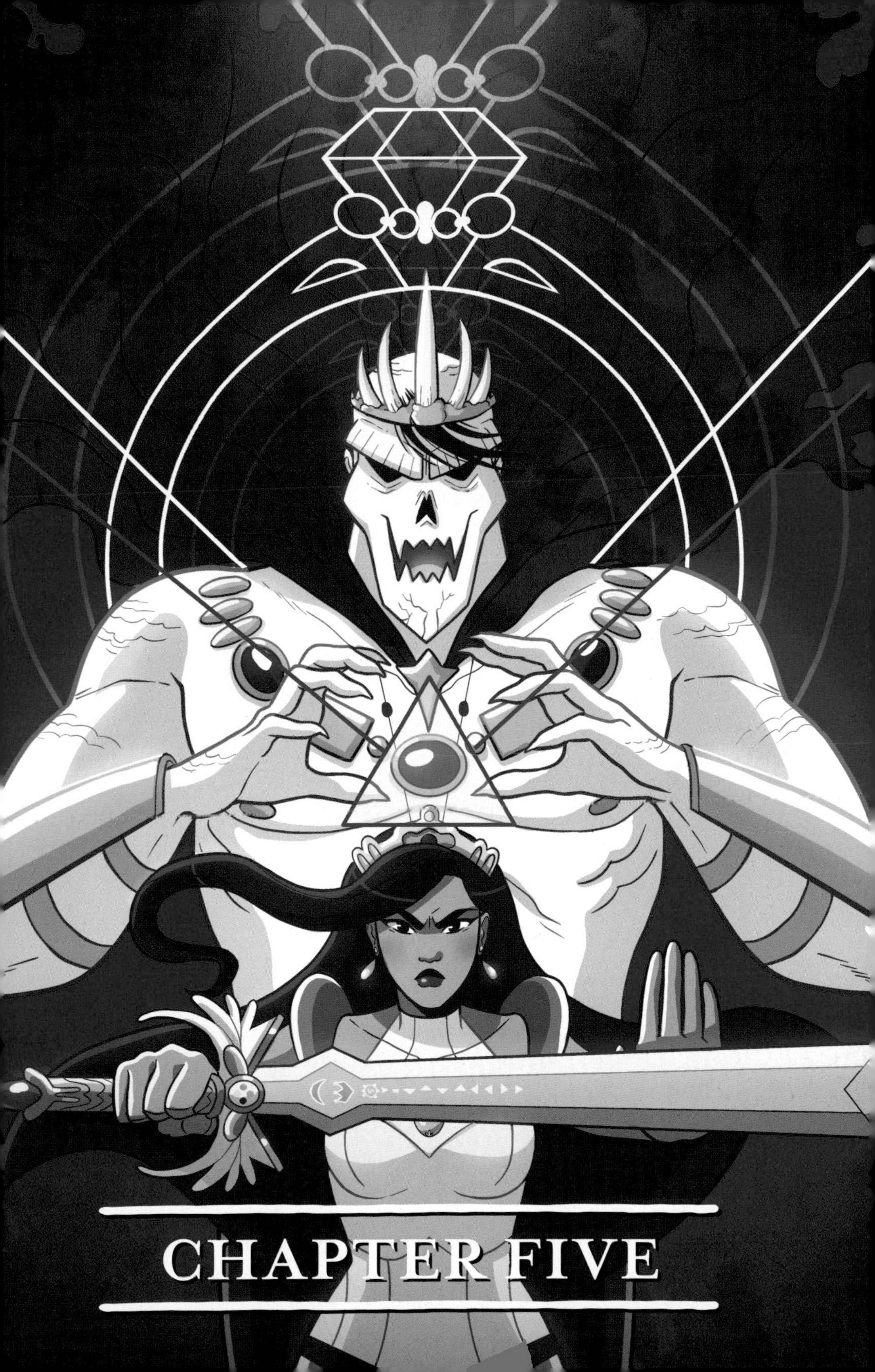

CHAPTER FIVE

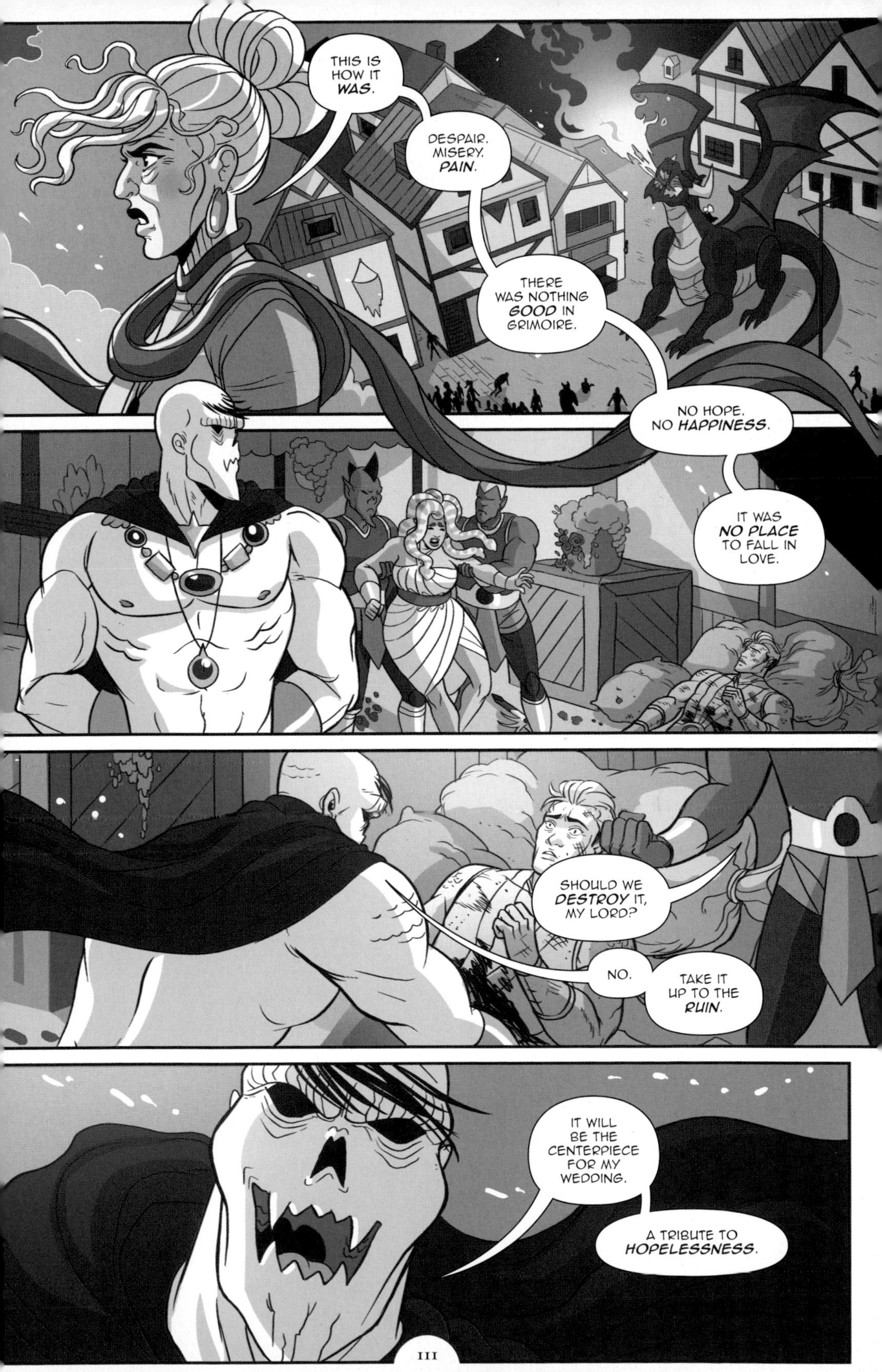

THIS IS HOW IT WAS.
DESPAIR. MISERY. PAIN.
THERE WAS NOTHING GOOD IN GRIMOIRE.
NO HOPE. NO HAPPINESS.
IT WAS NO PLACE TO FALL IN LOVE.
SHOULD WE DESTROY IT, MY LORD?
NO.
TAKE IT UP TO THE RUIN.
IT WILL BE THE CENTERPIECE FOR MY WEDDING.
A TRIBUTE TO HOPELESSNESS.

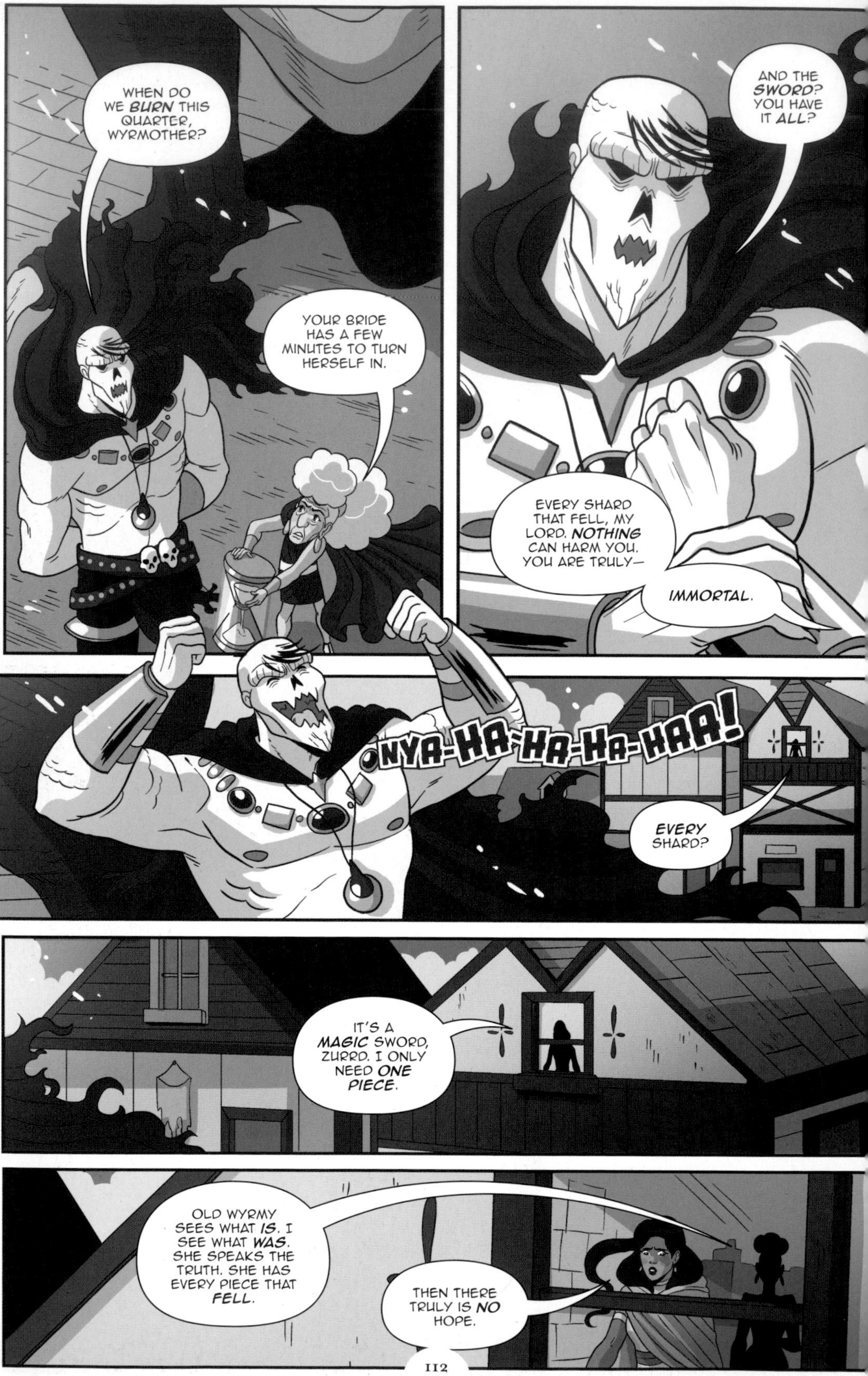
WHEN DO WE BURN THIS QUARTER, WYRMOTHER?
YOUR BRIDE HAS A FEW MINUTES TO TURN HERSELF IN.
AND THE SWORD? YOU HAVE IT ALL?
EVERY SHARD THAT FELL, MY LORD. NOTHING CAN HARM YOU. YOU ARE TRULY—
IMMORTAL.
NYA-HA-HA-HA-HAA!
EVERY SHARD?
IT'S A MAGIC SWORD, ZURRD. I ONLY NEED ONE PIECE.
OLD WYRMY SEES WHAT IS. I SEE WHAT WAS. SHE SPEAKS THE TRUTH. SHE HAS EVERY PIECE THAT FELL.
THEN THERE TRULY IS NO HOPE.

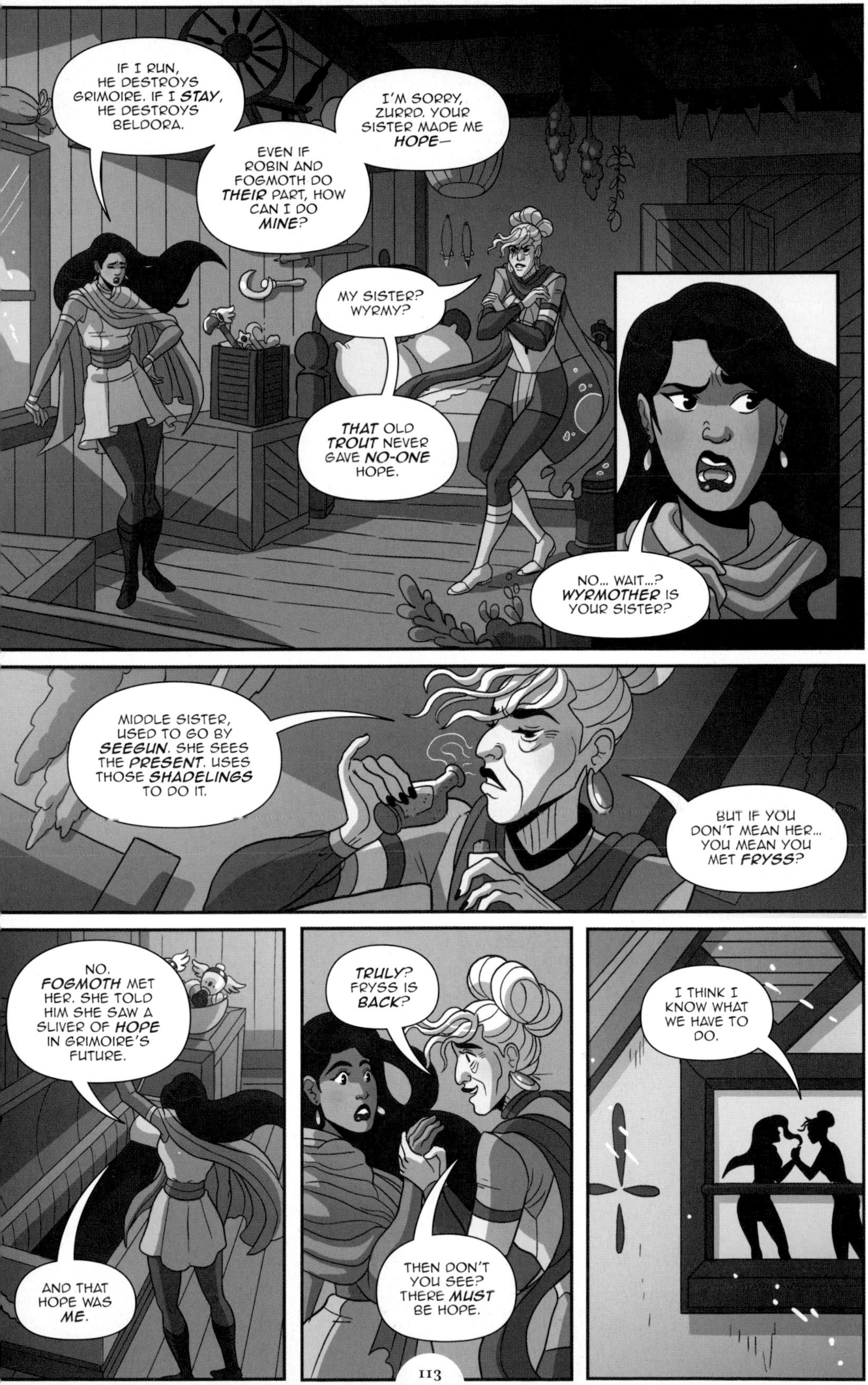
IF I RUN, HE DESTROYS GRIMOIRE. IF I STAY, HE DESTROYS BELDORA.
EVEN IF ROBIN AND FOGMOTH DO THEIR PART, HOW CAN I DO MINE?
I'M SORRY, ZURRD. YOUR SISTER MADE ME HOPE—
MY SISTER? WYRMY?
THAT OLD TROUT NEVER GAVE NO-ONE HOPE.
NO... WAIT...? WYRMOTHER IS YOUR SISTER?
MIDDLE SISTER, USED TO GO BY SEEGUN. SHE SEES THE PRESENT. USES THOSE SHADELINGS TO DO IT.
BUT IF YOU DON'T MEAN HER... YOU MEAN YOU MET FRYSS?
NO. FOGMOTH MET HER. SHE TOLD HIM SHE SAW A SLIVER OF HOPE IN GRIMOIRE'S FUTURE.
AND THAT HOPE WAS ME.
TRULY? FRYSS IS BACK?
THEN DON'T YOU SEE? THERE MUST BE HOPE.
I THINK I KNOW WHAT WE HAVE TO DO.

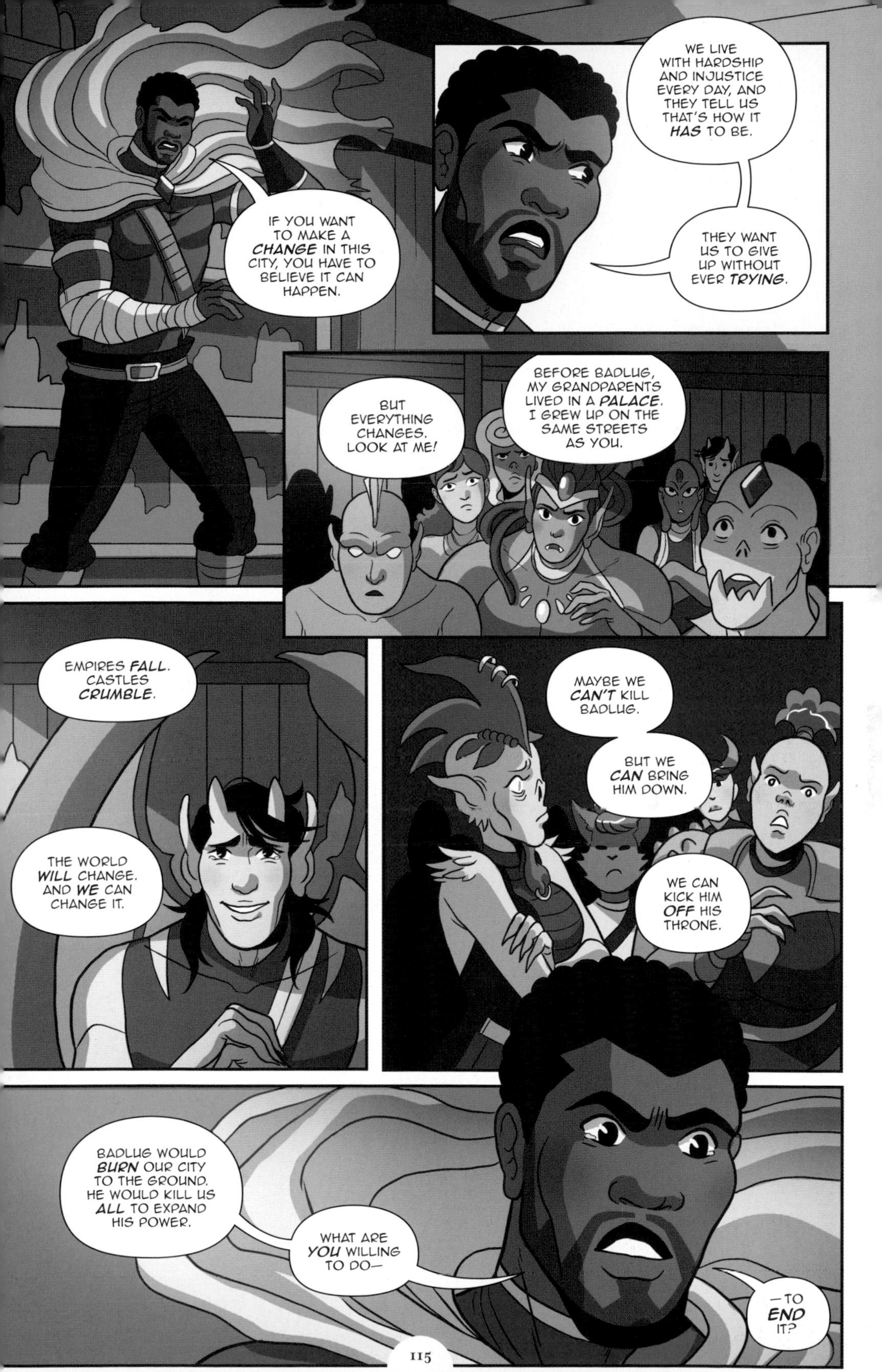
IF YOU WANT TO MAKE A CHANGE IN THIS CITY, YOU HAVE TO BELIEVE IT CAN HAPPEN.
WE LIVE WITH HARDSHIP AND INJUSTICE EVERY DAY, AND THEY TELL US THAT'S HOW IT HAS TO BE.
THEY WANT US TO GIVE UP WITHOUT EVER TRYING.
BUT EVERYTHING CHANGES. LOOK AT ME!
BEFORE BADLUG, MY GRANDPARENTS LIVED IN A PALACE. I GREW UP ON THE SAME STREETS AS YOU.
EMPIRES FALL. CASTLES CRUMBLE.
THE WORLD WILL CHANGE. AND WE CAN CHANGE IT.
MAYBE WE CAN'T KILL BADLUG.
BUT WE CAN BRING HIM DOWN.
WE CAN KICK HIM OFF HIS THRONE.
BADLUG WOULD BURN OUR CITY TO THE GROUND. HE WOULD KILL US ALL TO EXPAND HIS POWER.
WHAT ARE YOU WILLING TO DO—
—TO END IT?

122

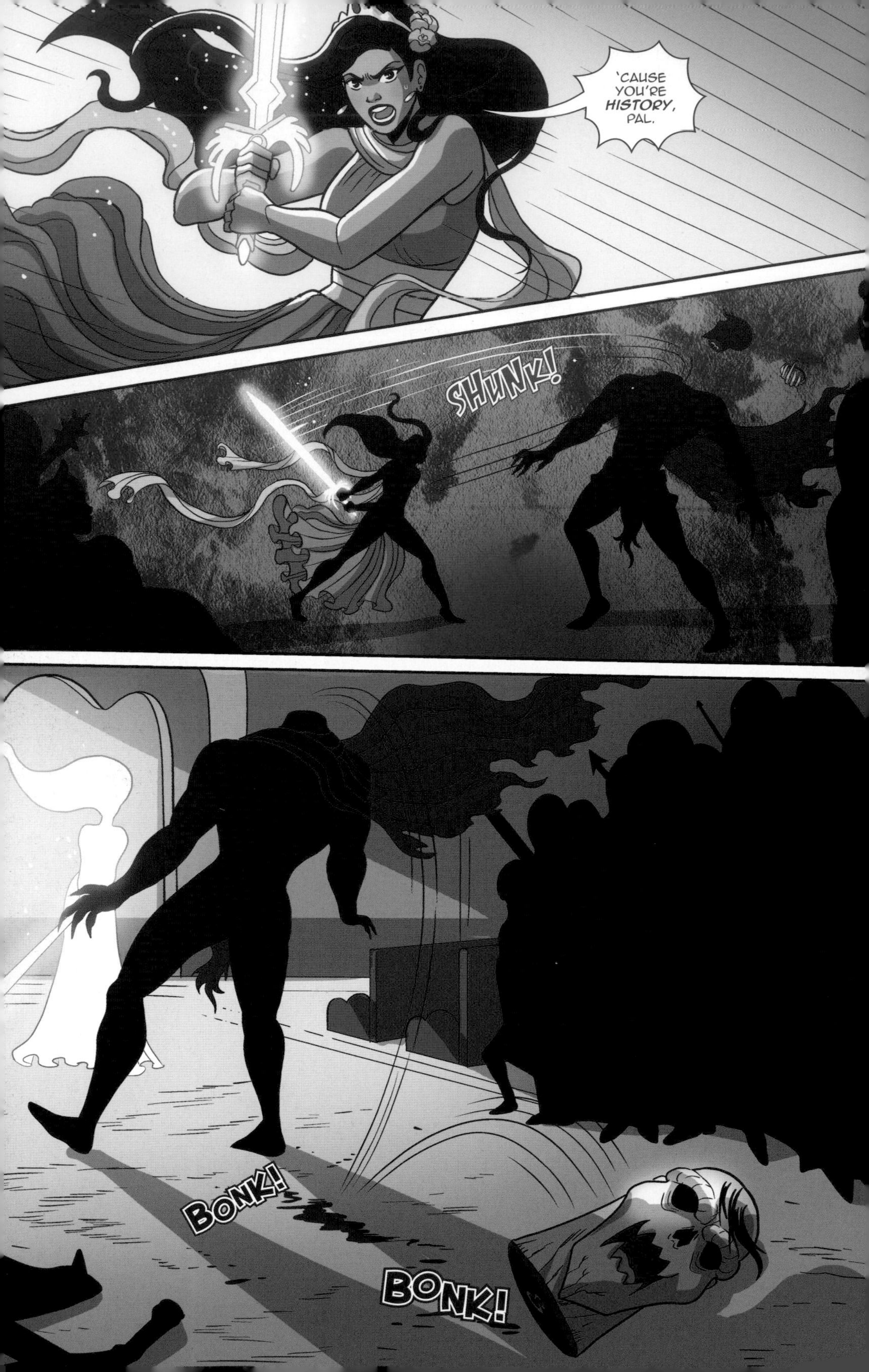
'CAUSE YOU'RE HISTORY, PAL.
SHUNK!
BONK!
BONK!

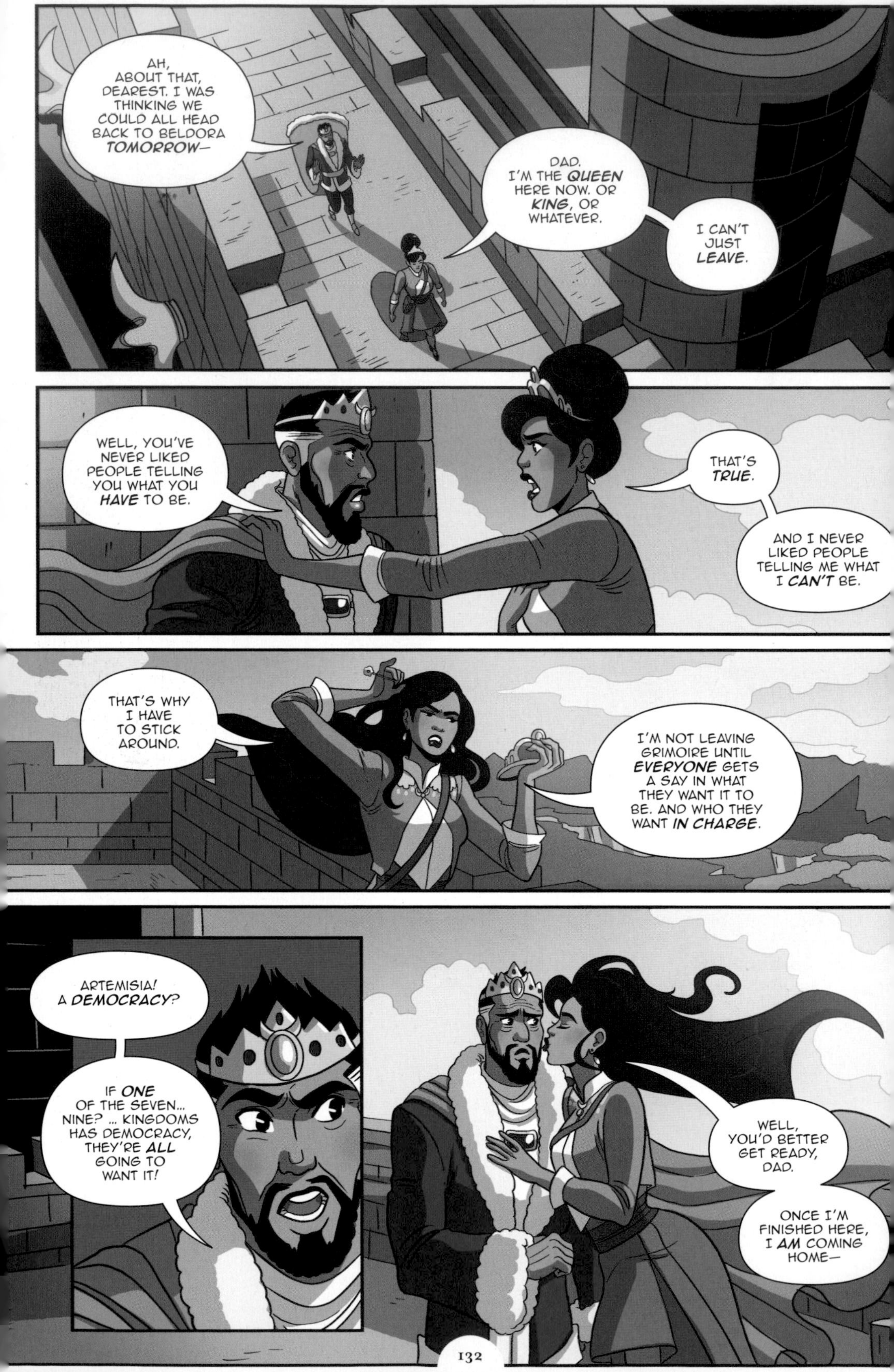
AH, ABOUT THAT, DEAREST. I WAS THINKING WE COULD ALL HEAD BACK TO BELDORA *TOMORROW*—
DAD. I'M THE *QUEEN* HERE NOW. OR *KING*, OR WHATEVER.
I CAN'T JUST *LEAVE*.
WELL, YOU'VE NEVER LIKED PEOPLE TELLING YOU WHAT YOU *HAVE* TO BE.
THAT'S *TRUE*.
AND I NEVER LIKED PEOPLE TELLING ME WHAT I *CAN'T* BE.
THAT'S WHY I HAVE TO STICK AROUND.
I'M NOT LEAVING GRIMOIRE UNTIL *EVERYONE* GETS A SAY IN WHAT THEY WANT IT TO BE. AND WHO THEY WANT *IN CHARGE*.
ARTEMISIA! A *DEMOCRACY*?
IF *ONE* OF THE SEVEN... NINE? ... KINGDOMS HAS DEMOCRACY, THEY'RE *ALL* GOING TO WANT IT!
WELL, YOU'D BETTER GET READY, DAD.
ONCE I'M FINISHED HERE, I *AM* COMING HOME—

PROPHECY IS *EASY* WITH KINGS AND DESPOTS. THEY DON'T LIKE CHANGE.

ALL OF THIS? THIS IS *NEW*.

THE PAST IS A *LANDSCAPE*, LITTERED WITH *KINGS* AND FALLEN ARMIES. RUINS OF PALACES. BORDERS *BURIED* WITH FRESH-TURNED MUD.

BUT IF YOU DON'T REPEAT THE *SAME* MISTAKES, IF YOU LET PEOPLE *CHOOSE* WHAT THEY WANT TO BE, THE FUTURE IS A *MYSTERY*, EVEN TO *ME*.

SOME PEOPLE THINK THAT'S SCARY.

BUT IT'S SCARIER IF PEOPLE *DON'T* GET TO CHOOSE.

The end.

THE FUTURE IS A LANDSCAPE AS WELL, AND WE CAN BUILD *WHATEVER* WE LIKE THERE.

WE DON'T HAVE TO BUILD ANOTHER *CASTLE*.

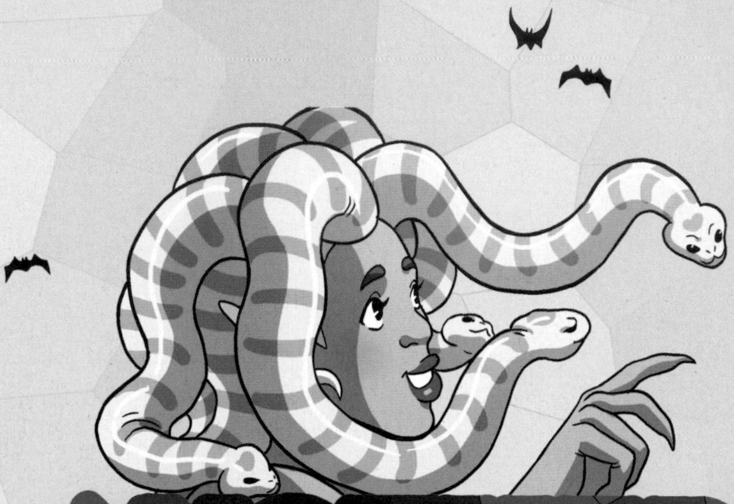

ANOTHER CASTLE

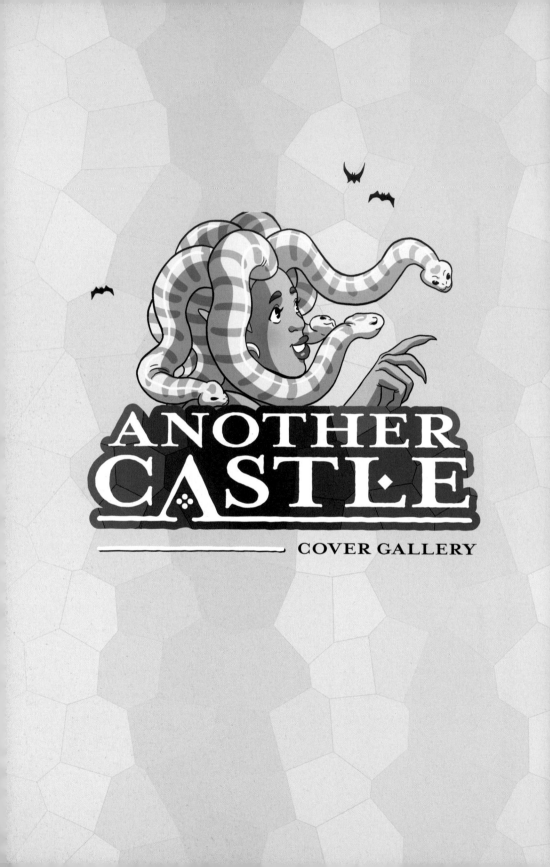

COVER GALLERY

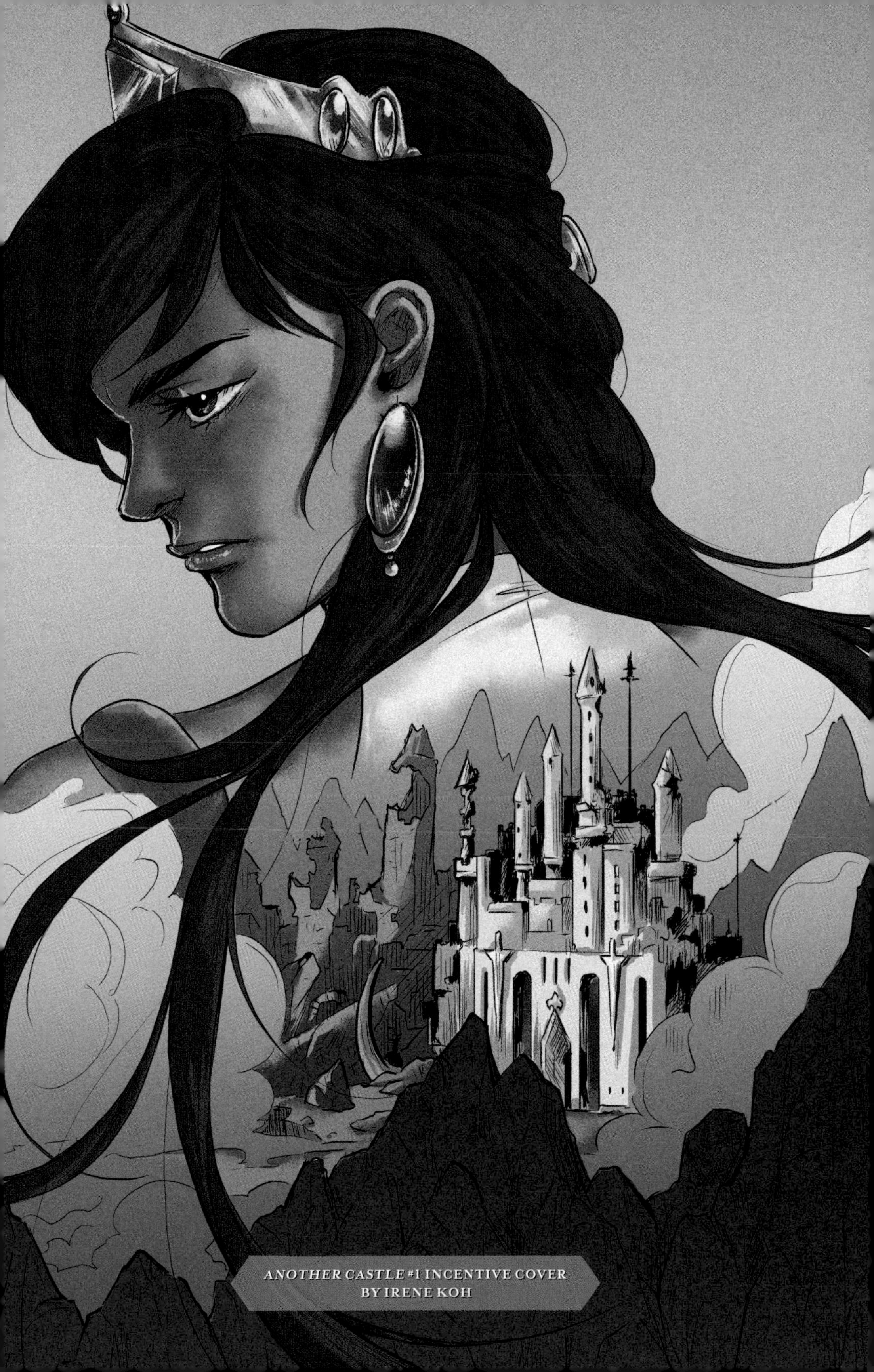

ANOTHER CASTLE #1 INCENTIVE COVER
BY IRENE KOH

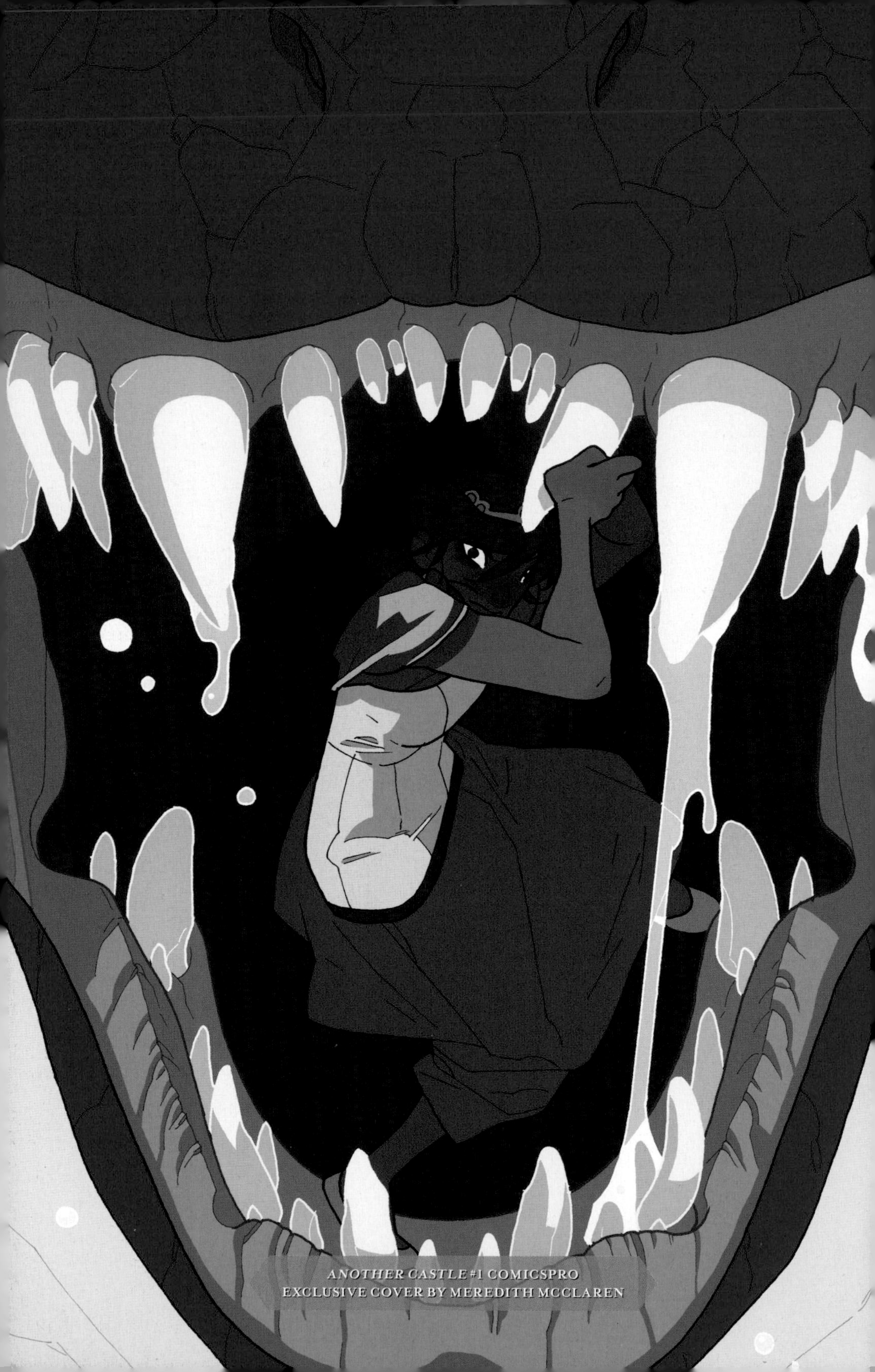

ANOTHER CASTLE #1 COMICSPRO
EXCLUSIVE COVER BY MEREDITH MCCLAREN

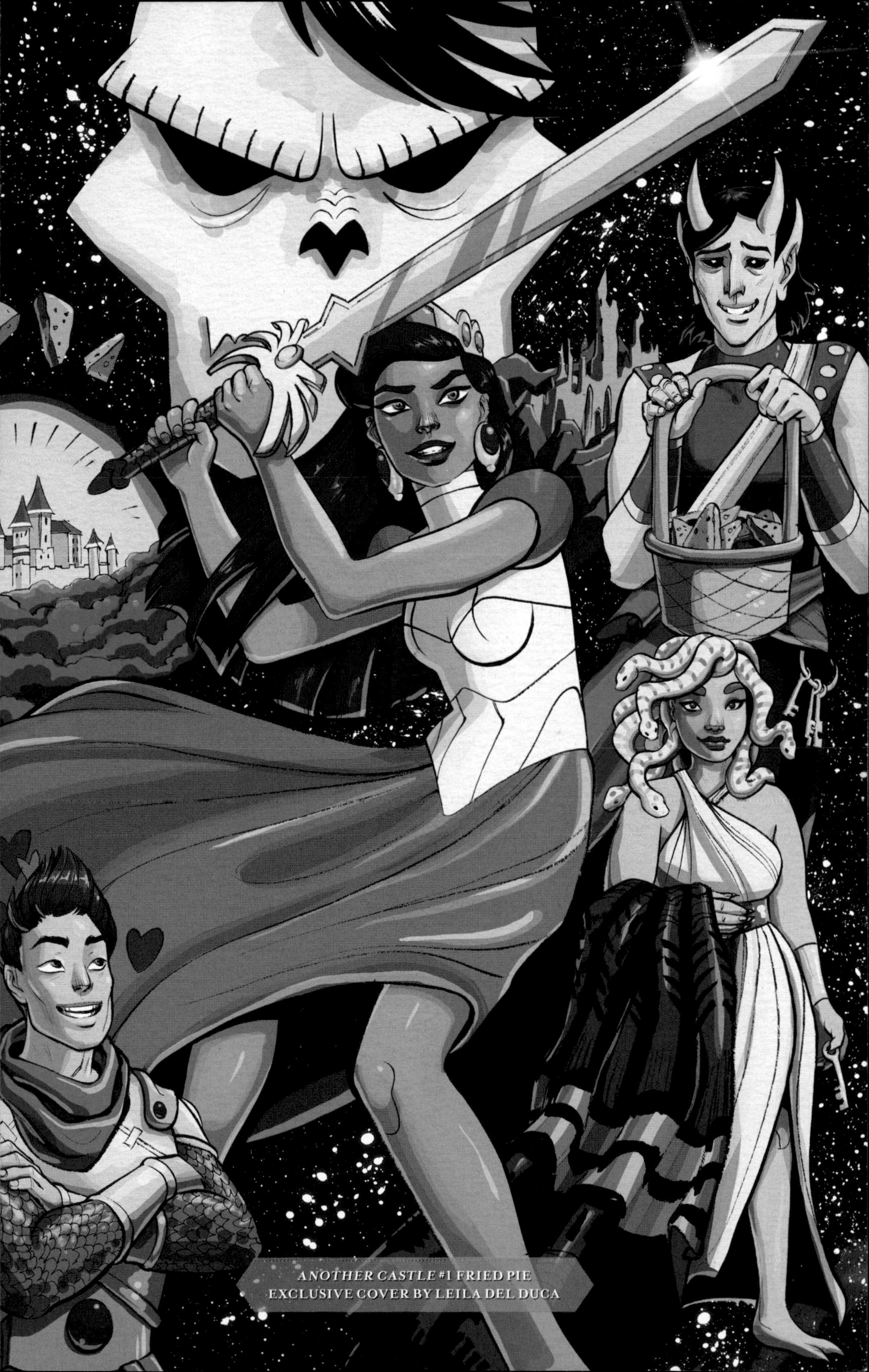

ANOTHER CASTLE #1 FRIED PIE
EXCLUSIVE COVER BY LEILA DEL DUCA

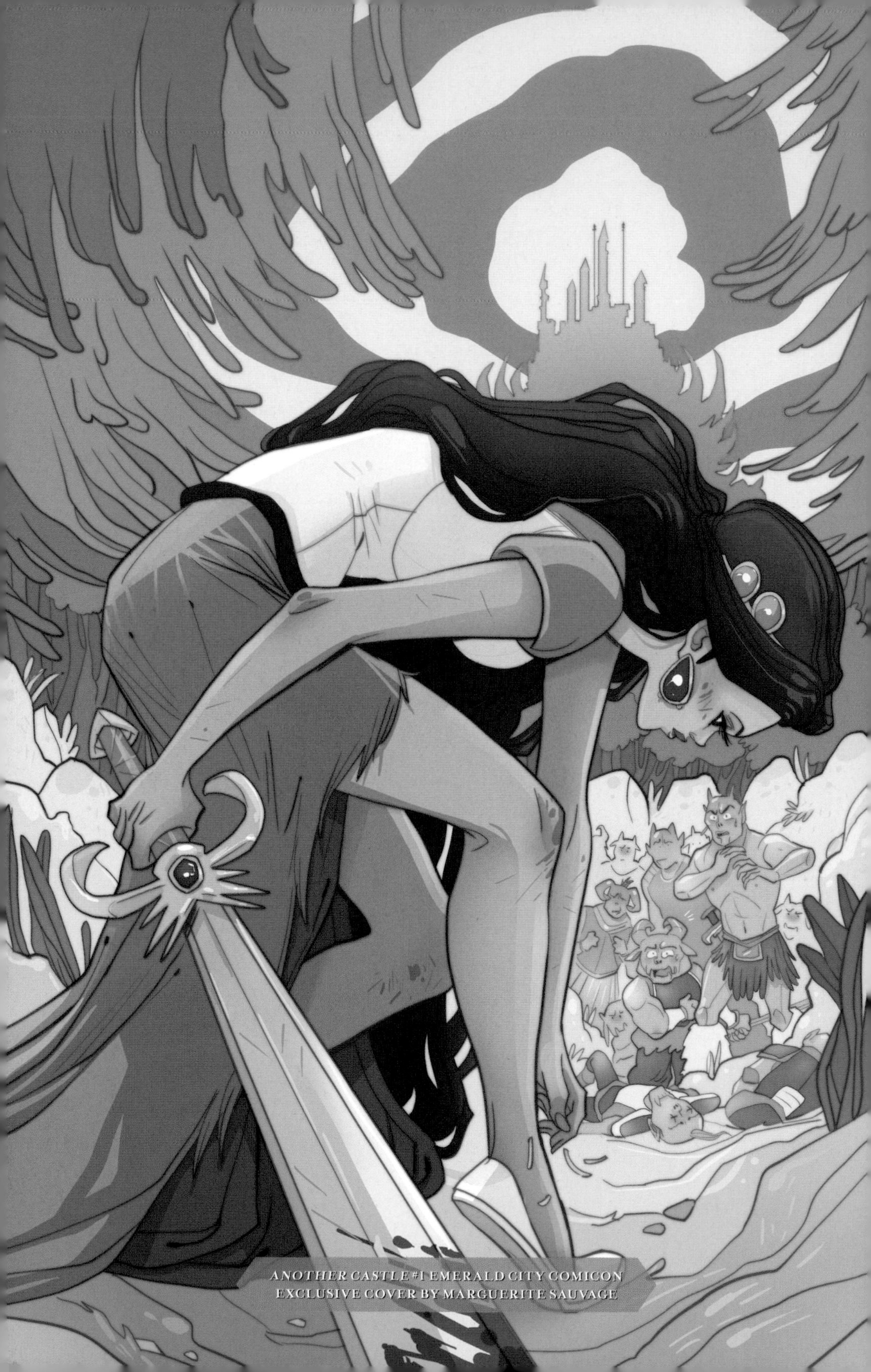

ANOTHER CASTLE #1 EMERALD CITY COMICON
EXCLUSIVE COVER BY MARGUERITE SAUVAGE

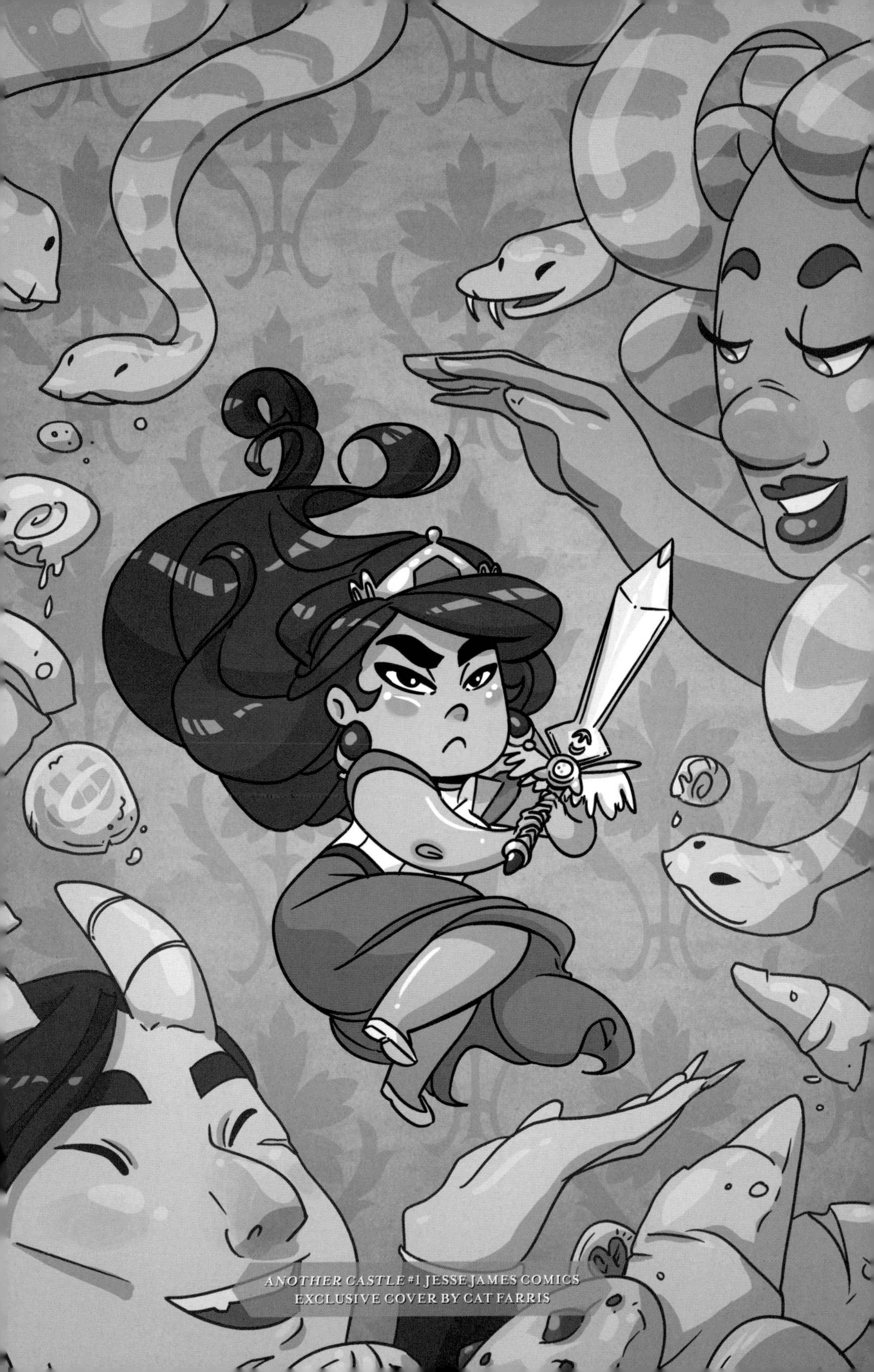

ANOTHER CASTLE #1 JESSE JAMES COMICS
EXCLUSIVE COVER BY CAT FARRIS

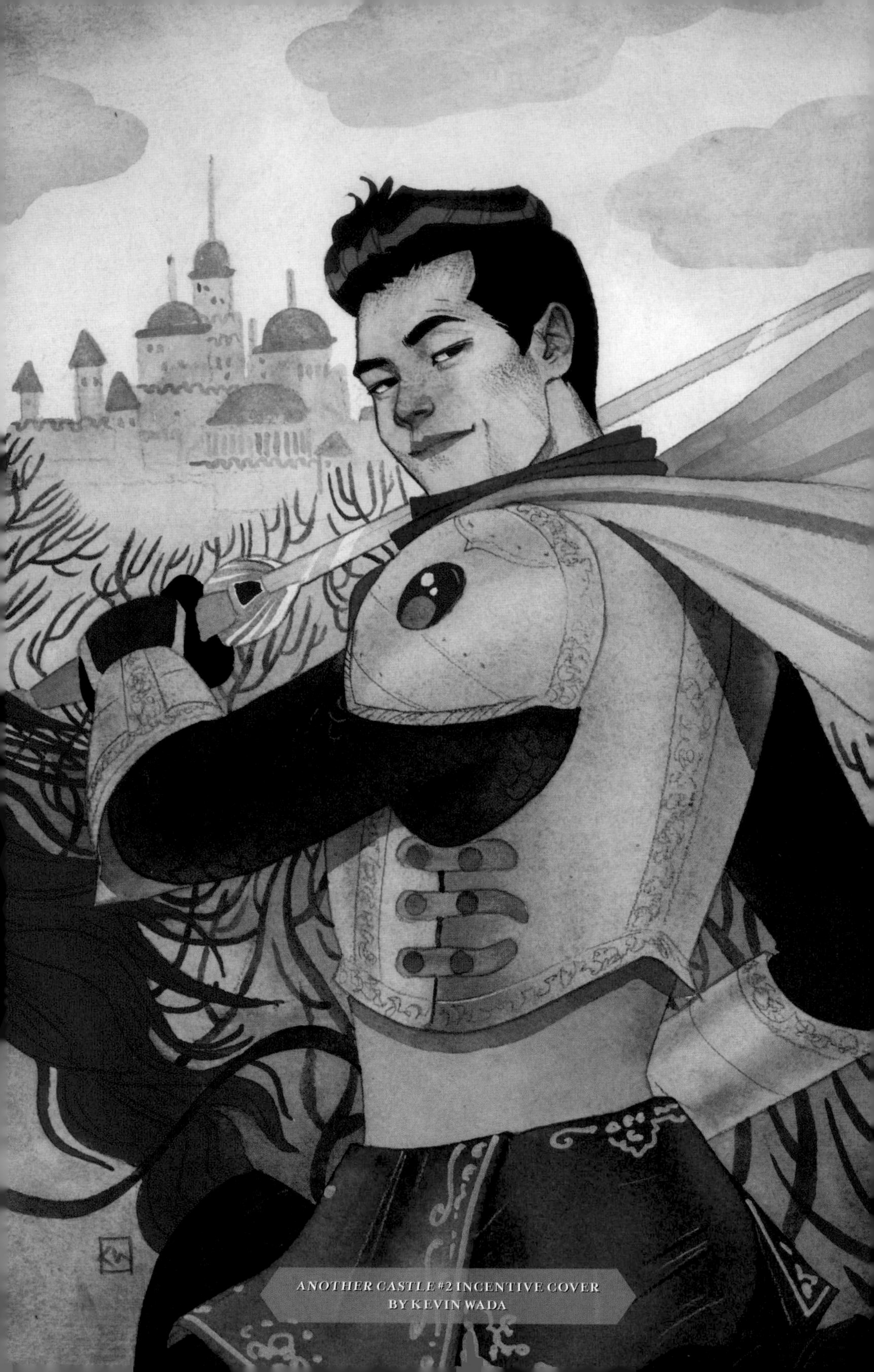

ANOTHER CASTLE #2 INCENTIVE COVER
BY KEVIN WADA

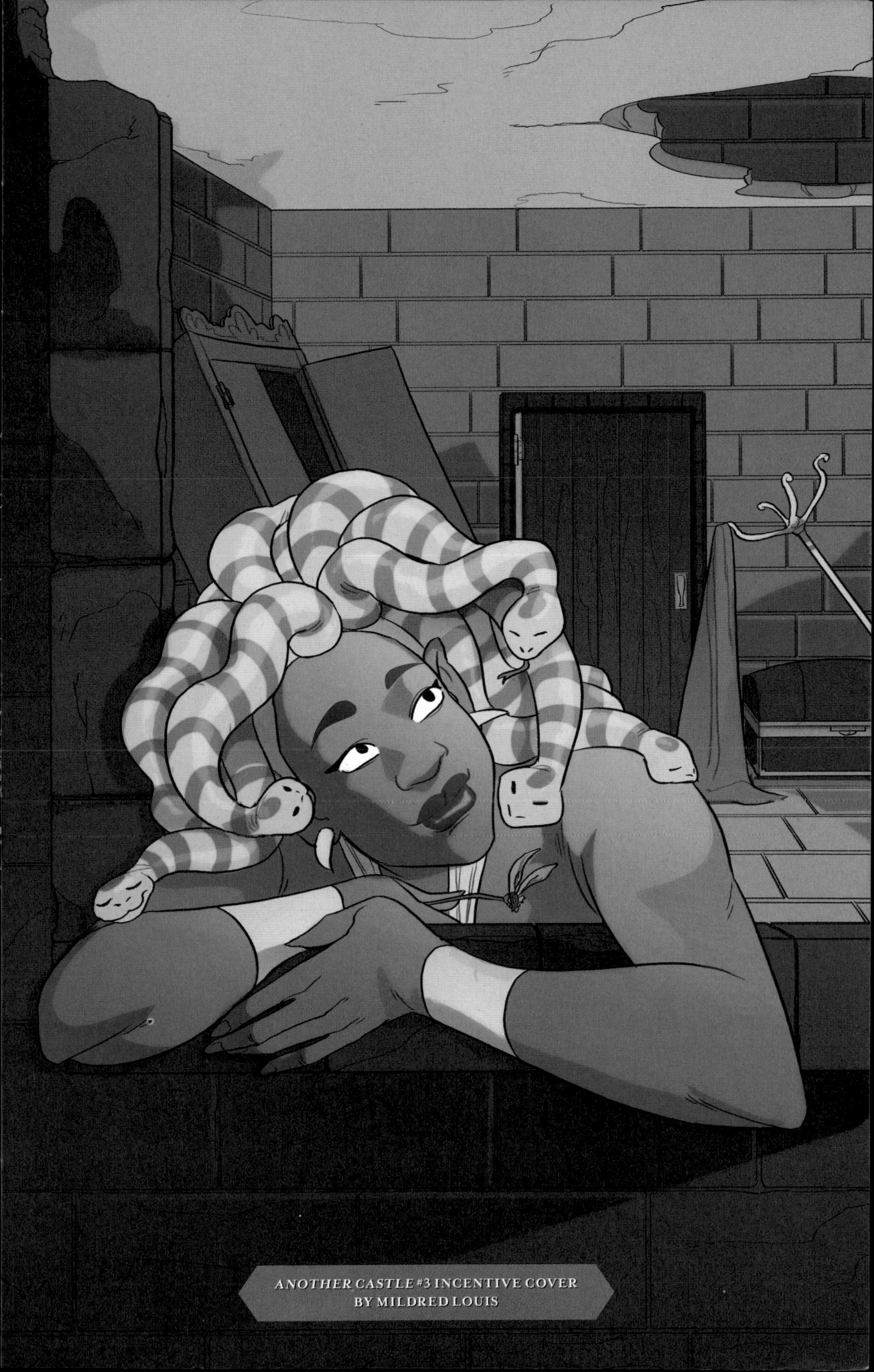

ANOTHER CASTLE #3 INCENTIVE COVER
BY MILDRED LOUIS

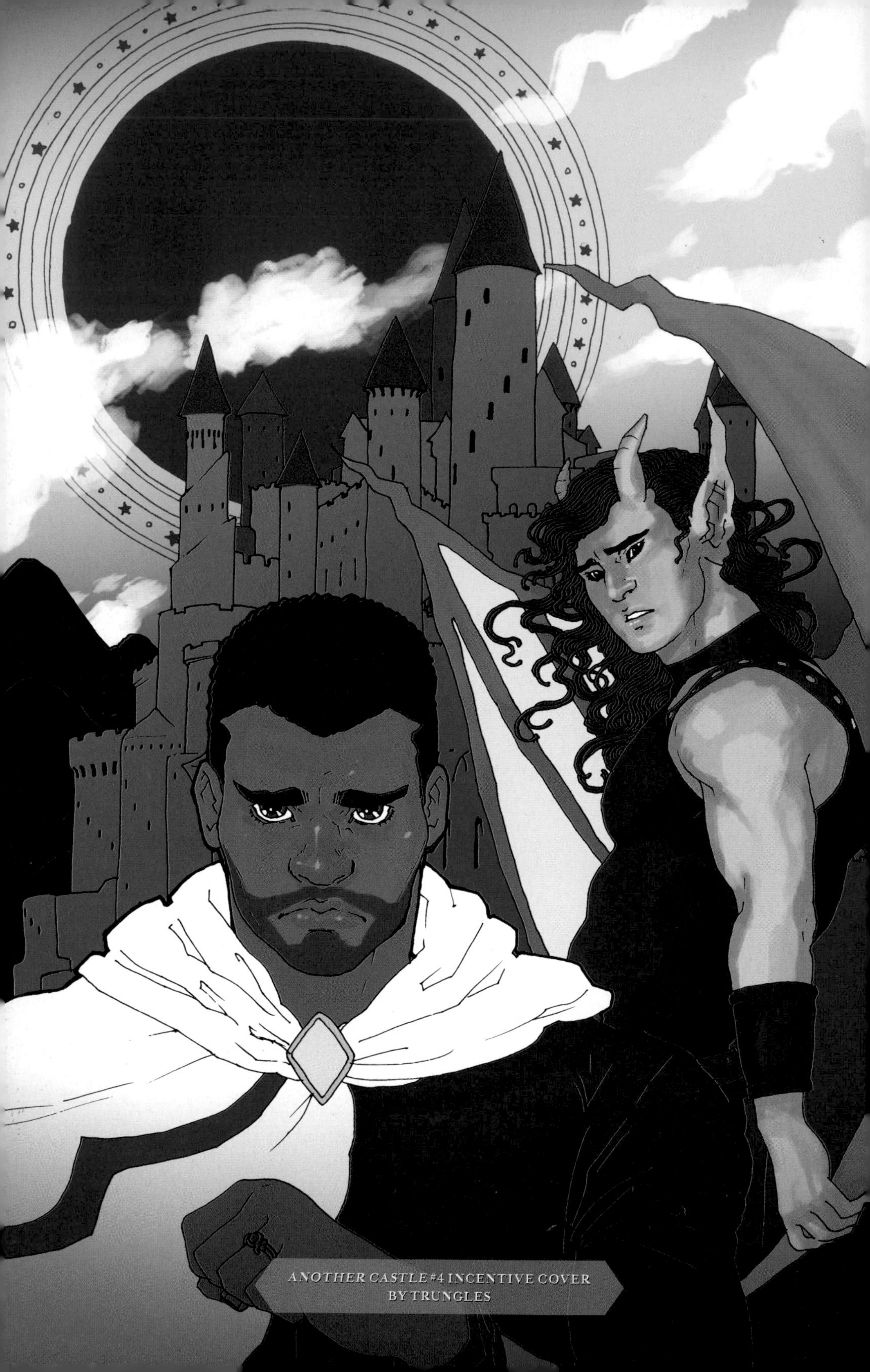

ANOTHER CASTLE #4 INCENTIVE COVER
BY TRUNGLES

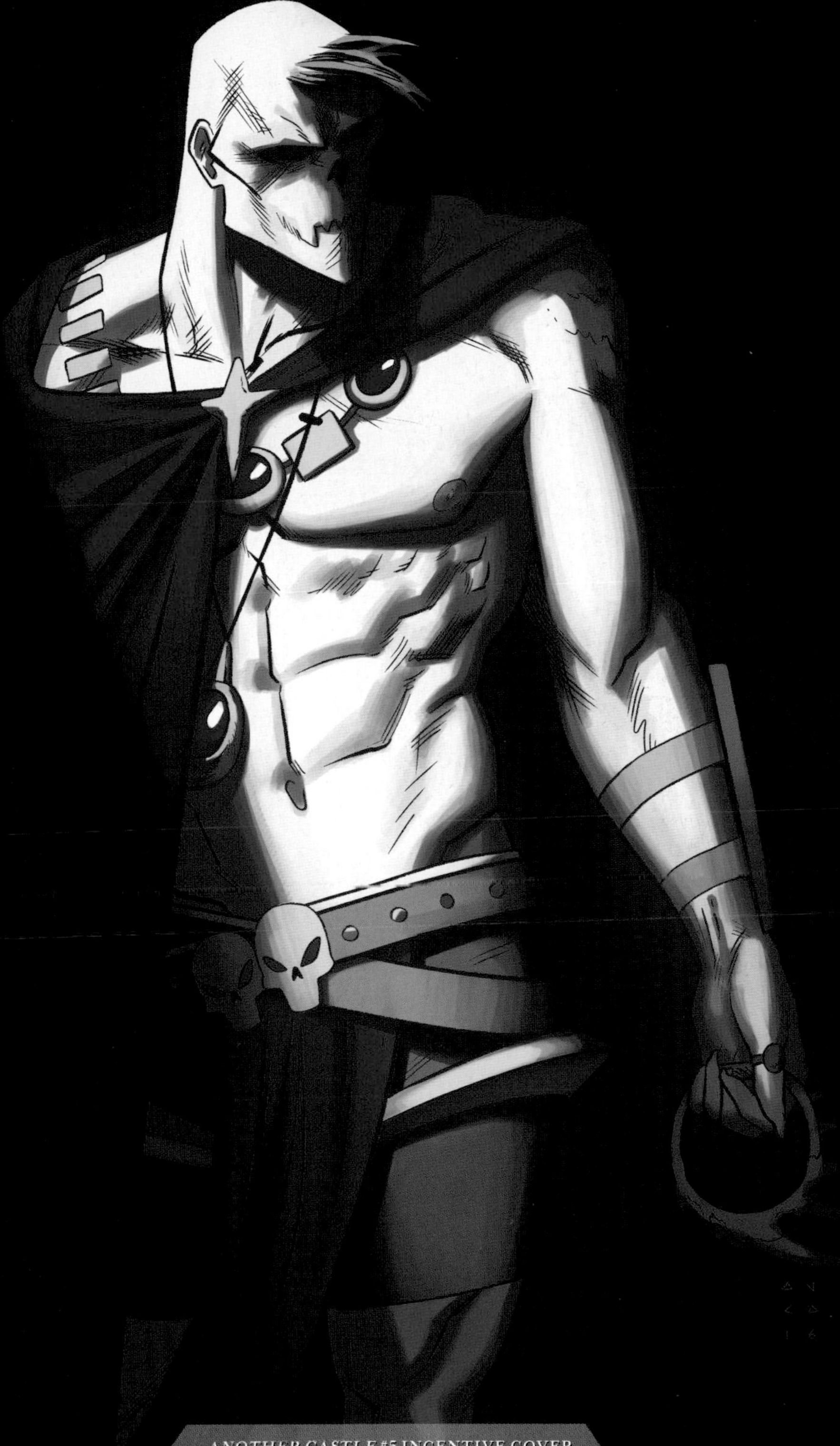

ANOTHER CASTLE #5 INCENTIVE COVER
BY KRIS ANKA

INTERVIEW WITH
Andrew Wheeler & Paulina Ganucheau

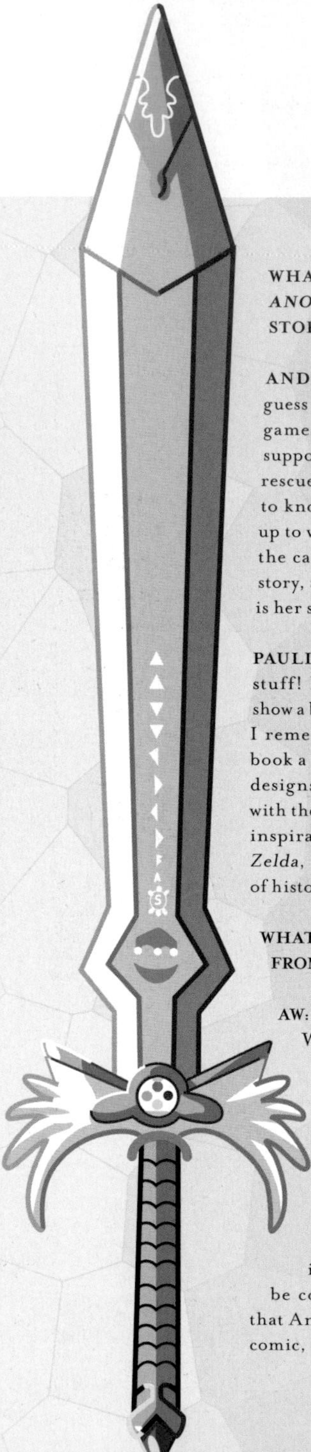

WHAT WAS THE INSPIRATION FOR *ANOTHER CASTLE*, **BOTH IN THE STORY AND THE ART?**

ANDREW WHEELER: As you might guess from the title, it started with video games, and how the princess is always supposedly just waiting at the castle to be rescued. I didn't like that idea; I wanted to know what else the princess might be up to while the hero fights his way toward the castle. But Misty is the hero of this story, and the only thing she's waiting for is her sword.

PAULINA GANUCHEAU: Jeez, so much stuff! I think most things I love always show a bit in my work. Specifically, though, I remember looking at the *Tangled* art book a LOT when I started the character designs. I mean, how can you go wrong with the fluidity of Glen Keane? But other inspirations are *Dragon Age*, *Legend of Zelda*, *Magic Knight Rayearth*, and a lot of historical art, surprisingly.

WHAT IS SOMETHING YOU LEARNED FROM MAKING *ANOTHER CASTLE?*

AW: I learned that this is so much fun. Working with Paulina, working with the Oni crew, and having this idea turn into something I can share with the world, it's incredibly exciting!

PG: That I still love princesses as much as I did when I was a five-year-old and how amazing it is to draw a feminine pink princess be completely fierce. Also, I learned that Andrew is crazy good at writing this comic, haha.

WHAT'S YOUR FAVORITE ASPECT OF CREATING THE COMIC?

AW: Getting the pages back, definitely. Always so gorgeous! But also, whenever Paulina gets to design another character, I really love that. Her costumes and her designs are phenomenal. I always think I know what these characters look like in my head, and then I get Paulina's version, and I think, "Nope, that's what they look like."

PG: Character building is definitely up there for me, but also just showing the relationships between the characters. Acting and emotion is so crazy important for me. I love it.

IF YOU LIVED IN BELDORA OR GRIMOIRE, WHO DO YOU THINK YOU WOULD BE?

AW: Oh boy. Maybe I'd try my hand at being a bard in Beldora? I bet the squires all swoon for a good bard.

PG: I'd be Misty's best friend back in Beldora that you never see 'cause she's too busy drawing tapestries of the kingdom's history.
> Misty: *"Hey, you want to hang out today?"*
> Me: *"Naw, girl, I'm on a deadline. Go save the kingdom, tho. Love ya!"*

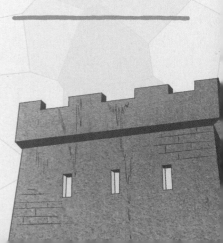

How a Cover is Created

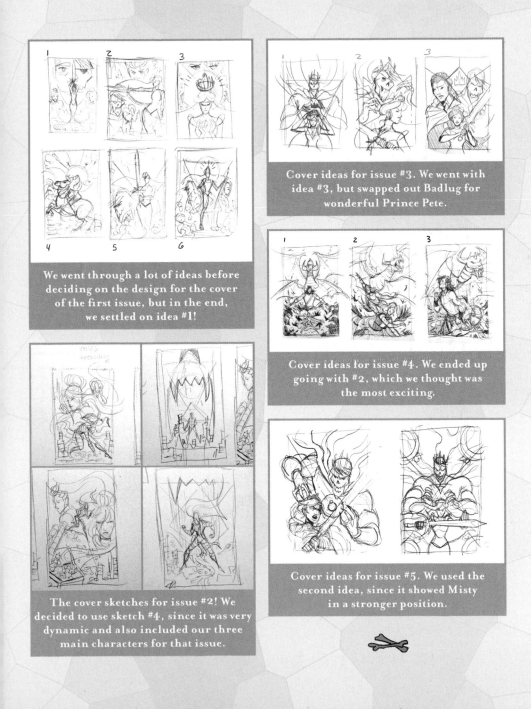

We went through a lot of ideas before deciding on the design for the cover of the first issue, but in the end, we settled on idea #1!

Cover ideas for issue #3. We went with idea #3, but swapped out Badlug for wonderful Prince Pete.

Cover ideas for issue #4. We ended up going with #2, which we thought was the most exciting.

The cover sketches for issue #2! We decided to use sketch #4, since it was very dynamic and also included our three main characters for that issue.

Cover ideas for issue #5. We used the second idea, since it showed Misty in a stronger position.

CREATING A COVER

Step-by-Step

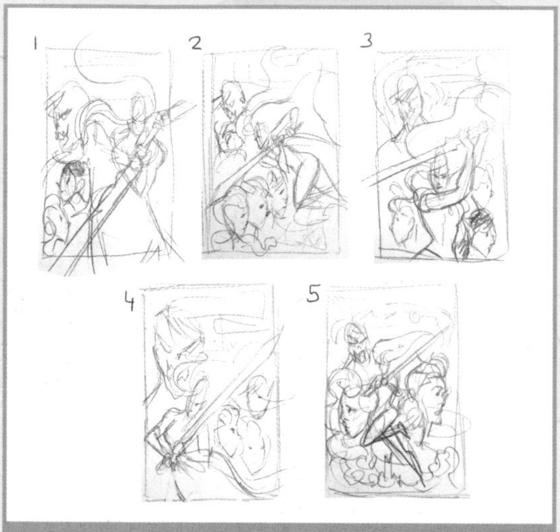
1
2
3
4
5

First, a few sketches of different ideas.

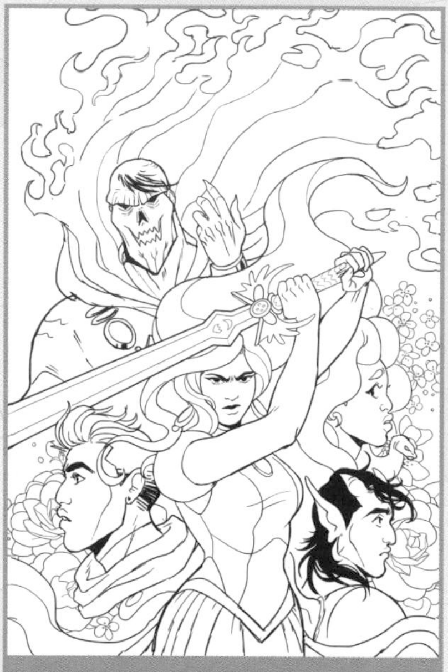

Then pencils!

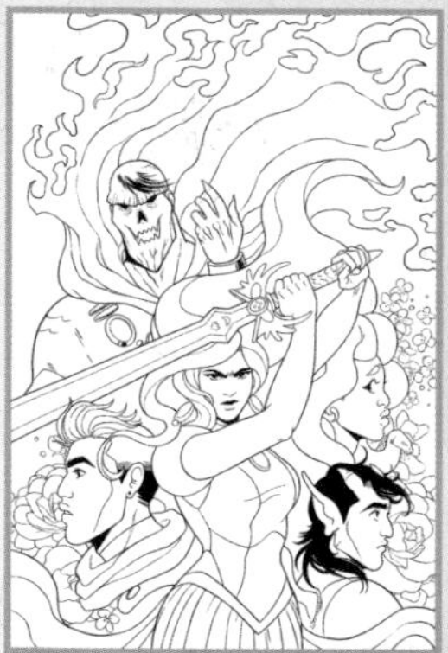

Then inks!

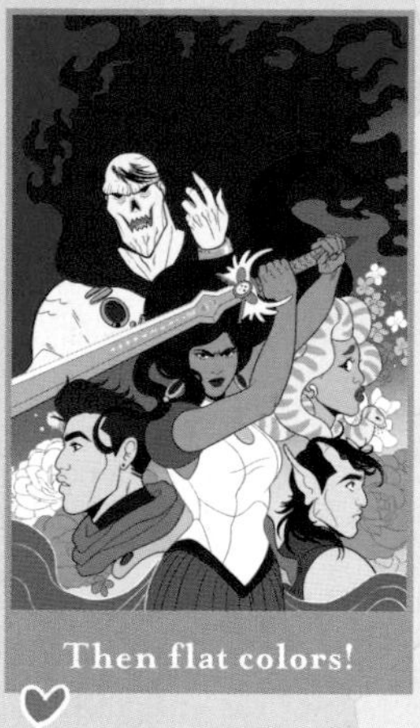

Then flat colors!

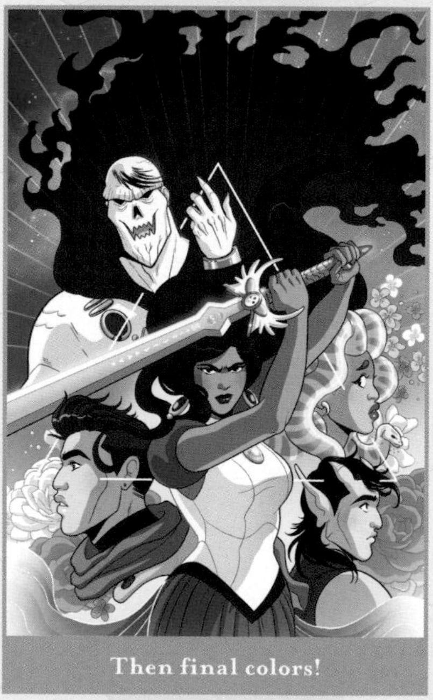

Then final colors!

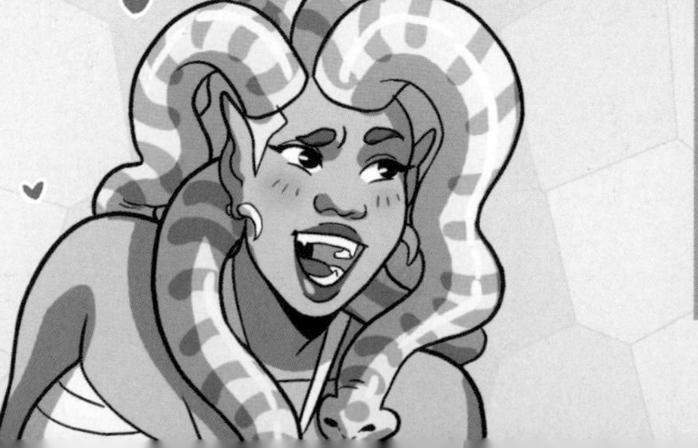

Characters & Set

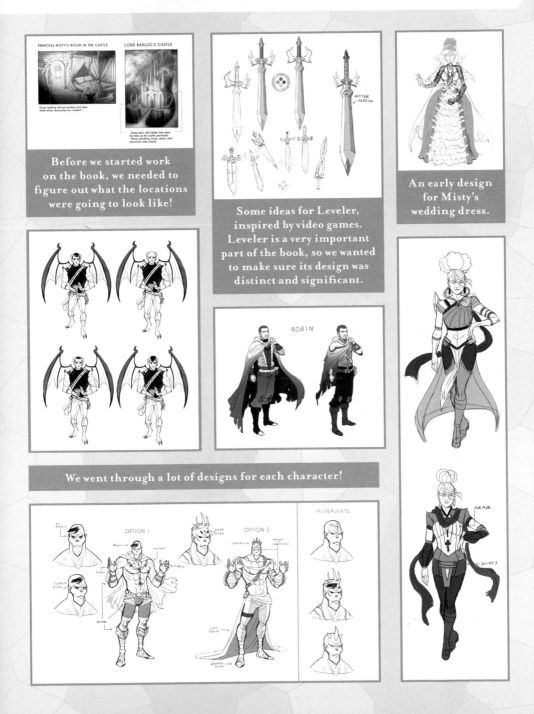

Before we started work on the book, we needed to figure out what the locations were going to look like!

Some ideas for Leveler, inspired by video games. Leveler is a very important part of the book, so we wanted to make sure its design was distinct and significant.

An early design for Misty's wedding dress.

ROBIN

We went through a lot of designs for each character!

OPTION 1

OPTION 2

ALTERNATE

DESIGN PROCESS

Characters & Set

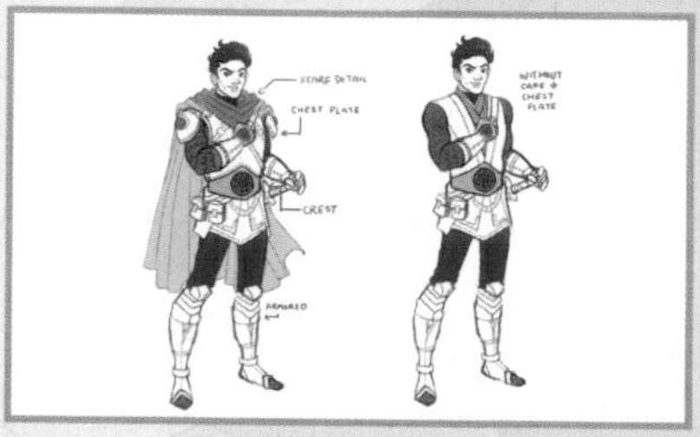

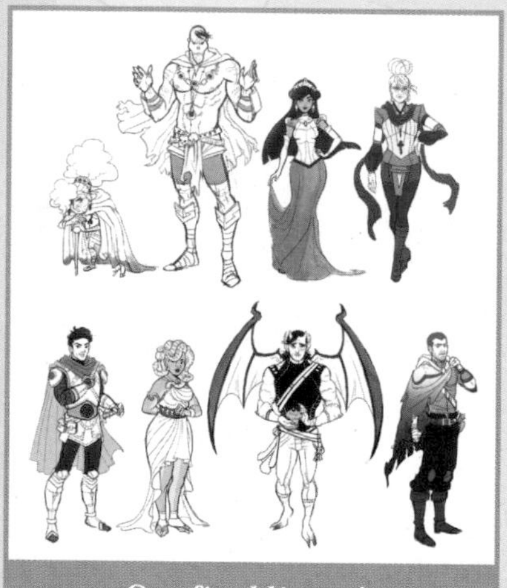

Our final lineup!

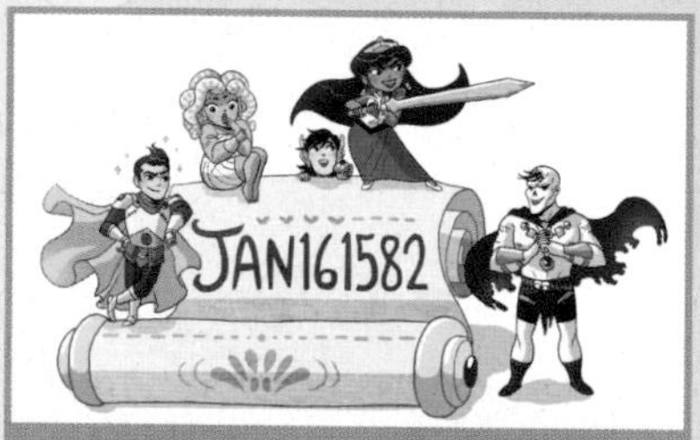
JAN161582

When you publish a comic book, readers can preorder it through their local comic shops by using an unique code. This was the code for *Another Castle* issue #1!

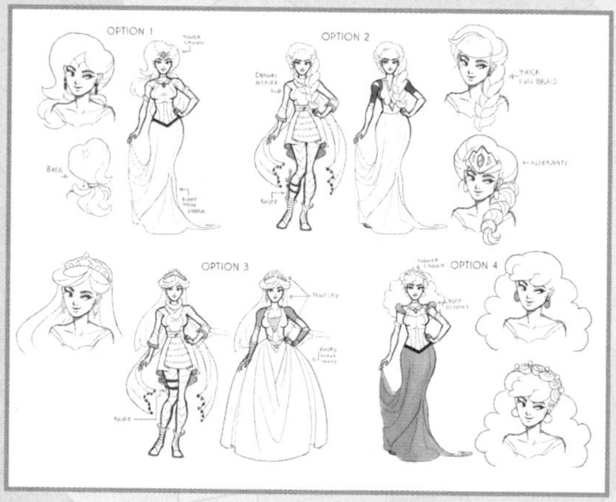
OPTION 1
OPTION 2
OPTION 3
OPTION 4

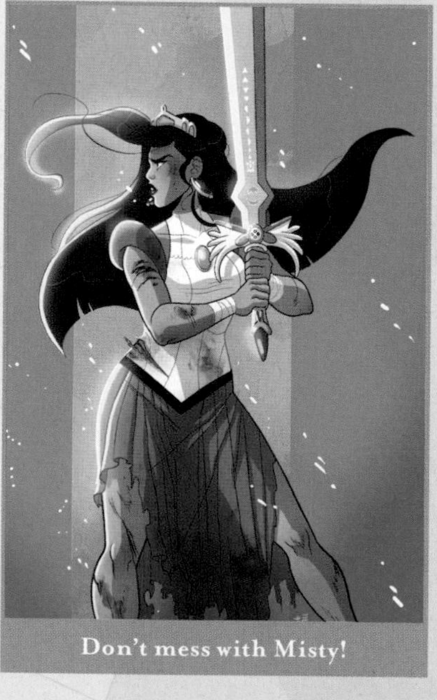

Don't mess with Misty!

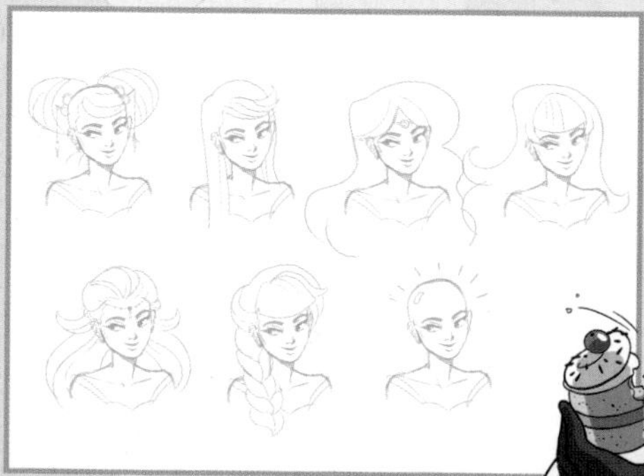

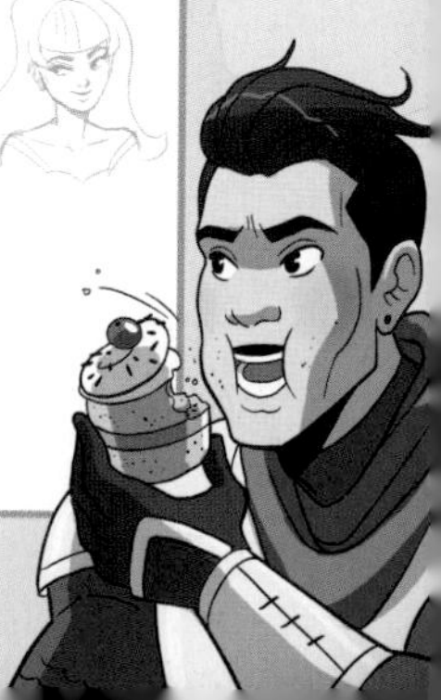

ANDREW WHEELER is an award-winning comics writer and editor whose works include the *Dungeons & Dragons Young Adventurer's Guides, Wonder Woman: Agent of Peace,* the queer superhero series *Freelance,* and *Shout Out,* the Prism-nominated LGBTQ+ anthology for young readers. Andrew was born in Hastings, England, and now lives in Toronto with thousands of raccoons.

PAULINA GANUCHEAU is a comic artist and illustrator based wherever her computer lives. She is the creator of *Lemon Bird,* with an original graphic novel out in 2021, and co-creator of *Zodiac Starforce,* published by Dark Horse Comics. Her hobbies include watching pro-wrestling, cloud photography, and following cats on Instagram.

JENNY VY TRAN is a graphic designer, cookie aficionado, and knows a lot of big words thanks to watching every episode of *Frasier.* She discovered her love for drawing at the age of five, but forgot about it until five years ago. She has worked on other Oni Press books such as *Hopeless Savages Break* and *The Lion Of Rora.*

MORE MYSTICAL & MYTHICAL ADVENTURES FROM ONI PRESS!

"Mooncakes is spellbinding!"
—Tillie Walden, Eisner-winning creator of Spinning and On a Sunbeam
Mooncakes
Wendy Xu
Suzanne Walker

MOONCAKES
By Suzanne Walker and Wendy Xu

A story of love and demons, family and witchcraft. Nova Huang knows more about magic than your average teen witch. One fateful night, she follows reports of a white wolf into the woods and comes across the unexpected: her childhood crush, Tam Lang, battling a horse demon in the woods.

PAX SAMSON
THE COOKOUT
RASHAD DOUCET • JASON REEVES

PAX SAMSON
By Rashad Doucet and Jason Reeves

The Cookout is the first volume in a new action-packed, modern fantasy trilogy that depicts a world struggling to find peace in the midst of threats, and a young superhero chef torn between following his passion and following in his family's footsteps.

CHEER UP!
LOVE AND POMPOMS
"Sweet, lovely, and wonderful..."
—Seanan McGuire, author of October Daye
Crystal Frasier · Val Wise · Oscar O. Jupiter

CHEER UP!: LOVE AND POMPOMS
By Crystal Frasier and Val Wise

Through the rigors of squad training and amped-up social pressures (not to mention microaggressions and other queer youth problems), two girls, Annie and Bebe, rekindle a friendship they thought they'd lost and discover there may be other, sweeter feelings springing up between them.

THE BLACK·MAGE
DANIEL BARNES • D.J. KIRKLAND

THE BLACK MAGE
By Daniel Barnes and D.J. Kirkland

When a historically white wizarding school opens its doors to its first-ever black student, everyone believes that the wizarding community is finally taking its first crucial steps toward inclusivity. Or is it?

ONI PRESS

For more information on these and other fine Oni Press comic books and graphic novels, visit www.onipress.com. To find a comic specialty store in your area, visit www.comicshops.us.